Waiting for Joe

By the same author

Children of the Day
The Russländer
The Two-Headed Calf
The Chrome Suite
Agassiz, A Novel in Stories
The Missing Child
Ladies of the House
Night Travellers

For children
The Town That Floated Away

Plays
The Revival
A Prairie Boy's Winter

Waiting
for Joe

a novel

Sandra
Birdsell

Random House Canada

www.randomhouse.ca

Random House Canada and colophon are registered trademarks.

This book is a work of fiction. Names, characters, places and incidents either are the product of the author's imagination or are used fictitiously. Any resemblance to actual persons, living or dead, events or locales is entirely coincidental.

Library and Archives Canada Cataloguing in Publication

Birdsell, Sandra, 1942–
Waiting for Joe / Sandra Birdsell.

Issued also in electronic format.

ISBN 978-0-307-35916-2

I. Title.

PS8553.I76W33 2010   C813'.54   C2010-901389-1

Design by Paul Dotey

Printed in the United States of America

10 9 8 7 6 5 4 3 2 1

Once again,
for
Jan Nowina-Zarzycki

Waiting for Joe

One

It is early morning when Joe Beaudry awakens to a droning sound, the ceiling fan, he thinks. His father has left it going again in his room at the back of the house. But when Joe opens his eyes, the greenish light is seeping in around the edges of the blind and he remembers that he and Laurie are parked on the Walmart lot in Regina. The cold is like a hovering presence above the bed, alert and waiting for his next move.

"What time is it?" Laurie asks, and she feels the sudden tension in Joe, his surprise that she's awake too. She sees his arm rise and the glow at his wrist lights the bottom of his stubbly face.

"You don't want to know." It's near to three o'clock, Joe doesn't say. When he came to bed around midnight unsettled by the red wine they'd drunk with supper, Laurie was already asleep. She lay completely still, hands folded and tucked under her chin, the rise and fall of her breathing barely perceptible. He'd often been jealous of that stillness, of whatever took her away. Soon after, he'd heard the clatter and dull rolling sounds of the skateboarders at the far end of the lot, and then the sweeper making its nightly pass of the shopping centre parking lot, beginning at Safeway and working its way toward them. He must have slept though, because the droning had awakened him, maybe a turboprop warming up at the airport.

He sits on the side of the bed for a moment thinking of Pauline. By now she'll know he's left. He didn't call to say goodbye. He didn't want to suggest there was more to them other than that she was sometimes lonely and he was in no hurry to go home. They found themselves agreeing to meet for a drink, to talk, Joe doing most of the talking once it became apparent that his RV business, the Happy Traveler, was failing. He turns to flip the blanket over Laurie to double its warmth, regretting their haste to leave Winnipeg, their lack of foresight in not thinking to look in the drawer under the bed to make sure there was adequate bedding, their not having hung on to the sleeping bags.

When Joe gets up and crosses the room Laurie smells the garlic—the pizza they had for supper. She fights the ache in her chest while she watches Joe in the closet mirrors, the glowing rectangle of the window lighting up the space around him, his buttocks tinged green as he bends to collect his clothes. How quickly he pulls on his jeans, T-shirt and hoodie. He leaves her without speaking.

Like Joe, she'd heard the sweeping crew, their shovels scraping up the debris the machine left behind. The noise receded when the work crew and machine went round the back of Walmart. She'd slept again, only to be awakened now by the muffled drone. The Meridian was supposed to be well insulated against the elements and noise, but it's damp and chilly, and she hears what could be an airplane. Or it might be the city, two hundred thousand people breathing. Then comes the electric whirr of the Meridian steps unfolding, Joe opening the door, the woof of air compressing as it closes behind him.

She listens for his footsteps and hears none. She heaps his pillow onto her head to shut out the light, tells herself, Laurie, do not think. Do not think about Joe turning away from her yet again. She puts the thought in a jar, screws the lid down tight and imagines setting it on a shelf up near the ceiling.

Don't think about the house, its vibrant rooms like a jewel box, the colours of mustard and the Mediterranean; the geranium-red kitchen only just renovated, the warm sheen of its cork floor. That about now she would be washing the winter dust from the upstairs veranda, preparing it for the summer months when they liked to leave the door from the bedroom open throughout the night and they would awake to the tap-tapping of the nuthatch daubing the inside of the gourd she'd hung in the ornamental crabapple tree. To the thick odour of the Assiniboine River rising in a cloud at the foot of the street, the smell like fish and rust.

She tries not to think of Joe's father, Alfred, of going past Deere Lodge the evening before they left and seeing him at the window, outlined in that little square of yellow light in his little square room, among a myriad of lights along Portage Avenue. His liver-spotted coconut of a head framed by the window. She puts the thought of Alfred in a jar, screws down the lid, sets it up on the shelf. Within moments the pillow, warmed by her breath, is a cave of comfort she can safely fall asleep in.

Joe stands in the parking lot taking in the dazzle of frost scalloping out from the bases of the concrete parking stops and light standards, emerging on the side of a nearby garbage container, while the Meridian remains untouched. When they'd arrived in Regina three days ago, he'd parked where the manager suggested, at the front of the lot and close to its perimeter, parallel to Gibson Road. By the end of that first day a couple of employees had erected a chain-link enclosure nearby.

It's filled now with bales of gardening supplies, bags of soil, containers of herbicides and pesticides, chemicals he sometimes gets whiffs of. The enclosure is the source of the greenish light, while above Joe, the orange glow of the sodium vapour lights obliterates the stars. He thinks of the Happy Traveler lot, how in the early years the rows of trailers and RVs were lit by a single light, until he came upon the remains of a bonfire in a thicket behind the storage Quonset and installed a security camera and two more lights. He regretted having done that when it came time to take the Meridian, which was parked inside the Quonset near the gate, the shortest distance between his need for wheels and a place to live.

He'd carried his .22 rifle in a duffle bag. Worried that it looked suspiciously light, he'd waited until the taxi merged with the glowing stream of tail lights going into the city before setting off along the road bordering the industrial park. He felt dwarfed by the security fences around the sprawling complexes, some of those lit-up yards as large as two city blocks and filled with long-distance hauling rigs and trailers. He passed by ATCO and its mountains of prefab office structures and workforce housing; a pipeline and drilling company, it was a major supplier to the oil patch and several Arab states. Then the newest complex, the company making Portakabins, the trailers that were used by the military at the Canadian base at Doha during Desert Storm and now in Afghanistan.

When he reached the most northerly section of the park he turned onto the dirt service road and then veered into the ditch, cursing as he plunged through a film of ice and his tassel loafers filled with frigid water. The bank was slippery underfoot and he grabbed at dried weeds to haul himself up the slope. The barbed wire fence bordering the field behind his yard was alive with shredded plastic bags, like tethered dogs leaping and snapping at his face when he stepped down on the bottom strand and swung the duffle bag through the space onto the frozen ground. Then he ducked between the wires and carried the bag toward a clump of bushes whose crown was clotted with more plastic that rippled in the wind. He was still in the business suit he'd put on in the morning for his meeting with the loans manager of the credit union, hardly dressed for the bite of spring on the northwesterly edge of Winnipeg.

There was a hollowed-out space inside the bushes where branches were broken off, and the ground was lined with cardboard. He dropped to his knees and slid the bag inside, thinking that someone had called the bushes home. Could be the man in the oil-stained parka, whom Joe had caught picking through the garbage at Pauline's restaurant. He'd swung round at Joe as though he expected to be chased off and was prepared to object. The skin on his hands looked smoked and thick, his feral eyes like a windstorm. That man in the thicket, watching Joe shut down in increments, his four employees gone, one after the other. By the time winter arrived, only Joe going about the yard, the air hazed with snow sifting off the motorhomes and trailers, the roofs growing higher each day with perfectly shaped domes of snow that he'd had to punch through before he could clear them off.

The cold penetrated through the cardboard where he sat in the hollowed-out bushes, his knees drawn up, trench coat pulled tightly around him, hands shoved into its sleeves for warmth while he waited for the lights in Pauline's to go out. For Pauline to lock up her diner, get into her van and drive off to her acreage in the south end of the city where she kept horses. He didn't want Pauline to have to lie, to say she wasn't aware of anything unusual happening next door, even though she'd made it clear that he was welcome to store whatever he wanted in the shed at the back of her property. She wouldn't talk, he knew, although people were talking, the men in the diner going quiet whenever he came in, the bank clerks avoiding eye contact with him.

The Winchester .22 that Joe cradled against his chest was his father's gift to him on his sixteenth birthday, but like most of what Alfred had given him, he'd seldom had a use for it. This morning when Joe got up, Alfred had been awake, sitting at the kitchen table over a mug of tea. He'd been unable to sleep through the night, he'd said, and Joe heard it as an accusation, that it was his fault Alfred had been up and knocking about his bedroom at the end of the hall. His father knew something was in the air and Joe knew he would soon need to tell him about the arrangements he'd made for him to take up residence at Deere Lodge.

Pauline's van started up and backed off the diner lot, its headlights sweeping across the bushes as she passed by. When she reached the gravel road she turned and sped away. She had gone bankrupt twice, it was not a big deal, she told him, her cigarette rising in an arc above the bed. The first time, her husband had left her with three small kids and a pile of debts, the second was a business venture, the Chocolate Shop, a downtown café that offered tarot readings, tea and chocolates. There are ways around it, she said. Both times her credit was restored within a few years.

"I don't know," Joe said, staring into the chasm of air that had opened up inside him. He was alone now. Alone as anyone could be who had once believed that nothing happened to him without it being part of the grand design.

Within weeks, perhaps a month, people would come to take an inventory of his business and he didn't want there to be any video evidence of him driving away in the Meridian. It was the last of the high-end Class C motorhomes he'd sold, to a farmer who'd used it once and had been storing it with him ever since. Even after the several eviction notices he'd received, Joe had been electrified the morning he came to work and saw the notice posted on the door and discovered that all the locks on the main building had been changed. But not the lock on the yard gate, however, and he knew immediately how to make use of that oversight. He shouldered the rifle and sighted the security camera at the corner of the building under the eaves. The thin sharp crack, the sound of the camera shattering were covered by the rising swirl of wind and the roar of shredded plastic lashing out from the fence and in the air above his head. Three lights, three more cracks, and the Happy Traveler yard fell into darkness.

"I don't know," Joe says now as he paces along the perimeter of the Walmart parking lot, gazing at the bungalows across Albert Street. All the windows of the houses are dark, except the glow of one front-door fanlight. He imagines the light is left burning for a kid. Just as the light was always left on for him. He wants to call home and reaches for his cell, knowing there's nowhere for him to call. He turns away from the thought only to be confronted by the gleaming hulk of the Meridian.

He could call Alfred. Not even the threat of a sensor pad being installed on his bed has stopped his father's nightly wandering at Deere Lodge. But it is too late. His scalp throbs with his rising pulse as he enters a number. When Maryanne Lewis answers he can only say, "It's me. Joe."

"Oh, I had a feeling it was you. You've been on my mind for days. I said to Ken, 'We're going to hear from Joe.'"

Joe leans into Maryanne's familiar voice, wants to sink into it.

"I've been meaning to get in touch with you for ages," he says. It's his way of acknowledging that he's not replied to their many telephone and email messages; the years of silence passing between them.

"It's Joe," she calls out, and Joe hears a phone being picked up.

"Joe," Pastor Ken exclaims. "How's it going, little brother?"

Joe listens for disappointment or regret and fails to detect either. "What time is it there?" he asks. They sound as though they've been asleep, and he realizes that even with the time difference, it's past midnight in Vancouver.

"Listen, Joe, any time you want to call is the right time," Pastor Ken says.

"I've lost my business." Joe gets it out there before he can't. *I've lost the house, my father.*

Lost, as though the Happy Traveler, his home, his dad, wandered off and he's been unable to find them.

"Joe. Oh, no," Maryanne says.

"How?" Pastor Ken jumps in to ask.

"It's been coming for a while now. Last year business was really bad, but ever since 9/11, things haven't been great."

"People stopped travelling then," Pastor Ken says.

"Yes." Joe does not say that although he'd incorporated, when the business began to falter he'd taken out a mortgage on the house. The small property Laurie had inherited from her grandmother, along with a time-share in a townhouse in Tofino, had gone as collateral against his line of credit.

He does not say he'd driven past the entrance to the industrial park on some mornings to head out along the highway, his eyes following the zinging arc of the frost-silvered hydro wires as they dipped down and up from poles, driving out a bit farther each time. Sometimes he would pull over and sit for a moment before heading back, watch for the doe and her yearling to emerge from the scrub bush near the city dump.

"I got behind on things. Behind a year on the lease of the shop. And then the bank foreclosed on the house."

He receives their immediate outpouring of condolences, as waves swell and threaten to crash over his head. Those two lifeguards. They had rescued him at a time when he'd most needed someone to be there.

He takes a deep breath to calm his voice. "You should see the area now, you wouldn't recognize it. They call it the Juba Industrial Park."

When he'd first opened the Happy Traveler, it had been the largest of the single proprietorship businesses in the area, the brake and carburetor shops, sandblasting and paint garages. Then the land was sold and developed and most of those enterprises moved, or shut down. Spur rail lines bringing in tons of crushed vehicles, scrap metal being turned into gold—he couldn't understand, get a handle on how any of this worked. But he'd stayed and incorporated. Expanded. Went into boats and ATVs, RV storage and repairs.

"You know what, Joe? It's like you've lost a child," Maryanne says. "A man's business is like that to him. It's his child. You're grieving."

The yellow light shining in the fan of the front door of the house becomes a blur, and Joe turns away, shivering now with the dampness and cold emanating from the asphalt.

"Where are you?" Pastor Ken asks and when Joe tells him, he says, "So are you heading this way, then? We'd sure love to see you, guy. It's been far too long."

"Well no, I wasn't planning to. I've got a job right now at Canadian Tire. For a few days, anyway. Until me and another guy finish putting together the garden centre. I should have enough cash by then to get to Fort McMurray. You remember Steve? He's living there now. I'm hoping he'll have some leads on work."

"Steve Greyeyes," Maryanne says. "Of course we remember him."

"I need to find a job, and fast," Joe says, thinking of the promise he made to his father—the move to Deere Lodge is only temporary. This is the lie he also tells himself—that no matter where he is he'll return to Winnipeg and set the record straight. When he has the means he'll make whatever arrangements are necessary to move Alfred in with them, wherever that may be.

"Is that what you want to do, Joe? Go to Fort McMurray?" Pastor Ken asks.

"It'll do for now," Joe says and gives a ragged laugh.

"Remember, Joe, you're God's kid. He wants only the best for you," Maryanne says, echoed by Pastor Ken's "Amen to that."

"Can we pray for you, Joe? Ken and I have been thinking about you so often lately. Now we know why."

"I haven't got much time left on this phone," Joe says quickly, thinking they mean to begin praying now.

Maryanne laughs. "It's okay, Joe. You don't need to be in on this. God is, and that's what counts."

"Promise you'll keep in touch," Pastor Ken adds. "And if there's anything we can do, all you have to do is ask, little buddy. Anything at all."

"Thanks," Joe says. Although he wants to hold onto their voices for a while longer, he needs the time he's got left on the cell to stay connected to Alfred. He hangs up without saying goodbye.

He turns toward the motorhome and sees his own foot-prints in the sheen of frost. He can smell it, like wet saw-dust and must. Like the odour of the tin-sided garage whose earth floor hadn't been exposed to sunlight for years. The scent sometimes clung to his mother's sweater when she'd been out there cleaning storm windows, or refinishing a piece of furniture. It is a time he can scarcely recall, although he'd lived all his life in his parents' house on Arlington Street.

Once inside, he undresses quickly, knowing from Laurie's stillness that she's asleep. He climbs into bed, careful not to wake her. There's a sudden sharp snapping, the skin of the Meridian contracting in the dropping temperature. He closes his eyes, remembering how the walls in the empty showroom would snap during winter, startling him so that he would sometimes go and see if someone had come in without him knowing. He recalls then, how in late after-noon the sunlight retreated from the land out back, the wind-sculpted snowdrifts looking like waves on a sea. That's when the doe and her yearling would emerge from the scrub bush, like faint beige brush strokes as they minced along the deep ruts worn through heavy snow and down into the ditch beside the road where they would be sheltered from the wind. Minus thirty without the wind chill, while inside the Happy Traveler the heaters hummed and surged.

When Joe comes down the steps of the Meridian the next morning on his way to Canadian Tire, the traffic on Albert Street is already heavy, a steady one-way flow toward the city centre. Although the sky is overcast, he squints against the brightness of daylight, shivers as he tugs the cords on his hoodie to draw it snug against his neck. He goes round the front of the Meridian, its broad windshield running with moisture, and then down along its side, startling several gulls into flight. He inspects the motorhome for deflated tires, scratches, the chalky spatter of bird feces. Should there be any damage he has no recourse, and so he practises vigilance, hoping it is enough to ward off an attack.

He looks up to see if the pot of greenery has appeared on the third-floor balcony of an apartment building across Gibson Road. Last night when he went to pick up the pizza, the plant was gone. Whoever puts it out in the morning gets up early. A woman, he thinks. Hell of a struggle, given that it's the size of a small tree. Maybe she came out onto the balcony in a terry robe. He thinks of Laurie sprawled across the bed, her breasts a surprise of white in contrast to the deep tan of her body; the welcome in Maryanne Lewis's voice.

Here and there cars are parked on the lot, belonging to employees, he guesses, and beyond Walmart at the entrance of Sunrise Mall, he sees the blocky figure—mall security—standing just inside the doors waiting to check the employees through as they arrive. The windows of Walmart and the shopping mall are like mirrors and conceal what he imagines goes on before opening, the quiet scurry of employees rearranging the merchandise to create the impression that every day is the first day of business, as others keep their eyes fixed on computer screens placing orders and checking inventory.

He runs his hand along the side of the Meridian as though it's a horse, thinking that he'd like to be able to say he left it in the same condition as when he stole it. Except, of course, for the mileage. He squats and peers into the wheel well, reassures himself that he has some time before the receiver takes an inventory of his defunct business and discovers that the Meridian is gone. When he hears Laurie moving about in the motorhome he rises from his squat.

He crosses the short distance between the parking lot and the sidewalk beyond it, and then Gibson Road, empty of traffic at this time of day. The lights flash amber in all directions, as they will until the shopping mall opens in an hour, and again in the evening after it closes.

Several blocks beyond the traffic lights, Gibson Road comes to an end in country where the Trans-Canada Highway curves west past the airport and rises through a gentle ridge of smoke-blue hills. After they fled Winnipeg, Joe at first stayed clear of the highway. He took a longer route through a winding valley, under a sky that looked heavy and threatened rain. But when the fuel gauge hit the halfway mark and began sinking rapidly, he joined up with the Trans-Canada, where he was more likely to find diesel.

He reaches the parking lot at Boston Pizza, thinking that the air smells like high altitude, like the mountains, clean and thin. *Are you heading this way?* If he left now he could be in the Rockies within a day and a half.

"Joe," Laurie calls, and he turns to see her, her robe a flash of purple satin as she tiptoes alongside the motorhome and over to the sidewalk where she stops, crimps the robe closed at her neck and holds out a paper bag. His lunch, the sandwiches she made last night. *One loaf of bread: $2.35, Ham: $3.49*, she entered in the notebook she had bought at Walmart the day they arrived. *Walnut Crest, $11.95*, Laurie jotted in the notebook, giving herself a pat on the back for not having bought a more expensive Australian shiraz.

As he retraces his steps he sees that her lips are stained with the wine she drank while watching *24* last night, the *kachunk kachunk* soundtrack accentuating the quickness of their pulses. Joe sat at the dinette, the remains of the pizza and bottle of wine on the table before him. Laurie curled up on the lounger, rising now and again to top up her glass, the scent of Wish, her perfume, lingering. She came across it years ago in a duty-free. She likes the bottle, a heavy piece of glass shaped like a diamond. Wish, a state of desire. A wish for something more, for a happy ending.

He takes the bag from Laurie without speaking or meeting her eyes, but he notices that she's come after him without stopping to put on shoes and that her toes are scrunched up against the cold.

"You're going to freeze, you'd better get inside," he says, without the usual undertow of anger.

"Should I come down and meet you later?" Her green eyes roam across Joe's face in a fruitless search for warmth.

"Do whatever you want," he says.

He sees her lips come together and stretch across her face in a prelude to crying. He suddenly wants her heat. His need to move beyond the ache in his body causes him to reach out and haul her in against himself, wrapping his arms around her.

"Joe," she says, caught by surprise, then she slumps into him, her knees giving way in relief.

He scoops her up into his arms and as he carries her to the door of the Meridian, sunlight breaks through the wind-driven stratus clouds. The wet parking lot shines, gulls call out as they wheel across the clearing sky. The apartment blocks along Gibson Road look as though they've just been freshly coloured in with white chalk.

Laurie sees a woman standing at a balcony railing, her long beige tunic and dark head covering blowing sideways in a brief tide of wind. Joe sets her down at the foot of the steps and moves his hands to her buttocks, urges her to hurry up and get inside.

They fall together on the bed. The long spell of silence between them has made them hungry for each other. Just so much has happened to them, and in such a short time. It's as though a pyramid has come crumbling down around them and they're buried, hardly breathing, and unable to think how they might begin to dig themselves out. Joe on top of Laurie, as he wriggles free of his jeans, and then Laurie on top of Joe, struggling to undo the buttons on his shirt, feeling the thickness of his penis against her stomach. Again they roll, Laurie beneath him now. She takes his face between her hands and says, "Hello."

Hello, hello, Laurie thinks, as Joe moves inside her, her nose turning red, as it always does when she cries.

Moments later they lie side by side, their bodies slick with perspiration. Laurie begins to feel the chill, like a hand sweeping across her. She turns to Joe and rests her head on his shoulder, listens to the large thump of his heart. Yes. Thick dark curls hug the nape of his tanned neck, intermingled with a mat of white wiry frizz that creeps up the back and sides of it. Sometimes when he was between haircuts she had shaved the frizz off with his razor and scattered it across the yard, thinking the birds would gather it for their nests.

She thinks to tell him that in the mall Winners has a sign advertising for help and that she wants to apply, although she knows that he'll object, that they aren't going to be in Regina longer than several more days. And what does she know about retail sales? Nothing. But she believes that a life spent being a consumer is qualification enough. There are also signs posted for waiters and kitchen help at Kelsey's and Montana's, and for part-time ticket sellers at the Galaxy Theatre.

She needs to find ways to spend the day, other than going from store to store in the mall, passing time in the food court nibbling on biscotti and sipping burnt coffee, imagining the lives of the people congregating at the tables as though they're one large gregarious family. She watches the security men, most of them oversized and red-faced, their bodies thick as greasy sausages stuffed into their navy polyester uniforms. They lounge about the security office door, or stroll through the food court ogling the half-dressed schoolgirls shoplifting at the Dollardrama. She silently vows not to spend a nickel more than what's necessary.

Joe sighs so deeply Laurie feels the shudder in the mattress. When she went to meet him last night at Canadian Tire, she didn't recognize him for a moment. He was still the same, tall, yes, lean and well-muscled, but his arms hung at his sides while he listened to the man talk. Pete, a Métis, Joe had said, who never shut up. What made Joe stand out among others were his eyes, as brilliant a blue as she'd ever seen. With the light in his eyes gone, he looked ordinary.

Joe lies on his back, head propped in his arms. He'll need to call Steve soon. Let him know that they are headed his way, and why. Men older than Joe have been hired on in the tar sands. He's heard the stories, seen the news, the Newfies, fishermen, packing up and driving thousands of miles, six beefy guys crammed into a Honda Civic, their gear strapped on top. Kids and wife bawling on the doorstep. *We're just going to have to learn to do without him. He'll come back with enough money to see us through for years.* A young single man vowed not to return until he chalked up a million. Six guys living in a one-bedroom apartment in Fort McMurray, taking turns cooking and sleeping in the bed. He bets those fishermen don't have any more qualifications than he does. He has some welding. He and several of his buddies once restored an old Chevy from the frame up and he took a welding course at Red River College to do it. It might be enough to get him hired. What he'll make at Canadian Tire added to the credit remaining on their one card will pay for the fuel, with enough left over to see them through to a first paycheque. All he wants from Steve are his contacts, nothing more.

A vehicle drives past the motorhome and stops nearby. Its doors open, and then slam shut. The murmur of voices seems dreamlike and far away. What I would like to do, a woman says, but the remainder of her words are lost. A man laughs in response, which brings Laurie to the surface. She recognizes the high-pitched cackle of the white-haired greeter at Walmart, a man who looks to be in his late sixties.

"Welcome to Walmart," she says. "I think that's the man who greets people at the door. He looks like he's past retirement age." Though he's elastic in the way he can dip sideways, bend backwards to try and peer into her tote bag.

"He likely is. They'll hire anyone," Joe says.

She wants to tell him that she was awakened by the cell-phone this morning. Maryanne Lewis, her voice as sugary and bright as a jar of jelly beans. How was Laurie doing? Fine. *How's Joe this morning? When he called us last night he sounded pretty down. Ken and I just know that something good is going to happen for Joe. Will you tell him to get in touch?* I'll tell him, Laurie promised, but when she saw Joe had left the sandwiches on the dinette she went tearing after him and forgot to relay the message. Something good is going to happen for Joe. Which means either he'll find a million dollars lying in the gutter, or he'll find twenty-five cents. Or he will find nothing. That too could mean something good has happened.

Joe becomes aware of the heavy scent of Laurie's hair. When she met him at work last night, she looked different, her usual strawberry blonde hair was the colour of a new penny. Her hand lies across his chest and the sight of the moisturized sheen of her tanned skin, the perfect white crescents of her French polish are an irritation itching at the base of his skull. Throughout the past winter, these early months of spring, while he's been locked in his racing thoughts, she's been able to think of things other than the end of life as they've known it. He pushes away from her, up and off the bed, and goes into the bathroom.

Laurie hears water running, Joe scooping it up from the sink and splashing it into his face, his underarms, his scro-tum. They are not to use any more water than necessary, no showers. As if she wants to, given there's no hot water. She had to use the microwave to heat water to rinse away the hair colour, the shampoo.

Don't think, she tells herself.

Don't think about Joe setting the big screen television down against the garage wall and ramming into it with the Explorer. Smashing with the sledgehammer the things that failed to sell on eBay, or in the *Bargain Hunter.* He would rather smash them than let her put them in the garage sale where they'd sell for such a small fraction of what he'd paid for them. There's my profit, Joe said, only a small fraction of what he was thinking, she knows. *What shall it profit a man, if he shall gain the whole world, and lose his own soul?* She'd seen that line of scripture highlighted in his Holy Horoscope, her name for the book of daily meditations he used to keep on the bedside table, its pages loose and its cover gone soft like a chamois.

He gestured to the appliances on the parking pad, the Cuisinart Power Prep and her Chi Vitalizer machine, the Bose sound system she'd just bought for the kitchen, the espresso maker and crushed ice drink maker she'd hunted down and found on sale at Home Outfitters, the small appliances lined up there on the parking pad, shining and wet from a light rain, looking as though they'd just been taken from their boxes.

She'd gone into the basement and covered her ears to shut out the noise as Joe smashed the appliances to smithereens. She sat on the floor, back against the stone wall, consumed by guilt and not knowing why. Joe could have waited until night, but the smashing would have brought lights on in the neighbourhood, the houses on either side of them being so close that sometimes they'd hear quarrels, music played too loudly, a hoarse cry in the night. In those final weeks she'd hardly seen anyone though. It was like they knew the Happy Traveler was no longer in business and were avoiding them, fearing that what they were going through might be contagious. But of course, the neighbourhood came out in droves to their garage sale, cockroaches swarming over the leftovers of a feast. We're moving to the new Waverly subdivision to be closer to the business, Laurie had thought to say should anyone ask, but no one did.

Joe enters the bedroom, his nakedness shielded by the wastebasket. "I sure as hell hope this isn't what it looks like," he says, the words compacted between his teeth.

She realizes her mistake. The price tags and sales slips should have been tucked down into the garbage out of sight. Through the years she'd learned to bury them beneath vegetable peelings in the can under the kitchen sink. When rushed she'd sometimes stuck them into potted plants, or under the mattress in a hotel room.

He upends the wastebasket and a shower of garbage drops onto the bed, the tags, the tiny plastic envelopes containing spare buttons and loops of thread, the flattened packaging from the skin care products and cosmetics, the crumple of tissue that had been wrapped around the purple robe. The gloves she wore while colouring her hair are stuck together, the latex mass smeared with what looks like dried blood. They give off an acrid odour that quickly permeates the air between them. She winces as he flings the wastebasket aside and plucks up several of the tags.

"Did you record these in the notebook too?"

His voice is unbearably caustic. Only moments earlier she'd embraced the full weight of him, borne his collapse. She still holds his semen. She wants to point out that she coloured her hair herself instead of going to a salon, but remains silent. "I'll need to look half decent when I start job hunting," she finally says.

"Job hunting in that." He indicates the purple robe lying on the floor at the foot of the bed.

"I've had that for years," she lies.

Laurie had also bought a black linen sundress printed with large green ferns. When she tried it on she imagined wearing it on a summer night. The three of them, Steve, Joe and herself, seated on a café patio overlooking a busy downtown street. Buying the dress was insurance that there would be better times ahead for her and Joe. And when she saw herself in it, she remembered, too, the way Steve used to look at her.

"Dammit, Laurie. Where's your head? We've got to get to McMurray first." He gathers his clothing from the floor, dresses quickly, snatches up the cellphone from the dinette table and is gone.

Two

"HEY, DAD. IT'S ME," Joe says. Alfred, gripped by coughing, puts the receiver down. A moment later a young woman speaks into the phone.

"Mr. Beaudry? Your father will be just a minute."

I'll call back, Joe intends to say, but she's already gone. He walks along the lane beside Boston Pizza, waiting for his father to come back on the line, skirting crumbling potholes iridescent with oily water. From a nearby tree a bird calls its name, chick-a-dee-dee-dee buzzing through the rumble of traffic on Albert Street. Joe spots the bird, wondering why something that small needs such a large voice. At the side door of Boston Pizza, two men and a woman in white caps and aprons huddle under a canopy having a smoke.

He takes in the greasy-looking ponytail of one of the men, his arms covered in tattoos; the startled slack-jawed look of the other, a kid really, his thin face riddled with acne; the woman, overweight and half asleep. He wouldn't have hired them, not even to sweep snow from the roofs of vehicles, hose away the grit in summer that could corrode paint, and sometimes split open the skin on his hands.

He senses their growing and calculating interest in him and stifles a sudden paranoia. Likely they saw him leave the Meridian and are noting his leather bomber jacket, looking for the bulge of his wallet in his hip pocket.

In his ear he hears the young woman gently scolding Alfred, and his anxiety shifts to his father's cough, which sounds rough, and then he worries that the time on the cell will expire before they'll be able to talk.

The lane grows wider as he walks, becomes more of a service road that provides access to the parking lots of the businesses along Albert Street. On one side there are the backs of commercial enterprises, identical square buildings painted stark white, and on the other, brown brick apartments, their wide predictable balconies looking like yawns. The clearing sky is criss-crossed with a grid of wires, the lane opening up in the distance to a street, and a fringe of trees beyond it in a residential neighbourhood. The Lakeside District, Pete, the Métis he works with, had said. But what's called Wascana Lake is only a man-made pond, and is nowhere near enough for the inhabitants of the Lakeside District to see. Or to smell either, a good thing, Pete said. Algae, goose poop, sometimes so thick you can walk across it. His grin revealed the gaping space in the front of his top teeth.

When Joe enters the parking lot at Canadian Tire Pete is slouched in a lawn chair beside his small truck, legs splayed, the bill of his cap pulled low. He's been watching for him, Joe guesses, and notes the gate to the garden centre is closed. Something is up. At that moment Alfred comes back on the line and Joe stops, turns away from the noise of traffic and hears Alfred ask, "Is it raining there?" Meaning, where is Joe?

Their house on Arlington Street is walking distance from Deere Lodge and so, for a short time, they'd shared the common bond of the weather and the traffic along Portage Avenue.

"No, it's not raining, but it sure looks like it wants to," Joe says, having to speak loudly to make himself heard.

"I don't understand that. It's pouring here. It has been for hours," Alfred says, annoyed. "It was five o'clock this morning when I went to the bathroom. It was raining then, and it still is." When Joe doesn't reply, his father's voice softens. "If this keeps up, don't come today. More than likely the underpass will be flooded."

Joe takes a deep breath. "But, Dad, you know I'm away right now. Laurie and me? I told you that. We'll be back at the end of the month. I won't see you until then." He winces inwardly as he recalls the way Laurie and he had to struggle to get Alfred across the lobby at Deere Lodge, his suitcase falling open, the hollow clatter of the tea-stained dentures tumbling from the plastic bag and skittering across the floor. Alfred's spares, the several pairs of dentures he'd hung on to throughout the years in fear something might happen to the current ones. The sight of them had taken the wind from Alfred's sails, jolted him from his tantrum and sent Joe to his knees. He'd gathered them up, vowing to himself, and later to Alfred, that his stay at Deere Lodge was only temporary.

"That's right, you told me," Alfred says, his voice thinning to squeeze back another paroxysm of coughing, and failing. "I'm here," he says a moment later.

"That cough of yours sounds pretty serious."

"You'll be back when?" Alfred asks.

"The end of May, first week in June at the latest," Joe says above the sudden blare of a car horn, the screech of brakes. He looks up to see the near rear-end accident at the intersection beyond. Antsy, he thinks. Everyone's antsy this morning, including him, to finish talking, to get on with what he needs to do next. Call Steve. Get to McMurray and find some work, fast.

"I'll get the girl to write that down," Alfred says and calls to the woman attending him.

"Not now," Joe interrupts.

"What?"

"I've got to go now, Dad. I'll call later on in the day."

"When?"

"Later."

"It's the girl here, wants to know what time. They've tried reaching you at the house and the shop, and both of the phones are down."

"I gave them this number," Joe says, exasperated. "I told them to call me on my cell."

"You're not exactly answering that phone either," Alfred says. "Where's Laurie?"

"She's here with me. Why?"

"She wasn't there yesterday. Clayton Wells went by the house looking for you and no one was home."

Joe's mind reels with confusion for a moment. "That's because we're travelling right now. I just told you that. Of

course Laurie wasn't at home, she's here with me, Dad."
Why was Clayton Wells at the house? he wonders. *Was* he
at the house, or is Alfred confused?

"Well, put her on then," Alfred says. "I want to have a
word with her. She should stop sending flowers. I'd do
better with a shot of brandy now and then, and the chance
to see her ugly puss."

"I can't put her on. She's up in the hotel room. I came
down to get some breakfast," Joe lies.

"You've been gone four days, you must be in BC by
now," Alfred says. His moment of lucidity is unsettling.

"Why did Clayton go to the house?" Joe asks.

"He says you still owe him a couple of months' wages."
Alfred's voice is clear and strong. "He came round yester-
day looking for you. I said I didn't know where you were.
And I don't know why the damned phones aren't working
either. He's a good man, Joe, you can't afford to lose him.
What the heck is going on?"

Nothing, Joe thinks. He'd paid Clayton as much as he
could, a good chunk of the garage sale cash went to him
when he came begging, his three kids hanging out the
car windows wanting to give Uncle Joe a hug. Crafty son
of a bitch. His face grows hot and he loosens the neck of
his hoodie, welcomes the shock of cold air at his throat.
It's easier to start a business than it is to stop one. It's a
voracious machine that needs to be constantly fed. People
become dependent on you for their mortgage and car
payments, their kids' hockey careers, their ex-wives' support; their various habits. What comes out at the end is
such a small turd for the number of hours, the amount
of effort, the uncertainty. The only people who profit

from a small business are lawyers, accountants and lending institutions.

"I've got to go," Joe says.

"Yes, this must be costing money."

"I'll call around eight tonight," Joe promises. He's seen a Shoppers drugstore nearby. He will buy more time for the cell there.

"The girl is going to take me down to X-ray now," Alfred says.

"X-ray? What for? Let me talk to her, will you?"

There's a muffled riff of sound, and then the woman says, "Mr. Beaudry?"

"What's this about my father needing an X-ray?"

"A chest X-ray. The doctor ordered one. Your father has a bit of a temperature. When you call this evening, would you please call through the desk? The supervisor will be there. She'd like to talk to you."

"Your chest?" Joe says when Alfred comes back on the telephone.

"Yah. Smoke eighty-some years, what else could it be?"

"You should have said something sooner about wanting brandy, Dad. I'd have brought you some."

"I didn't want it sooner."

He'll get in touch with the liquor store in Osborne Village, they'll deliver. There's still enough room on the one credit card to make that happen.

"Let me see what I can do," Joe says.

"Good. I'll have a shot of it before going to bed, maybe it'll warm me up."

"Talk to you later, Dad," Joe says.

He's barely pocketed the cell when Pete is at his side.

"We're not working today. Probably we won't get any more hours."

"You saw the boss?" Joe scans the parking lot for the man's SUV.

"He's not in yet. That's how come I know. He'd be here if we was to work. After you left last night the university kids came by. They're done writing exams. It's supposed to warm up this week, and as soon as it does, the boss will hire his son and his pals. Same as last year." He grins, reaming the space where his front teeth should be with the tip of his tongue.

The windows across the front of the store reflect the sky, Pete's truck, which looks cumbersome and top-heavy with its unpainted plywood cabana, the solitary lawn chair set beside it, Joe and Pete. Joe is a head taller, and near to ten years older, but he looks younger. He can't see into the store to know whether or not the lights are on at the customer service desk.

"What do you say I buy you a coffee?" Pete says.

Joe concentrates on Pete's forehead to avoid looking at the wet space between his teeth. He doesn't particularly want to spend time with Pete, but going for a coffee will delay his return to the Meridian and the decision about what to do next.

"You're on," he says.

He waits as Pete folds up the lawn chair, unlocks the aluminum door on the cabana and tosses the chair onto what appears to be a narrow cot covered in a red blanket. He shuts the door quickly but not before Joe has seen an assortment of tools hung on the walls on either side of the small window above the cot. "Home sweet home," Pete says with an apologetic grin.

"You live in that?"

"Sometimes." Pete turns away toward Albert Street and Joe notices for the first time his bowlegged gait. His jeans are too long and his heels have worn holes through the backs of both pant legs. Joe catches up to him and together they wait on the boulevard for a break in the traffic.

Pete casts him a sideways glance that takes him in from head to foot. "Where're you from?"

"Winnipeg," Joe says with reluctance, knowing that he's opened the door to the questions Pete's been burning to ask.

"So, you're visiting, or what?"

"Visiting," Joe replies and waits for the next question. Why would a person in his situation be working as casual labour? But Pete remains silent as they cross the street and approach Robin's Donuts. Two women shiver with cold as they perch on the edges of wrought-iron chairs on either side of the door, smoking cigarettes.

"Don't you say a thing," one of the women warns Pete with mock severity, her eyes hidden behind white-framed sunglasses, her mouth a wilted pucker of rose.

"Don't need to," Pete says and smiles at her. "Amanda here is trying for a Guinness World Record for the number of times a person has tried to quit," he tells Joe.

The smell of coffee and the din of male voices in Robin's Donuts are familiar. Men of all ages are crammed thigh to thigh around the small square tables, just as they would be in Pauline's diner at this time of the day. As Joe makes his way to the back of the room several of them give him the once-over before returning to their newspapers and laptops, their heated opinions about what they'd like to do to a pedophile who has abducted a young boy at a bus depot in Brandon, Manitoba, and is reported to be heading west.

Joe finds a table near the rear of the coffee shop, adjacent to a window, while Pete takes his place in the lineup at the counter. Where once he would have faced the early morning crowd, Joe chooses to turn his back to it, staring at the window, opaque with mist, obliterating sight of the strip mall beyond. A chest X-ray, he thinks. He looks down at his hands spread across the table, fingers stiff and the knuckles enlarged and scuffed from the recent marathon of getting rid of what amounted to fifty-one years of his and his father's life. He imagines Alfred's hands, his father's fingers shiny with slime as he tears the entrails from a fish. *Look here, Joe, our supper.* Joe smells kerosene and wood smoke, the time of the yellow canoe.

Pete makes his way slowly among the tables, his eyes fixed on the tray he carries, intent on not spilling the coffees. He unloads the brimming mugs and two bagels with exaggerated efficiency. "At your service."

"Hey, what's this?" Joe asks and indicates the bagel, the container of cream cheese tucked in beside it on the plate.

"You don't eat bagels?" Pete looks worried.

"Sure, but you said just coffee. Thanks, buddy."

"The tip's not included." Pete grins. The gum between his missing teeth is purplish and swollen. Joe busies himself with the sugar and cream.

Pete takes a wad of papers from his chest pocket, unfolds them carefully and smooths them flat against the table. "Take a look," he says and slides them across the table to Joe.

On the top page are drawings of boxes of various shapes and sizes, dimensions neatly noted. On the next page, there's a drawing of a garden arbour inset with a bench, and again, all the measurements are noted. In shaded block printing at the bottom are the words, "Designed by Peter Lavallee." The final page proves to be a hand-printed list of building materials and the cost of each item.

"I made a grape arbour for a lady last year and the word got out. So far I've got orders for three more and half a dozen planters," Pete says. "Over there, in Lakeside," he says and nods in the right direction.

"You can actually make these things cheaper than the Chinese?"

"Better, not cheaper. And I make them to order, whatever size they want," Pete says. "One lady took me down the street to look at an arbour in someone's yard, told me she wants this and that different, higher, wider. Mine are stronger, too. And don't cost much more than what you see at the garden places." Pete's voice is strong with conviction.

"Looks like you've got your work cut out for you." Joe slides the papers back across the table to him.

"That's what I wanted to talk to you about. You and me, we could put this order together inside two days."

"Me?" Joe says.

"Yah. I seen you work."

"Oh, god, no. I'm not going to be here long enough."

"I'd go halfers with you on the profit. You'll make a couple of hundred bucks. That should be worth anyone's time to stick around."

Pete said *you'll make a couple of hundred bucks*, the same way more polished men might have said, *a couple of hundred thousand. A couple of million.* Among the men who had the time to frequent a place like this, there weren't any who would not have relished being able to say *a couple of hundred thousand.* The men around him were likely grease monkeys from lube joints, mechanics, farmers, grocery store clerks, or at most, managers.

"Why give away half the profit when you can have it all?" he asks Pete. He notices that a large man sitting at a nearby table is taking an interest in their conversation.

Pete dumps sugar in his coffee, stirs, empties several containers of cream into it, again stirs, while his eyes flit nervously about the room. "I only got my dad's garage for two days," he says finally. "That's where I build them. I can't do it by myself in just two days. And I got deposits for the orders, but only about half of what I need to buy all the supplies."

"And you'd want me to put in the other half? I don't think so."

"Look, I only do cash," Pete says quickly. "You could come with me when I deliver. I use a trailer, and I'll need help loading and unloading. Them things are heavy as hell. Everyone pays cash, that's the deal. I'll pay you out right on the spot. We work two days and deliver them one night, and it's over."

When he sees Joe is not convinced, he says, "I can take you around, show you some of the things I've built."

"Go for it, Pete," the overweight man at the nearby table says *sotto voce*, and then to Joe, sending him a look, "You should go and see what he can do."

An unlikely shill, Joe thinks and nods to Pete as he gets up to leave. As he heads for the door he sees movement in the mirror behind the counter—himself. Not the trim and broad-shouldered person he knows himself to be, in a Tommy Hilfiger polo shirt and chino pants, what he'd come to think of as being his uniform. He sees an unkempt man whose features are dark and puffy from lack of sleep. His black leather jacket makes him look defensive and stiff. A loser, he thinks with some chagrin, and then a couple of hundred bucks would help to get him to McMurray. It's a quicker means to an end than slogging away for hours on the minimum.

"Hey, you going to show me, or not?" he calls to Pete over his shoulder.

Pete leaps from his chair and is halfway to the door when he stops short, returns to the table, wraps serviettes around the bagels and stuffs them into the side pockets of his vest.

Moments later they're driving along a wide street lined with elm trees whose branches are a lime-green canopy above them. Near the end of a block Pete pulls in close to the curb and nods, "That, there." He inches the truck forward so Joe can look over a fence and into the side yard of a stately looking buff stone house towering over a corner lot. Its striped green awnings are down, shading windows, and anyone who might be at a window watching. A beat-up truck like this, two scruffy guys casing the neighbourhood—he'd call the police.

Pete points at an octagonal cedar gazebo in the yard. "I built that. And the fence. The fence darn near took me all of one summer. Because of the trees, I had to do most of the postholes by hand."

As they turn at the corner and move down the side street

Joe whistles at the length and height of the cedar fence. The gate is a full-size wooden door with narrow glass panels through which he can see the turned-up garden beyond. At various intervals and heights along the side of the fence, squares have been cut into the boards and framed.

"What are the holes for?" he asks.

"The dog," Pete says and chuckles. "So the dog can see what's going by. That was my idea."

"That must have set them back a few bucks," Joe says, thinking of the cost of the modest fence he hired a company to build along the back of the house on Arlington Street.

"It didn't cost them anything but the lumber," Pete says. "That's my dad's place."

Within moments they're back on Albert Street and going past Canadian Tire. There are several vehicles parked on the lot now, the manager's black SUV in its usual spot. Joe thinks to say they should stop and see what's up, but Pete revs the engine and they lumber through the green light at the intersection, the small truck swaying precariously beneath the weight of the cabana as they gradually gain speed, their destination the ring road at the end of Albert Street that leads to the Trans-Canada Highway and a Home Depot store.

As they pass the Sunrise Mall, Joe sees Laurie looking tall and fit in a beige and brown sweatsuit, her coppery froth of hair gathered on top of her head and bobbing with her energetic stride. She has his bag lunch in her hand and he concludes that she's heading for Canadian Tire to bring it to him.

"As far as my old man goes, I can't do anything right." Pete has been going on about his father ever since they left the Lakeside District. "He's been on my case my whole life."

She's marking time, Joe thinks, waiting for this to blow over, as though what's happened to them is only temporary and not a life sentence. He thinks to tell Pete to pull over so he can let her know where he's going.

"How do you think I lost my teeth?" Pete asks.

"What?"

"My teeth. How do you think I lost them? My old man, that's how. He winds up and plows me one. I was eighteen years old, right? He still thinks he can push me around. Chips my teeth. I showed him. I took the money he gave me to get them fixed and had the dentist yank them out. He's never laid a hand on me since."

Joe watches in the side mirror as Laurie and the city fall away behind him.

There's a pay phone near a row of shopping carts just inside the door to Home Depot, and when Pete heads into the store, Joe calls out that he will catch up with him.

He pecks out the information number for Manitoba, asks for the liquor store, then clenches the receiver under his chin while he fishes for change in his pocket and pools it on the metal shelf below the phone. He wants to reserve what time is left on his cell in case Alfred calls after the X-ray, in the event that he's unable to buy more time before calling Deere Lodge in the evening.

The phone rings as he looks out across the parking lot through the tinted windows, the sky darker than it really is, the sun a splotch of putty behind the clouds. He thinks of the brutality of Pete's father. He's heard similar stories, knows how lucky he's been.

When a clerk answers the telephone, Joe tells him what he wants and where to send it and then gives him his credit card information.

A moment later the clerk says, "It looks as though you've exceeded your limit. Do you want to use another card?"

Laurie, Joe thinks. The clothes, the hair, the flowers. Laurie, Laurie, Laurie.

Pete stands just inside the Home Depot waiting for Joe, hands on his hips. You idiot, Joe says, and when he slams the receiver into its cradle it falls out and dangles round his knees. Again he slams it into place, and again it falls. He picks it up and smashes it against the number panel. Idiot, he says to Pete waiting beyond the doors, to himself, to Laurie going off down the street.

Three

Laurie can't help but be elated by the growing brightness of the morning, the way Albert Street, wet with melted frost, mirrors the traffic, and daylight convulses like a heartbeat between the passing vehicles. Yes, she says to that pulsing of light, the music playing on her iPod, and the residue of Joe's angry departure vanishes.

As long as she says yes she's moving forward, bringing Joe's lunch to him, and not backward to their old house on Arlington Street, to the six months paid in advance at Curves, to her little blue Zoom Zoom hanging off the back of a tow truck. She isn't without hope as she imagines that somehow, in the near future, their life will continue to be, more or less, what it's been for the past eighteen years. She's not someone who wants much, she only wants enough. Enough not to have to worry, or think twice before spending money. Enough.

Across Albert Street the buildings lined up in a row leap forward in their wet vividness, colours vibrant and primary like plastic pieces on a Monopoly board. The jittery movement of light, the gleaming sprawling city, are a backdrop to Van Morrison playing on her iPod, achy, melancholy, as though he's underground and calling out to be rescued from his past.

She thinks of Van Morrison, a small man in a grey fedora emerging from the dark at the back of the stage into the spotlight at the concert she and Joe had attended only weeks ago. How he became a large man the instant he opened his mouth and sang. The air was thick with the smell of weed and musk, and she remembers Joe's arm touching hers, his thigh, his body humming. I'm seeding the economy, maybe we'll get a return, she'd joked when Joe had voiced concern over the expense of the tickets. She felt vindicated when he gave himself over to the music.

Lost now in the soundtrack in her head, she sees herself and Joe going arm in arm along the street after the concert as though they aren't hanging on by their fingernails to a life that's made them thick around the middle, as though they aren't down to their last real dollar. Morrison's songs seem to begin midstream and go on in a way that suggests they may never end. But of course every song has an end, and the concert ended as abruptly as it began, only this time with Van Morrison exiting into the dark at the back of the stage while the band played on. What a way to go, Joe says, as though Morrison has died and not just left the building. A bloody feast, Joe says, struggling to describe the effect of the music on him.

Two children on bicycles sweep past her and she pulls out the ear buds to let the brisk little city inside. In bringing Joe's lunch to him she hopes to restore the truce that bound them for moments earlier in the morning. *Did you write these down in the book too?* After she drops his lunch off at Canadian Tire she plans to continue on downtown where she'll find the bronze buffalo in an open square, and in a street near the square, the flock of stone geese. Just keep going toward the towers, the woman at the information centre in the mall had said, which this morning are a dull patina of light against the clouded grey skyline.

When she and Joe were approaching on the Trans-Canada Highway, Laurie had seen how Regina seemed to rise up from the earth as though it'd been summoned. From the highway, at sunset, the twin green glass towers are like beacons of fire and during the day like columns of lead crystal. She passes a strip mall featuring a cheque-cashing establishment, a tanning salon, and a pet supply store whose portable sign advertises in Day-Glo letters a sale of authentic Saskatchewan homemade dog biscuits. In another strip mall the Western Baptist Union office shares one wall with a pizza takeout and the other with Oral Arts, which proves to be a denture clinic. Beside the clinic there's a tobacco and pipe store.

There doesn't seem to be any rhyme or reason for the variety of services being offered in such close proximity to one another, although she allows that pipe smokers are usually older people, as are denture wearers, and for that matter, people who might have business at the Baptist Union would be older too. Perhaps she'll find more than the usual farther down Albert Street, beyond the man-made lake, downtown among the life-size statues of the buffalo and the stone geese.

When she enters the parking lot at Canadian Tire she

sees the manager unlocking the gate to the garden centre.

"Where's Joe?" she asks.

"You tell me," the manager replies.

"He hasn't come in?" In all the years they've been married, any unforeseen absences on Joe's part have always been benign. Her friends have envied her Joe's steadiness, his thoughtfulness. Until recently, nothing about Joe has given her cause for alarm.

The manager takes in Laurie's expression and offers her a crumb. "I was late getting in this morning, so maybe he was here and left. Could be he's across the street at Robin's. I'll bet you a donut Pete's there too. If they are, why don't you tell them it's time to get shaking and baking."

"Will do," Laurie says.

She waits for a break in the traffic then jogs across Albert Street. The door to Robin's swings closed behind her and she knows instantly Joe isn't among the people lingering over coffee.

"I'll bet you're looking for someone," a huge man calls out from a table near the back of the room, peering in her direction overtop his glasses. In comparison to his body, his face looks inordinately childlike. "Dark hair, about six feet tall, a good-looking fella? He's wearing a black leather jacket with a crest on the back. Wildcats. Right?"

Honing his skills for Crime Stoppers. "That'll be him," Laurie says.

"He and Pete just left," the thin-faced woman behind the counter calls out, her sharp nose made even sharper by the visor she wears.

"About fifteen, twenty minutes ago," the other waitress chimes in.

"Less than that," the thin-faced woman corrects.

"Well, pardon me. I'm just the one wearing the watch," the waitress says, and resumes unloading a tray of donuts onto the rack of shelves.

The thin-faced woman grins at Laurie and jerks her head in the direction of the other woman. "PMS. Watch what you say. Cheri, here, keeps a chainsaw in the back."

"Ever funny," the other waitress says.

"They went to look at a job," the fat man calls out.

"Pete's always got some scheme going," the thin-faced woman says with what sounds like exasperated affection.

"Did they say where?" Laurie asks.

"Nope," the man says.

"He's my husband. Joe," Laurie says, sensing that he wants something from her before he'll give her more.

He takes a large handkerchief from his pocket and wipes perspiration from his face before stuffing it back, the entire production striking her as a means to keep her waiting. "This place is Pete's office. If I know him, he'll be back sooner or later. You want me to tell your husband you're looking for him?" he asks.

"If you don't mind, just tell him I was here."

Laurie leaves the donut shop feeling optimistic, and drops the rather soggy bag of sandwiches into the trash can at the side of the door. Joe wouldn't have gone with Pete if he wasn't on to something more lucrative than Canadian Tire. She takes in the Help Wanted sign taped to the window. Judging from the faded look of it, it's been posted for a while. Everywhere she goes in this city, there seems to be Help Wanted notices. Opportunities.

She hesitates, debates whether to return to the Meridian

in the event Joe might stop by. On the boulevard, a row of newly planted trees are tethered to the ground as though to prevent them from flying away, the spindly branches knobby and greening with unfolding buds.

She'll still go downtown, she decides, go and see the buffalo beside the glass towers. And near the towers is a park and a coffee shop, a place called Roca Jack's where the coffee is just as complicated but cheaper than Starbucks, the woman at the information centre said, a woman who seemed to take a single question as an opportunity to start up a lifelong friendship.

Within moments she comes upon yet another strip mall and beside it, a store whose windows are filled with several mannequins. Clara's Boutique, the sign above the entrance says in flourishingly pink script. At last, something worth stopping for. She sees herself in the door as she approaches, her tall beige and brown figure, strands of bright copper hair that have pulled loose from the alligator clip being lifted and twitched about by the wind, the ring of keys swaying between her breasts. Like a house on fire, she thinks, recalling Alfred's description of her. Next to New Fashions, a smaller sign in the window informs her.

She doesn't expect to find anything of interest in a second-hand shop, but she has all day, and curiosity compels her to investigate. She's reassured by the bulging heaviness of the knotted sock in her side pocket, which holds the cache of garage sale change, her copy of Joe's credit card, the roll of bills fastened with an elastic band, a lipstick.

A brass bell tinkles as she enters the brightly lit store, and the young clerk, hanging clothing on a rack, glances up at her. The skirt of her iridescent blue dress is made of strips of fabric that sway around her legs when she moves. Like in a car wash, Laurie thinks, and notes her sixties-era yellow and blue platform shoes. She's almost certain she won't find anything here.

Several women chat among themselves over a rack of dresses; one of them exclaims loudly as she holds up a garment and the others rush over to her. "The wrong colour green for me?" she asks.

"You won't really know until you try it on," the youngest of the three women says with some authority, a small-breasted woman with narrow hips.

"Right," the woman with the dress concurs.

They're dressed in a mishmash of styles from various decades. Three generations, Laurie decides. Grandmother, a grey-haired woman wearing stylish red-framed glasses, mom holding the green dress, and her daughter, all heading to the back of the store and the corridor to the dressing rooms.

Nice. She's never had the experience of going shopping with her mother, and over the years she's vacillated between thinking she has missed something vital or nothing of consequence.

Laurie comes upon a white jean jacket, and soon after that a black linen bolero that could have been made for the sundress she'd bought the day before. She takes both garments to the three-sided mirror at the back, slips out of her sweat jacket and tries them on. The colourful and well-ordered store opens up behind her, the mannequins in the windows facing the street as though guarding the entrance.

The three women emerge from the dressing rooms, the oldest stopping to look at Laurie's reflection in the mirror.

"It's perfect," she says.

"I don't usually wear white," Laurie demurs, thinking that at least someone in this city has style. The jacket is cut in panels and trims her waist, accentuates the curve of her back.

"But that's such a warm white. You look great," the woman says and goes away to join the others.

Liar, Laurie thinks, but she keeps the jacket and the bolero over her arm as she wanders among the racks. This place is nothing like the dingy, jam-packed used clothing store she and her grandmother frequented, a sour-smelling place. The real bargains, her grandmother said, were to be found in the barrels, among a tangle of assorted items that were often torn and mismatched.

At the shoe racks she comes upon a single brocaded black flat with a rounded toe, and looks for its mate. When she finds it on a rack behind the counter, along with the mates to all the other shoes, she's surprised that a second-hand shop would need to protect itself against shoplifting. She calls to the young clerk to bring her the other shoe, and immediately the three women are interested. The clerk comes toward her, and Laurie notes the yellow silk flower pinned to her dress, the too earnest attempt to try and pull her outfit together. The three women watch as Laurie strips off her running shoes and socks and slips into the shoes. A perfect fit.

"Awesome. How did I miss those?" the daughter moans.

"You want to try them on?" Laurie asks and takes off the flats, slides them toward the young woman with her foot.

"Oh, I want these," she says after she has them on and does a short tap dance that makes them all laugh.

"They're yours," Laurie says with only a twinge of regret. She would have worn them with rolled-down white socks and a short skirt.

The door opens now and several women enter the store, one carrying a garbage bag of clothes she unpacks on the counter. The three women go over to see what she's brought, while Laurie sees the sign, REDUCED, 50 PERCENT, hanging from a rack of sweaters, and goes over to browse.

"Check this out, it just came in." The tap dancer rushes toward Laurie holding up a leopard pattern knit dress.

Holy. Shades of Maryanne Lewis, the pastor's wife. "Does it come with a matching pillbox hat? Never mind," Laurie adds with a laugh when the young woman looks puzzled.

"I'll bet it'd look great on you. Why not try it on?"

"No thanks," Laurie says too quickly and adds, "but thanks, anyway."

She continues browsing among the sweaters, remembering Maryanne Lewis in the leopard-spotted suit and pillbox hat, stationed at the church entrance greeting parishioners on one of those rare occasions when Laurie let Joe talk her into going. Maryanne in a zebra-striped sheath dress conducting the children's choir. For a time Joe kept a photograph in his meditation book as a marker. A picture of himself as a boy, holding up a Bible he'd won in a Sunday school contest. Maryanne is at his side, in a faux wolf vest and pencil skirt, plastic daisies clipped in her platinum hair, her arm about his shoulder.

That woman didn't resemble the person Joe used to go

on about, the pastor's wife who had slaved away in the church basement teaching young women to sew. While with the other hand, apparently, she baked half a dozen or so loaves of bread to send home with them. He and Pastor Ken would launder the clothes that piled up in boxes and bags on the church steps, while Maryanne ironed and patched, the clothing destined for the drawers and closets of families known to be less fortunate than most. Maryanne had gone knocking on doors for donations of rice and raisins, sardines and flannel blankets. She'd raised a tractor-trailer load of care packages that she and a committee of women assembled and shipped to World Vision for their orphanages in Vietnam; and when Saigon fell, she organized an ecumenical city-wide day of prayer for the safety of the children.

Laurie grew to dread picking up the telephone and hearing the woman's jelly bean voice. She would call to remind Joe of a church meeting, and then again, if he'd happened to miss it. *Why don't you tell her you got tangled up in my pyjamas?* Which, on the occasional Sunday morning when Laurie brought breakfast to bed, was what did happen—a leisurely, long sex-saturated morning, the clock radio turned up to cover the sounds of their lovemaking. After the Lewises left Winnipeg, the calls continued for a time, but less frequently—praise the Lord, as the pastor was forever saying—and then stopped. Their contact with Joe had been severed, or so she thought. *Something good is going to happen for Joe.* Of course, Maryanne's prediction hadn't included her.

Her cheeks are hot, her legs shaky from trying on clothes in the cramped cubicle in the corridor of cubicles, the

47

doorways hung with brightly printed curtains. The usual moans are coming from behind the curtains, the exclamations, the disconcerting heavy sighs. The tap dancer has ventured out from her refuge to preen in the three-sided mirror, and as Laurie emerges from hers the young woman looks at her as though expecting a compliment or a least an envious glance. That trim figure is not going to last long, Laurie tells her silently.

At the counter she unknots the sock and spills her loose change, feeling that in purchasing second-hand merchandise she is doing penance for what she spent the day before. She unrolls the bills and realizes that she's not going to be able to buy everything. She decides between two sweaters and sets one, and a black tulip skirt, aside.

"Well, you did good," the young clerk remarks cheerfully. "Is this the first time you've been here?"

"It's the first time I've been to Regina. My husband and I are travelling and we decided to stop here for a few days." Laurie suddenly feels the weight of her words come to rest on her shoulders.

Joe's gone. The thought is a dart flying across the room and lodging in her chest. A sudden outburst of laughter from the dressing rooms is like a rain of pebbles thrown against the window. She has just lost Joe.

"I hope you enjoy the rest of your visit," the clerk says as she pushes the large plastic bag toward her.

The bag knocks annoyingly against the side of her leg as she walks out the door, and immediately she feels chilled. It's not Joe who's gone, she reassures herself, zipping up her sweat jacket. It's Alfred she's missing. She woke up mornings still expecting to hear him moving about in his room.

Getting downtown is one thing, but getting back will be another. Her body is beginning to feel the lack of food, the early morning workout in bed, the walk. Pointless, she thinks, when she comes upon yet another strip mall that houses an insurance broker, a hearing aid store, and a florist. Within moments she's inside and ordering flowers to be sent to Deere Lodge. And then she's outside, her thoughts churning as she wonders how to go about telling Joe that the last of their credit is gone. *Laurie, you are such a fool,* she tells herself. Then she squares her broad shoulders and retraces her steps to Clara's Boutique.

The women in the store are startled by her abrupt entrance, her grim impatience as she waits for the clerk to be finished with the woman in front of her.

"I want to return what I've just bought." Laurie plunks the bag on the counter, as though the clerk is somehow responsible for her impulses.

"You've read our return policy?" the clerk replies carefully. She gestures to a sign on the wall behind the counter. "We don't refund cash, but we'll be happy to give you a credit. You have six months to spend it on anything in the store."

"I'm not from here, and so I won't have a chance to use the credit. Couldn't you take that into consideration?" Laurie feels the women listening.

"I'm sorry, I can't make an exception," the young clerk says.

"Pardon me for asking." Laurie turns away, and when she wrenches open the door, the bell above it jangles sharply.

She takes off at a brisk walk down the street, her stride made long and quick by anger, the bag thumping against her leg. Within moments the shopping centre comes into sight and with it, the motorhome, and her anger turns to relief. The Meridian's silver length is interrupted by whirlwind swirls of purple and white, and by the slide-outs jutting from its sides that allow space for the queen-sized bed and a drawer chest in the bedroom on one side, and the dinette suite on the other. She's grateful for its relative spaciousness. She's grateful that the owner gave Joe a break on the rent, otherwise they might be living in a smelly and rusting dinosaur. Otherwise, they might be homeless.

As she steps inside she's enveloped by the almost overpowering odour emanating from the Formica and carpeting, the maple veneer and pressboard of the cupboards, closets and storage spaces. She drops the bag on the floor and sinks down into the leather lounger. The wine glass with its bridal etching is in the cup holder in the lounger arm, its rim printed with the boysenberry shape of her lip. The empty wine bottle and Joe's glass are on the dinette table, as are the postcards she bought when they arrived, intending to send one a day to Alfred.

At the sound of voices she gets up and slides in behind the dinette table where she can look out the window. Coming across the parking lot is the woman she saw on the apartment balcony earlier in the morning, wearing the long beige tunic and the head scarf. A little girl in a pink sweatsuit lags behind, her dark hair shining as though lacquered. She's trying to take in all the sights at once, as her mother tugs at her hand to hurry along. As they pass by the motorhome, the girl peers up at it, her eyebrows scrunched in concentration. A gust of wind plasters the woman's skirt against her body, revealing the outline of her long slender legs. She's wearing orange plastic clogs, a surprising shot of colour.

They continue on toward Walmart, the girl walking backwards now to stare at the Meridian. Although Laurie is certain she can't be seen at the window, she feels the power of the child's scrutiny. She lowers the blind and goes over to the media centre above the cab of the motorhome where she keeps a folder and returns to the dinette with it. She takes out her notebook, and a bundle of photographs secured with a red ribbon slides out onto the table. She opens the notebook. *Postcards, $18.49, Walnut Crest, $11.95,* are the last entries she's made. Beneath that she writes, *Clara's Boutique, $88.87.*

Her eyes stray from the page and come to rest on the bundle of photographs. On top is a picture of her grandmother with Joe's mother, Verna. *Pals forever,* someone wrote in black ink across the bottom. They pose in front of a café in winter in the small northern town where they grew up. Her grandmother's hair is curly, like her own, while Verna's hair is stiff and blunt, cut in a style that makes her look like a sphinx. Her grandmother was already a widow when the picture was taken. She'd been left to raise Laurie's mother alone before Verna was even married. When Alfred returned home from Japan, he'd come upon Verna and Laurie's grandmother having a coffee in that same café, and Verna swept him off his feet, according to the story he liked to tell.

Laurie unties the ribbon and shuffles through the pictures, finds the one she's looking for and cradles it lightly in her long fingers as though it's brittle and in danger of crumbling. Her mother, Karen Rasmussen. While Laurie doesn't often contemplate her future, she does contemplate her past, the young mother she never knew, her sliver of a smile like a new moon suggesting there's much more to her than what meets the eye. In the photograph she rests a drinking glass on top of her pregnant belly, her long fingers, like Laurie's fingers, wrapped around it.

It's the only picture she has of her mother and herself. Verna took it on the veranda steps of the house on Arlington Street, the day Laurie was born. The day her mother, and Verna, also died. In the picture, her teenage mother looks as untroubled and unsubstantial as a paper doll, although only minutes after it was taken she went rushing off toward the river—and Verna went rushing off after her.

All three women are gone now. Laurie's grandmother, who raised her, struck down by a terrible stroke several years ago while still living in her cramped three-room house in the northern town, collapsed on the kitchen floor. The neighbours found her when Laurie alerted them that she hadn't answered their usual Sunday afternoon telephone call. Verna drowned trying to rescue Laurie's mother after she fell from the train trestle bridge. *Fell*, Laurie's grandmother preferred to say, although it was well known around town that Karen Rasmussen had got herself pregnant, been sent to a girls' home in Winnipeg where she threw herself off a bridge. On the twenty-seventh day of July, 1967. The year Trudeau proclaimed the government had no business being in the bedrooms of the nation, people still thought they had the right to know the business of pregnant unmarried women.

The newspaper account of Laurie's rescue is near the bottom of the stack of photographs. She unfolds it and begins to read, although she knows by heart how the class of graduating nurses were having their picture taken on the lawn of the Misericordia Hospital when they heard her crying. They followed the sound down to the riverbank and saw her mother lying on the small island. Soon after Laurie was rescued by the river patrol who found her cradled between her dead mother's legs. The island she was born on, and where her mother bled to death, is within walking distance from Arlington Street, and when seen from the height and distance of the train trestle bridge, it looks no larger than a doormat.

Her hands tremble when she folds the clipping, gathers the photographs, her meagre history, and binds them once again with the red ribbon. Such a small bundle of pictures culled from the albums days before they left Winnipeg. She gave the albums to her friend Sandra, for safekeeping. Albums filled with pictures of Alfred and Joe taken throughout the years. Alfred and Joe, her linchpins.

She awakens hours later, sunlight flooding the bedroom's west-facing window. When she stretches to ease the tension in her body, the heat and movement releases the odour of their lovemaking from the sheets. She realizes she's hungry. Avocado and Melba toast. All the necessary building blocks her cells need for healthy and normal reproduction. Yes! she says, in the unlikely event that cells respond favourably to a positive frame of mind. Divide and conquer. Ha, she says, and grins.

But when she gets up and sees the plastic bag lying on the floor, she groans, then grabs it by the bottom and upends it, her folly dropping in a crumpled heap. What possessed her to buy the clothes? And where will she put them? The closet and drawer under the bed are already jammed; some of the clothes have never been worn, a blazer, blouses she'd bought on sale at Jones New York still have the price tags attached. Sell them. Take them to Clara's Boutique. The idea, at first startling, begins to grow. Of course. She could end up with more money than what she'd spent.

The silver fox, she thinks, as she rifles through the closet. She hasn't worn the fur jacket for years, given that fur is fur, and it makes her look like a bloated marshmallow. It was one of Joe's first real gifts, followed by the blue leather parka he paid too much for in an Edmonton leather store, and which she has also seldom worn because it's too heavy, like lugging a pregnant walrus around on her back.

In her search she comes across the fern-printed sundress and remembers the bolero she bought. She takes the dress out and drapes it across the bed, then quickly strips. When she reaches for the bolero on the floor, she sees herself in the mirror closet door.

She straightens, runs her fingers across the scar, the silver ridge on the bronze geography of her abdomen, silky smooth to the touch. What kind of mother would she have been? She thinks of the three shoppers in the second-hand store, the forbearance and generosity of the two older women toward the youngest. She remembers Joe standing at the foot of her hospital bed, white-faced, his lips moving as he prayed silently while Pastor Ken and Maryanne prayed aloud that her hemorrhaging would stop. They read from the Bible of the miracles performed by Jesus, including the one of the woman who had bled for twelve years, and who believed that if she only touched the hem of his garment, she would be healed. *Thy faith has made thee whole,* Jesus told her, and she was.

But Laurie's bleeding didn't stop and they lost their baby. And soon after that she lost her uterus, and the question: What kind of mother would she have been, had been answered for her. Oh ye of little faith. The Lewises were a constant reminder of her failure, and she was relieved when they left Winnipeg.

She returns the sundress to the closet without trying it on, then slips into a sweater and jeans, thinking that they'll soon need to find a laundromat. When she goes into the bathroom, the air is heavy with the incriminating smell of hair colour. She'd meant to take out the garbage after clearing it from the bed, and forgot. She reminds herself to do so now as she fills the sink with water, then dabs gingerly at her face, yearning for a stream of hot water against her skin. She's craving protein; perhaps if Joe is on to more lucrative work, dinner tonight will be more substantial. Seafood, or a thick rare steak at Montana's. Perhaps they'll celebrate with a bottle of their house wine, the Australian shiraz.

She unhooks the key lanyard from the drawer knob in the kitchen and loops it about her neck, carries the garbage can outside, weaving among the parked vehicles and over to the barrel set against the light standard. The lot is almost full now and like a circus the way people hurry toward the mall as though afraid they'll miss something. She takes the garbage can back inside, thinking that although Joe has his own set of keys, she doesn't want to go far, or for long. She'll browse her way through Walmart to the mall and to the food court, where she'll read.

She follows the people streaming toward the entrance, entire families, she notes, and realizes that it's Friday. There's a sudden pounding of feet behind her and several young men go galloping past, whooping loudly, all of them wearing tank tops and shorts, their flailing limbs startlingly white. Several people around her laugh, and she shivers for the half-dressed young men. She stops to feed coins into a newspaper box at one side of the entrance and tucks the *Globe and Mail* into her tote. Moments later the doors swing open before her to a collage of colour, a welcoming draft of heated air, and the tall white-haired greeter vibrating in a red vest and cobalt blue shirt.

"Welcome to Walmart," he calls out.

"Thanks," she says knowing that she's not expected to reply, but she likes the way his mouth turns up at the corners when she does, and is surprised now when he doesn't smile.

He sounds less chirpy too, as though he knows that she's come with no intention to buy anything. Rather she intends to wander among the aisles and continue to be disconcerted by the low cost of various items, and the fact that the quality seems to be almost as good as what she often paid twice as much for elsewhere.

"Are you returning something today?" The greeter has stepped directly into her path and holds up a little gun with a roll of green stickers attached. She sees his watery eyes are intently fixed on the tote bag at her side.

"No," she says. He's clearly reluctant to let her pass without being able to peer inside it, but he calls out, "Have a good day," as she goes past him. The words are like a finger counting the vertebrae in her spine.

Soon after, she's in the food court and feeling fortunate to have gained a table under the skylight, given the crowd. She sips at a smoothie. The long mid-morning sleep left her feeling wobbly inside and she's hoping the potassium in the banana smoothie will balance her electrolytes. She takes her notebook from the tote bag and writes: *Smoothie, $5.25. Newspaper 2.00. Picture frame $7.99. Glue $2.95.*

She bought the picture frame and squeeze bottle of white glue believing she would make a collage of the post-cards to give to Alfred when she sees him. It will add colour to his otherwise drab and small room. When next she sees him. Which may be never.

I *will* make a collage, Laurie vows, even as she admits to herself that likely she will not. It's not something Alfred would want, and yet he'd make a big show over it, knowing that she was hungry for his approval. She looks up at a loud sizzling and sees the cloud of steam rising from the grill at Edo, the people there lined up waiting to order food. Saliva fills her mouth. While the smoothie is filling, she craves the saltiness of a bowl of hot yakisoba noodles.

She sees the woman from the parking lot then, with the girl in pink. The woman moves away from the lineup at Edo carrying a tray of food, looking out of place in the dark head scarf, which narrows her features and turns her complexion sallow. When she reaches the edge of the food court, she hesitates as she looks about for a place to sit. The young girl darts off and quickly finds a vacant table and calls out to her mother, her voice sharp like a sparrow's, piercing the din of adult voices. When she sees a couple hovering nearby, intent on gaining the same table, she scrambles up onto one of the seats, leans forward and spreads her arms across the table, leaving no question that she's claimed the space.

An outburst of laughter draws Laurie's attention to a group of people across the food court. Seniors, she realizes, people years older than the woman who has parked her cleaning cart on the periphery and goes among them, clearing and wiping tables. In comparison, the seniors look youthful with their winter tans. Snowbirds. They've just returned from Arizona and Texas and are reconnecting now in the food court. Joe's clientele included people like them, women who often possessed a self-congratulatory air at having made it to their retirement with their health, marriage and funds intact.

She takes the newspaper from her bag and unfolds it. A square-jawed and sullen man glares at her from the front page. A pedophile, with a record of sexual assault on boys. Police in both Manitoba and Saskatchewan are hunting him, hoping to apprehend him before he harms the boy he's abducted. He's had the poor kid for two days now. Don't go there. She doesn't need to stick her nose in excrement to know how awful it smells.

"That's gross," she hears someone exclaim loudly.

"I know, but I can't help it," another person moans.

Laurie turns to see a couple of teenage girls nearby, colas and cartons of NY fries in front of them. Their attention is fixed on the hands one of them has spread across the table.

"If you don't do something about them, I'm not going out with you tonight. That's obscene."

The girl with the hands moans again. "Don't be mean. It happened before I knew what I was doing."

"You've got to go to the Nail Place and see if you can get in," the scolder says. "If you can't, I'm not going to be seen with you. That is, like, just so gross."

Laurie notes their low-rise jeans, the expanse of exposed skin, the wide studded belts that make them look as broad as hippopotamuses. One day they'll be going through pictures of themselves and screaming, how could we?

Beyond them, the woman wearing the hijab has been joined by other women similarly dressed, although their tunics are more colourful and of a lighter material. The woman is animated now as the women lean toward one another, gesturing as they talk, jostling small dark-haired babies on their laps. Behind them is the security office, where a uniformed man in the doorway speaks into a radio while he looks across the food court in the direction of the Dollardrama Store.

Laurie follows his gaze and sees Pete, the man Joe is working with at Canadian Tire, the man he was supposed to have gone off with on a job. Another security man in the Dollardrama is hustling him over to the counter where Pete opens the store bag wide and holds it up so the clerk can look inside. Then he plunks it down hard on the counter to free his hands, fumbles in his vest pocket and brings out a bagel, unwraps it and makes a point of taking a huge bite, as though to prove that indeed, it is a bagel, before stuffing it back into his pocket. He then produces what is likely a sales slip from another pocket. The security man studies it, then indicates with a stiff smile and wave that Pete is free to go.

Pete stalks away angrily toward the rear entrance of the mall. Laurie rises quickly and follows him. "Pete," she calls and again, louder. He turns and she receives the full brunt of his scowl. "You're Pete, right? You work with Joe, my husband?"

Pete's anger turns to disgust. "Not any more, I don't. And as if I haven't got enough trouble, those bastards are always on my case. I can't come into this place without being accused of something." The gap between his teeth causes his *s* sounds to whistle.

"I was at Robin's Donuts," Laurie says with a placating gesture. "They said Joe was there with you. Do you know where he went?"

"He took off. One minute we're at Home Depot and the next he's gone," Pete says. "When you see him, tell him I said he's a jerk." He turns, pushes through the doors and into the parking lot.

Laurie doesn't know what to think. She retraces her steps through the mall, weaves her way among the people milling about, passes by the lit-up shops without glancing inside, only dimly aware of the woman greeter in the mall entrance to Walmart, a small frizzy-white-haired woman whose sore-looking eyes are too large for her face, and weepy looking, like the eyes of an aging cocker spaniel.

She sees herself on the video screen, a tall woman with tangled hair on top of her head, walking with purpose, a tote bag swinging at her side. A woman with anxious eyes.

She goes across the parking lot, thinking of Joe. She hurries across a traffic lane, aware of a red car with a crumpled front fender coming toward her, thinking vaguely that she's seen it before, that she is beginning to see the same people over and over. The entire city of two hundred thousand cheerful people must pass through the doors of Walmart each and every day of the week.

She locks the door of the motorhome behind her, knowing immediately that Joe hasn't been there in her absence. The premonition she had in Clara's Boutique was real. Joe's gone.

Four

JOE STOPS TO UNZIP HIS JACKET and in that brief pause brings his eyes up from the ground to the far distance where the ridge of blue hills begins to take shape. It's almost noon and warm now, the morning cloud cover having moved off to the northeast where it rims the horizon in a band of pearl white. Released by the rush of air against his body, he continues to walk, keeping that faint elevation of land in sight.

When he'd hailed a taxi going past Home Depot, he'd felt as though he'd just punched his way out of a box. He paid the driver twenty dollars to take him as far as the money would go and after the taxi dropped him, he began to walk, needing to move, to wear himself down. Although his frustration is almost spent, he hasn't yet reached the point where he feels he has no choice but to turn round. He keeps close to the rim of the ditch, a trough of moisture greening with vegetation, and away from the sporadic charge of traffic whose drivers speed up as they pass by, as though to point out that he is on foot and they are not.

Moments later his thoughts are interrupted by the sound of a motor and he becomes aware of the farmhouse in the near distance, a well-kept two-storey house where a woman struggles to rototill a strip of earth that borders the gravel lane leading to the highway. He notes her awkwardness; the khaki parka that reaches her knees, likely a man's, and too large, judging from the way the sleeves are bunched up. It makes her look like a kid who's taken on a job beyond her capabilities.

She sees him now and stops working, then stoops over the machine and shuts it off. She straightens and pushes the parka hood down onto her shoulders, as though this will give her a better look at him. When he sees the wedge of dark bangs on her forehead, the way her short hair sticks out at the sides, he can't take his eyes from her. Grim determination, Alfred sometimes said when Verna tore into a job a man usually did to keep a house and yard going, including turning over the earth in the small back-yard garden every autumn and again in spring. Alfred's faulty Hong Kong heart, the result of incarceration in a Japanese prisoner-of-war camp, prevented him from doing anything strenuous. At any moment it might stop ticking. But Alfred was into his ninety-fifth year now, while Verna had been the one to die.

He guesses the woman is calculating the distance between them, the amount of time she has to get to the house, should she need to. If he hesitated in his pace, she'd turn and run for it. There's no traffic and the silence is so complete, it's a ringing in his ears. As he crosses the lane, the loose gravel shifts beneath his feet and he has to work to keep his balance, and he sees himself as the woman might see him, a middle-aged man walking along the highway, someone who has likely gone looking for trouble and found it. A moment later the Rototiller starts up; its whine follows him along the ditch like a dog sniffing at his pant legs.

He passes by a dug-out pond at the edge of the next field, its viscous surface wobbling with light. A row of wind-shaped trees border the field, their nude branches all crooked to the east and cradling scores of abandoned nests. Large egg-shaped stones are piled along the fenceline here and there, beige stones worn by the weather, porous and riddled with soil.

He stops for a moment to turn and take in the city behind him, which now looks like a chain of boxcars parked close to the sky. Laurie is worried, likely, and he's surprised to discover that the thought leaves him untouched.

He goes down into the ditch and up the other side and over to one of the piles of stones, leans into it, its heat radiating into the small of his back. He closes his eyes and listens to himself breathe. There were times when he was younger, out in the country, that he'd imagined he felt the nearness of God. Times like when he'd be lying in the grass as darkness came on, after a day of duck hunting, sunlight a faint jiggle of pink on the slough. He'd thought this was like paradise, a marshy place, the reeds alive with water animals and birds crying out at the end of the day. He lay watching the orange autumn moon rise up over his knees and thought, feed me, oh breath of God.

Our father, our father, our father, he breathes now, and opens his eyes when he realizes that he is trying to pray, something he stopped doing years ago when he heard his prayers rebounding off the inside of his skull.

He will call Steve. Steve's email message at Christmas lacked news. He'd just wanted to get in touch, to let Joe know he was back in Canada and working in Fort Mac. But he'd attached a picture of himself and his son, a kid with a mullet haircut whom Steve had in a headlock, the boy mugging pain for the camera. What leapt out at Joe from the photograph was the baseball caps they wore, the words *Space Raider 1* stitched on the bill of Steve's, *Space Raider 2* on the boy's, the names Joe had given himself and Steve when they were kids.

When the phone rings Steve's son answers. His dad isn't home, he tells Joe, and won't be until midnight when his shift is over.

"Tell him Space Raider 1 called," Joe says.

"Who?" the boy asks, and then he says, "Oh yeah. I get it." He promises to leave a note for Steve.

Space Raider, a name Joe had likely got from TV, given how much time he spent watching it, even sneaking downstairs after his mother had gone to bed. In the morning she'd find him asleep on the couch, the TV still on. *Your eyes are going to turn square.*

He pushes himself off the stones and climbs up to the shoulder of the highway, and when he lifts his arm, he promises himself to only give it ten minutes. If no one stops to pick him up, he'll head back to town.

Within moments a white service van with a rack of ladders strapped onto the roof passes by, and when it slows down and pulls onto the shoulder, Joe turns again to look at the city. If Laurie hadn't spent it, there'd been enough room on the credit card for a tank of fuel. And what he earned would have got them the rest of the way to Fort McMurray, bought groceries until the first paycheque. Let Laurie find her own way there. He jogs toward the van, and the driver seeing him coming in the mirror, rolls down the window.

"Keith," the man says and extends his hand for what proves to be a soft and half-hearted handshake. He's sweating and pudgy, and beside him in the passenger seat is an adolescent boy who glances at Joe once without interest and then not again.

"Joe," Joe says. "How far are you going?"

"Red Deer," Keith says. "You've got a valid driver's, buddy?"

When Joe nods, Keith says, "Okay, you're on."

Keith proposes that in exchange for the ride, Joe take on some of the driving. Joe already knows he doesn't want to spend too much time with this man and so he tells him he's only going as far as Medicine Hat. The boy crawls over the console into the back seat and Keith takes his place. In Medicine Hat Joe will get something to eat, and he'll call Alfred.

Within minutes of Joe taking the wheel Keith begins to talk. He's round in the face and pink-skinned, his hair falling in slick curls across his forehead. Although he appears to be in his early forties, he looks prepubescent. Pouches of breast fat jiggle beneath his T-shirt, his arms and face are hairless. He carries his spare tire below his belt, on his hips and lower stomach, like a woman.

He's a contractor, specializing in home and business renovations, he says. He's heading for Red Deer to put together a work crew in order to replace a flat roof on a house. He goes on to say that flat roofs aren't architecturally logical, although he allows that certain styles of buildings are enhanced by one. Flat roofs constructed in the sixties and earlier have asphalt roofing, which means there are seams and the roof is never entirely waterproof. People don't maintain a flat roof in the way they should and he sometimes finds moss and good size trees growing on them. "I've found lots of dead squirrels, and there was this cat once, it was like beef jerky, fried and dried out by the heat." He'd found a woman's diamond earring and wondered how it got up there. "I didn't ask, if you know what I mean," he says with a wink.

Joe doubts that Keith is really a contractor. He lacks the quiet self-assurance, the forbearance coupled with healthy skepticism that most professional contractors possess, which comes from years of being caught between the intransigence of tradesmen and the unrealistic demands of clients.

Keith says he resurfaces a flat roof with a synthetic compound that becomes a seamless membrane. The back of the van is loaded with gallons of the stuff, which explains why it pulls to one side.

"This is my right-hand man," Keith says, finally getting around to introducing the boy, whose name is Bryce, the son of a friend.

"Howdy," Joe says and receives a mumbled reply. He's thinking Bryce ought to be in school. "He's young," Joe says.

"He's old enough," Keith replies in a way that warns Joe away from the topic, and for minutes they don't talk, the silence filled by the back-and-forth chatter of a call-in show on the radio.

"Are you hungry, punk?" Keith asks the boy, the question tossed over his shoulder with mock toughness.

Bryce's reply is drowned out by the radio and engine noise. Joe takes Bryce in through the rearview mirror. The kid must be about fourteen, fifteen, given the hint of fine dark hair above his top lip. There's an evasiveness about him that reminds Joe of Steve at the same age.

Joe rounds a sweeping curve and the highway straightens out in front of them and stretches for miles, flat and mesmerizing. The hills lie behind him on the horizon now, thin and dark blue, like a murmur of thunder. On either side of the highway the fields are shorn and silver, hung faintly with mist that softens the bleakness of spring.

Keith rummages in a gym bag on the floor and comes up with a bag of taco chips, tears it open and jams it into the console between the seats.

"Help yourself," he says gruffly, in a way that suggests his generosity makes him uncomfortable.

"Thanks," Joe says. "Maybe later."

Bryce darts forward and claws up a handful.

"Hey buddy, how about leaving some for us?" Keith says and although he's spoken in a teasing manner, Bryce releases most of the chips into the bag.

"Sorry," he mutters and sinks back into the seat.

Joe takes another good look at him in the mirror, his long and narrow face and turned-down mouth, the adolescent moustache like a smudge of dirt making him look younger than he likely is. Impassive.

"You can have my share. Me and taco chips have never agreed," Joe says to Bryce.

"No thanks," he says.

"Don't be a prick," Keith tells Bryce, again in a jesting tone. "Kids," he says to Joe out of the side of his mouth, as though Joe understands what he means, an assumption that makes Joe uncomfortable.

"Come on, don't let me eat all these chips by myself," Keith says to Joe.

"I'll pass." Joe is light-headed with hunger but he doesn't want anything from this man other than a lift to Medicine Hat. He sees in the mirror that Bryce is staring at the back of his head with a glimmer of interest. When their eyes meet, Bryce looks away. The highway is mined with numerous spring potholes, crudely and randomly patched.

"Fine," Keith says tersely, startling Joe as he snatches up the bag of tacos and flings it into the back seat. "Go ahead, help yourself to a stomach ache."

Joe winces, feeling that Bryce has just been clouted one across the side of the head. Moments later the bag crackles and he hears Bryce nibbling at a chip.

The highway rises in a slight incline that seems higher and longer for the flatness around them. When Joe reaches the crest he sees the alarming blue flash of warning lights, several police cars in the distance, and he drops his speed. The tail lights of vehicles glow as the drivers, like him, begin to slow down.

"Radar," Keith says.

"I'm under the limit," Joe reassures him. He took the Meridian because it was in the Quonset and not on the lot where there was the chance the owner might go by on the road and see it was missing. But he can't help his sudden fear that it's been reported stolen and the police are now looking for him. Two officers randomly direct traffic over to the shoulder. He glances in the rearview mirror and is caught by the alertness—is it anticipation or fear?—in Bryce's face.

"Where's the registration?" Joe asks.

Keith reaches above him to slide a card from a plastic sleeve on the sun visor, and when he gives it to Joe there's a slight tremble in his hand.

Several vehicles are already lined up on the shoulder between the two police cars and an officer stands beside the driver's door of the first one.

"Some kind of spot check," Keith says and as they pass by, he nods and waves at the officer who signals with his arm that they're to keep moving.

Joe slips the registration back into the sleeve while Keith drums on the dashboard in a short burst of energy before leaning back again. "I haven't renewed my licence. I meant to do it before I left Winnipeg, but I ran out of time."

Joe lets this pass. "You're from Winnipeg?"

"Portage La Prairie. My dad's got a farm there," Bryce says. That he's spoken surprises Joe, and Keith too, given the way he turns to look at the boy.

"What kind of farming?" Joe asks wondering now why the boy's parents have allowed him to be absent from school, out on the road, working, and with a character like Keith, friend of the family or not. He's seen boys the same age as Bryce thinking they've got it made because they've got a job at a car wash or pumping gas.

Before Bryce can reply, Keith answers for him. "Yeah, that's right, his dad is a farmer. Raises llamas *and* a yard full of junk." He dips forward to turn up the radio in time for the news. "I want to hear this," he says.

The top item of the hour is the ongoing police search for the pedophile who has abducted a second boy and is believed to be heading west through Saskatchewan, a description of the van he's driving, a dark green older model vehicle with a dent in the rear fender; a caution not to approach the man for the sake of the safety of the boys. This is followed by a report of a bombing of a house in Iraq that took the lives of several women and children. Both items incite Keith equally; his expressed revulsion for the pedophile is as vehement as it is for the trigger-happy American military.

Joe remains silent during Keith's rant despite all the man's effort to draw him in. At one point his gaze meets Bryce's pale and red-rimmed eyes in the mirror, and again the boy turns away to look out the window. Moments later he covers himself with his jacket and closes his eyes. Keith, his righteous indignation spent, falls silent.

Joe welcomes the quiet, and then begins to notice the stiffness in his arms from clenching the wheel too tightly as the miles between him and Laurie slip by. He has no choice, really, but to do the right thing. Stop the van, get out and head back to Regina. Ride off into the sunset with Laurie and a prescription for Effexor, or some other drug.

If you ever get up this way, buddy, I'd sure like to see you. Steve's email, devoid of the tone of his voice, didn't really sound like an invitation. And yet, Joe thinks, recalling the picture Steve sent with the email, he went to the trouble to have *Space Raider* stitched on the baseball caps. Perhaps Steve recalled some of their childhood escapades and remembered the Indian sunburns, how they twisted the skin raw on each other's wrists and thought they were tough when they didn't wince or cry out. That they were like brothers from the start when Steve hiked over the fence and into Joe's yard, his dark eyes fixed on the Dinky toys lined up on the clothesline stoop. I can play, eh, Steve said, and snatched up the race cars and sent them crashing into each other.

Joe recalls Steve standing lookout in the churchyard, a summer day, the year he'd since come to think of as being the last of his childhood. Steve's barrel-shaped chest and huskiness made him look older than eleven. He'd shoved his hands in his jean pockets to affect a nonchalance, an innocence he worked at perfecting on adults, but never quite succeeded. Steve's mirth, his mischievousness, always shone through. While he, Joe, had been a sneaky kid. Sneaky enough to run water in the tub to convince his mother he'd taken a bath. To leave the house with his swimming trunks rolled in a towel, knowing he had no intention of going to his lesson. He imagines his young reflection in the basement window the day they broke into the church. Spiderman swings across the front of his T-shirt and his lips are shiny with saliva and working as he tries to open the window. His shoulder blades are knife-thin and stick out, looking sharp enough to break through his skin.

They'd come over the fence and through the bushes behind the church, and Joe's arms were criss-crossed with white scratches that were already fading as he knelt in front of the window. Although the window was rain-swollen, one of its hooks had been left undone. While Steve kept watch, Joe wedged the screwdriver between the casement and the frame, levering it hard, and the rotting wood began to splinter. Then the screwdriver slipped, and he felt a stab of pain. "I hurt myself," he moaned and threw the tool to the ground and sucked at the flap of skin on his knuckle where blood had begun to pool.

"Let me," Steve said, and after a curious glance at Joe's wound, he dropped to his knees and elbowed him aside. It was his screwdriver anyway, it was his idea, he should be the one to do it. And it was he who had seen the new man in the neighbourhood, the pastor, wheel the gumball machines on a dolly up the front steps of the church.

A trickle of blood hurried like a red worm across the back of Joe's hand. His mother would notice the cut and want to know how it had happened. If he said he'd got it at the pool, she'd worry about safety and call the city pool authorities.

The sound of a whistle spurted up from the park across the street, and the din of shrieking children subsided. The lifeguard was clearing the pool for a head count. That was where Joe was meant to be. He already knew how to swim, he just didn't know how to breathe while swimming. But he was not going to kneel in the cement wading dish with the little kids, put his face in the water and learn how to turn his head to take sips of air. He could hear his own heartbeat now, and then a dull rolling sound, like a bowling ball going down an alley. An instant later the sky filled with Tutor jets flying in formation, so low he could see the rivets in their underbellies.

"The Snowbirds," Joe yelled and pointed, the roar of the engines popping in his ears now, although the planes were already gone. The Snowbirds were going to put on a show at the airfield later in the week as part of the Centennial celebrations. When Steve didn't reply, Joe turned to see the window hanging lopsided from its hook and Steve on his stomach sliding through the opening. The air rushed out at Joe from the basement, musty cold, like a witch had yawned. I'm not going down there. Then Steve's head disappeared as his feet met the floor, and Joe had no choice but to follow.

He stood beside Steve beneath the open window, the throbbing in his knuckle forgotten. Dad. He could be going past the church right now. Or he might be delivering the six-pack to his wartime buddy, Earl, and cutting through the park to get to his apartment. He'd see that Joe wasn't at the swimming pool. As his eyes adjusted to the dark he noticed the wires overhead, and the curtains strung from them as room dividers, bunched up against the far wall. A silver chair glowed out from the semi-darkness at the centre of the room.

"See, I told you," Steve said and went over to the gumball machines at the bottom of the stairs. He twisted the handles of the money slots, hoping for pennies and gum, and got neither. Then he grabbed hold of one of the glass containers and rocked it, and the gumballs inside rattled noisily.

The ceiling above Joe squeaked. Steve heard it too and stared at the door at the top of the stairs, but there was no other sound. The silver chair, Joe thought. It looked like a spindle back kitchen chair, and should someone come he could easily pick it up and throw it in their path and gain enough time to reach the window. As he planned his escape, it occurred to him that getting out through the window wasn't going to be as easy as getting in had been. Even if he used the chair to stand on, he still might not be able to boost himself onto the ledge.

"There's no one up there," Steve said, sounding disappointed. "Let's go see what it looks like."

It was a poor excuse for a church. Verna had said this only days ago when she and Joe were going past the IODE hall and saw the new sign beside the front steps. The square two-storey building had been empty for years, and then for a short time it was a postal station, and now a church called "The Salt & Light Company." The stone-clad building was mottled with trace fossils and chain coral, and up near the top of the front door was a coral the size of Joe's hand that looked like a sunflower. He'd discovered it during a school field trip, had been amazed at the thought that the charcoal rubbings he held in his hands were of creatures who'd lived billions of years ago, and in a tropical sea, right where he stood. During a time when trees had looked like asparagus. Now, whenever he went past the building, all he felt was his mother's indignation. A church should look like a church. I'm not going up there, he told himself. But Steve had already reached the door at the top of the stairs and discovered it was open.

The carpet muffled Joe's footsteps as he followed Steve across the vestibule toward the double doors that opened to the large hall, which had become the sanctuary. Arranged about the room haphazardly was an assortment of old sofas and overstuffed easy chairs covered in denim throws, and among them were folding chairs. The blinds on the tall and narrow windows were drawn, and as Joe followed Steve further into the hall, one after another they lifted in a sudden swell of hot air, the pull rings rattling noisily. It was as though a ghost had walked along the length of the place and lifted each blind in passing.

"I think I'll have a sleep," Steve said and faked a yawn, then fell backward onto one of the sofas near the front of the room where he folded his arms behind his head and pretended to snore.

Joe went over to the table near the couch and the wooden box at its centre. There was a Bible on the box, and the back of the box was open. Inside was a collection plate, quarters, dimes and nickels scattered across its felt surface. Joe reached for the plate, thinking of the coins in his father's canoe jar, and how he might replace the money he had borrowed from it before Alfred discovered that his savings were not growing any larger.

"Boys," a woman exclaimed suddenly, her voice coming from behind Joe, and the shock sent the plate flying from his hand. The coins spilled across the floor, bounced down the single step in front of the table and spun to a stillness. Joe began to shiver. He turned to see the wife of the pastor, Maryanne Lewis. She was a young platinum-haired woman, her tanned shoulders bare, and she was wearing the same lime-green tube top as when he and Steve had seen her and the pastor going in and out of the house on Walnut Street the day they'd moved in.

"Sit down," she said to Steve who had jumped to his feet. The bangles on her wrist clacked as she pointed to the sofa he'd been lying on. "Now." Her voice became sharp.

Steve rolled his eyes, sighed heavily, and slumped down into the cushions. Joe went over and sat beside him, his heart hammering in his ears.

"It's okay, honey," Maryanne called out, her voice echoing in the vaulted ceiling. Joe turned and saw a balcony, heard a door up there close and someone descending stairs.

The pastor, likely. A chunky man with a brush cut, according to Cecil, the accountant, who boarded at Joe's house.

"Say, boys. Welcome to the Salt & Light Company. But I can think of better circumstances for us to have met, right?" Maryanne Lewis smiled suddenly, her mouth stretching across her narrow face to reveal large square teeth. "Now why don't you tell me what you're after?" She glanced down at the coins on the floor.

Gumballs. They'd planned on filling their pockets and throwing them at the kids in the wading pool to see if the water would turn colour.

"You think we were going to steal something," Steve said.

"What's it look like to you?" Maryanne said. Her tone remained friendly though, and her eyes softened as she took in Steve's dull hair falling across one side of his face to his jaw, jeans worn through both knees, no laces in his battered running shoes. Her grey eyes came to rest on Joe, lingered on his bloodied hand.

"I've seen you two around the neighbourhood. You live nearby, don't you?" Her voice was quiet now. When they didn't reply she looked directly at Joe. "You live in the yellow house, near Rosemont Place, right?"

"Right," Joe muttered, concealing his surprise.

"I thought so. So, guys, how's summer vacation going? It doesn't look like you have a lot of fun things to do. How would you like to go horseback riding?"

"Yes," Steve exclaimed, and struggled upright from his slouch, leaned forward now, his arms resting on his knees.

Yes, Joe thought, but it was unlikely his mother would allow him to go.

Maryanne laughed. "That's just one of the things we've got planned. We're going to have a summer day camp. Right here at the church. You boys should come. Listen, I've got an idea. How would you two like to earn a dollar?" She needed someone to stuff mailboxes with flyers advertising the camp, she explained. They should come to the church in the middle of next week. The flyers would be ready for delivery by then.

"What do you say? Have we got a deal?" She flicked a strand of platinum hair from the side of her neck revealing a pink hoop earring; freckles the colour of toast met the ribbed edge of her lime-green top.

"It's a deal," Steve said.

"Okay," Joe said.

"But you know, of course, that the pastor and I will need to speak to your parents about what went on here today. I want your names and addresses."

"Joe Beaudry," Joe said. She already knew where he lived.

"You should run some water over that hand, Joe Beaudry," she said and indicated that he and Steve should follow her as she went toward the foyer and basement stairs beyond, her stride long and her light paisley skirt flaring around her calves. Joe saw how her ankles dipped inward, that her sandals went one way and her feet another. As she was about to descend the stairs he noticed Pastor Ken at the bottom, looking up at them, hands at his hips.

"They didn't break the window," he said.

What Joe and Steve *had* committed was called break and entry. Joe heard Pastor Ken tell his parents this later on in the day as they talked in the living room, and Joe stood in the upstairs hall listening. The stairwell amplified their voices, as it did the television, his mother setting the table for breakfast in the dining room late at night, the last thing she did before going to bed.

"Break and entry," Alfred repeated as though he didn't quite understand.

"They used a screwdriver to get the window open, and came in through the basement," Pastor Ken said.

"Way to go, kid," Cecil sang out, and Joe turned to see the boarder in the doorway of his room. Butting in where he had no business.

"Joe and Steve are good kids, believe me, we know the difference, and so we didn't want to get the police involved," Maryanne said.

"Lucky for you," Cecil said and then closed his door.

"But they've got to understand that what they did was serious, and in another situation, it might have resulted in serious consequences." Pastor Ken picked up where his wife left off.

"Did the boys cause any damage?" Alfred broke in to ask.

"No, no damage," Maryanne said.

"Well, then," Alfred said.

"But if my wife hadn't caught them when she did, they might have stolen money. We keep a bit of change in the offering plate in case of emergencies, and the boys found it."

"Joe's got what he needs, he doesn't need to steal." From the sound of Alfred's voice Joe knew his father had stood up and moved toward the downstairs hall. He expected to be called to come and face the music, but his father sounded more angry at the Lewises than with him.

Verna cleared her throat and Joe imagined she was fingering the cigarette package in her pocket, wanting a smoke badly as she did when she was upset. He had explained his injured knuckle while she prepared supper, saying he and Steve had banged off a roll of caps with a piece of brick and he'd smashed his finger, all the while waiting for the phone or doorbell to ring.

"What if we hadn't been there?" Pastor Ken went on to say, the voice of authority now. "What if there'd been an injury and the boys couldn't get out of the basement?"

"Honey, it's okay," Maryanne said quietly, and then to Joe's parents, "Ken and I have been calling on people in the neighbourhood to introduce ourselves. I'm just sorry that our visit had to be over this. However, we want you to know that Joe is always welcome at our church. It would be great if he would come, by the way. We're going to have a day camp, for kids Joe's age and younger. We're planning a trip to the zoo to see the polar bear cub. And you folks too, we'd love to see you too, there's going to be something for everyone."

"Thank you, but we have our own religion," Verna said and Joe was surprised.

"Well, praise the Lord, that's good to hear," Pastor Ken said. "And so I'm sure you know that Jesus Christ died for our sins, and he rose up from the grave. He's alive, and wants to be your personal friend."

Verna interrupted. "Yes, well. Thank you for coming by. You can be sure Joe won't cause trouble again."

They had risen and were going toward the downstairs hall. Joe turned away from the stairwell and went into his parents' bedroom, their voices only a murmur as he hurried through it and out onto the upstairs veranda. Pastor Ken and Maryanne Lewis emerged from the overhang of the eaves, and went down the veranda steps. Joe saw Alfred then, the shiny bald spot on the back of his head like a yarmulke, as he stood for a moment watching the pastor and his wife go along the walk before he came back inside.

When the Lewises had moved in, Cecil had reported at the dinner table that the couple were not well off, judging from the quality and amount of furniture he'd seen being unloaded from the moving van. And they were Americans, he'd learned that from the waitress at the Hot Spot Café— the couple had been in twice for a fish-and-chip supper and both times, instead of a tip, they'd left religious tracts.

"God dammit, Joe. Get down here, now," Verna yelled from the bottom of the stairs.

She had rolled up the newspaper and shook it at him as he came down the stairs, in the way she shook it at cats scratching in the garden, sometimes throwing the paper at them, but more often, not.

"What in God's name?" she shouted.

Got into you, Joe finished silently, his arms feeling heavy now, as though he was carrying dumbbells.

"I could scream," she said, and flung the rolled-up newspaper into the boot rack. She sounded nearer to crying.

Alfred came up behind her and put his hands on her shoulders, steered her over to the stairs where she sat down and patted the step beside her. When Joe sat down, she snaked her sinewy arm round his waist.

"You know what this means, Joey. No TV for a week."

"Again," Joe said. In the last week of school he and Steve had spent an afternoon bumming around downtown, and the principal had called to tell his mother he hadn't shown up. His mother's stiff hair prickled the side of his face, the perspiration ringing the underarm of her blouse, smelled like vinegar. He knew she hated not being able to watch television almost as much as he did, but she would not turn it on until he'd gone to bed.

"Yes, again. You were faced with making a choice, and, again, you chose the wrong one."

There was a time you couldn't get a word in edgewise, and now, I've got to go at Joe with a crowbar to get anything out of him. Joe had overheard his mother say this during one of her phone calls to her friend up north. *And when I do, he tells lies, and with such a poker-straight face. I don't know what's got into him.*

"Joe and me are going for a walk, to clear the air," Alfred said. "Right now, Joe." He needed to be at work at the nightclub earlier than usual tonight as one of the bar refrigerators wasn't cooling.

"I'd sure like to go with you," Verna said as Joe got up. But she still had the supper table to clear, and she wanted to boil eggs for tomorrow's salad. She locked eyes with her husband and said, "We'll need to talk when you get back."

She followed them out onto the veranda and leaned against the pillar at the top step, and then pulled her blouse free from the waistband of her skirt and flapped the front of it to cool herself. I'm sorry, Joe thought, and suddenly, he was. He was sorry that he didn't know what had got into him.

"No TV for a week," she repeated and offered him her cheek.

"I know," Joe said and turned away.

He wheeled his bike across the veranda and bumped it down the steps. Alfred had already reached the sidewalk by the time he'd mounted it. But he soon passed Alfred by, wanting to ride fast, to pop a wheelie and take off, turn tight figure eights at the intersection at Portage Avenue and wait for Alfred to catch up. But he knew this was not the time to draw attention to his father's slowness.

They went along the sidewalk, the elm trees a tunnel of green, the aphids excreting sap that mottled the cement with dark grey stains. The stickiness tugged at the tires of Joe's bike as he rode over what looked like the shapes of bodies lying on the walk.

When they came near Vimy Ridge Park, several of Steve's younger sisters and a brother were trying to gain a toehold on the fence at the wading pool that had been locked for the night. There were eight Greyeyes kids in all, Steve being the oldest. Verna sometimes said she couldn't keep track of them, and likely that was the attraction of Steve, all those kids and an easygoing mother who, she joked, wouldn't mind if they played baseball in the house.

Joe looked about the park for Steve, thought he might be among the several boys leaning against the community centre building, passing a cigarette between them. He turned and saw Alfred had fallen far behind and so he got off the bike and waited. His mother was sitting on the veranda step now. Beyond her the girls from Rosemont Place were coming across the yard, all five of them bunching up at the gate when they reached it. Karen Rasmussen was among them. Some nights after Alfred had gone to work, Joe would hear voices and when he came downstairs he found Verna and Karen out on the veranda talking. The girl, seeing him at the door, called out like she was Ed Sullivan, "Ladies and gentlemen, let's give a warm welcome for Joey Boy."

Going for a walk with Alfred meant having an ice cream sundae at A&W, while Alfred laid down the law and the consequences of breaking it. "See my finger? See my thumb? See my fist? You'd better run," Alfred used to say, his fist descending to tickle a spot on Joe's belly. An ice cream sundae and a talk at A&W was a version of that baby game.

"Those young twits were having a cigarette. I'll skin you alive, if I catch you doing that. Smoking will stunt your growth," Alfred said when he reached Joe, speaking with a roughness Joe never felt.

Not if I don't start until I've stopped growing, Joe thought.

"You've caused your mother pain. Why did you want to go and do that?" Alfred said, walking alongside Joe now as he wheeled the bike.

"I didn't *want* to," Joe said, startled at the thought.

"Well, you have. And what were you and Steve thinking? Just what in tarnation were you hoping to accomplish?"

"We were just having fun."

"Fun." Alfred snorted. "You keep on having fun like that and you'll wind up in juvenile detention. You stay away from that church from now on. You hear?"

"I hear," Joe said, remembering Maryanne's promise of horseback riding, and that he and Steve had said they'd deliver the flyers.

When they reached Portage Avenue they left the shade of the elm trees and immediately Joe felt the simmering glare of the sun, a fireball hanging low above the city. He expected they would turn at the corner and was surprised when Alfred stopped to wait for the traffic light to change and then crossed over Portage Avenue. He wanted to see the yellow canoe hanging in the store window, but as they came near the Fuel and Supply store, the blinds had been drawn against the lowering sun.

"I'll go in tomorrow," Alfred said, worrying, Joe knew, that the canoe would be sold before he could save enough.

Joe saw their reflection in the store window, himself at eleven years old, prepared for a life of opposition. He'd grown up with old parents in an old house and had learned to put his shoulder to a sticky door, adjust his play to the tilt of floors, and his stories to his parent's outdated expectations. He straddled the bike, balancing on his toes while he waited for Alfred to decide what to do next.

The sun shone through Alfred's grey halo of wiry hair and his shaggy eyebrows met above his nose. He wore scuffed boots both winter and summer, socks rolled down now against the heat and looking like rings of sausages. His khaki Bermudas bagged at the rear, and the concave sag of his chest was compounded by the jelly roll of fat at his waist. Verna was proud that Alfred was no longer skin and bones, as he had been when they married. *There's nothing to gain but ridicule when you try to look like something you're not*, Verna had once said, when Joe wondered why his father did not dress like other fathers.

Alfred had sensed Joe looking at him and his mouth began to work. "I'll be right back," he said and took off for the entrance of the Fuel and Supply store, returning moments later looking as though he'd won an argument with himself.

They continued on to A&W on the opposite side of the street, where several cars cruised the lot in search of a vacant spot. A city transit bus lumbered by, its sides painted with the maple leaf flag in celebration of Canada's Centennial year. Flags hung limply from flagstaffs on buildings, and the light standards along Portage Avenue. Curlicues of decorative lights unfurled across the street and met at the median in the shape of a maple leaf. Sometimes after Alfred had gone to work at the nightclub, Joe and Verna would go for a walk to the intersection to see the Centennial lights along Portage Avenue, the icy white lit-up curlicues, the red maple leaves hanging at the centre of the street repeated into infinity.

"It might be some time before we even get near the door," Alfred warned as they took their place at the end of a lineup of people hoping to get into the restaurant.

The rhythmic boom of rock music reverberated in Joe's breastbone from car radios turned up high and to the same station, as though this had been agreed upon. The music broke off suddenly to the familiar voices of children singing the Centennial song. *Cann-aaa-daa- … we are twenty million*. If I had a dime for every time that song was played, I'd be a rich man, Cecil had said, and he and Joe had tried to calculate how much money, at ten cents a play, Bobby Gimby would make in a single day.

As the people in front of them failed to move forward and the lineup grew longer, Alfred's face became pale and slick, and Joe knew his father would soon lose patience. Especially over the rowdiness of several young men who had swarmed out of line and now milled about the entrance. From the Brazilian soccer team, Joe heard someone say. One of them managed to push his way into the restaurant and they all began shouting their food orders to him. Glass shattered and Joe turned to see that a waitress had dropped a tray loaded with mugs of root beer. Car horns blared, there were catcalls and whistling as the waitress skated to the order window and took down a broom and dustpan clamped to the wall.

A man who'd been leaning against a car came toward them, walking carefully, as though he was on a balance beam. He was slight and wiry, wearing white jeans and a baseball cap, and a yellow shirt printed with tropical birds.

The city was overrun with similar lithe, cat-like men who spoke Portuguese or Spanish, and with American-sounding athletes whose twangy voices Joe had overheard in the drugstore. And myriad volunteers wearing colour-coded pants and shirts, sunburned spectators, evangelists. People had driven for miles to attend the Pan American Games and all the campgrounds were filled with trailers and tents. Prostitutes and pimps mingled among the patrons at the Club Baghdad where Alfred was custodian.

"Hola," the man said to Alfred and lifted his baseball cap, pulled his fingers through his dark slicked-back hair, and jammed it back on.

"How's it going, fella?" Alfred asked.

Cheers rose up now as several people were allowed into the restaurant.

"It's like this all over. It's very difficult to get something to eat," the man said. His eyes slid from Alfred to Joe, and then back to Alfred. He rubbed his chin absently and then again looked at Joe. Joe braced himself for what he expected would be the usual embarrassing comment about the colour of his eyes.

"Is this your grandson?" he asked Alfred, and Joe knew that when Alfred explained he was his father, the man would say one thing while his eyes would say another.

When Joe was born Alfred had been forty-four years old, and Joe blamed his father's age for his own perceived inadequacies. The sight of the waitresses gliding effortlessly from car to car on roller skates took him back to the one time he'd been to a roller rink, his muscles cramping with the effort to remain upright while Alfred gripped him by the scruff of the neck. Forget it, I don't want to do this, Joe had said. Just forget it.

The man stared at him again, and his smile faded. Then the muscles in his face grew taut as he took Alfred by the elbow and turned him away from Joe. He spoke to him urgently, their faces only inches apart.

Alfred swore suddenly, and the man stepped away, then abruptly turned and went to his car quickly, and within moments he was backing it out of the stall.

"Let's get out of here," Alfred said, but his hand came down hard on Joe's shoulder, clamping him in place. "Listen here, Joe. You see that man again, you tell me right away. Don't you talk to him, don't you go anywhere near him."

The fierceness in Alfred's voice stopped Joe from asking why.

When they returned home Joe was surprised that the remains of supper were still on the table. When he went looking for his mother he came across her rubber thongs lying to one side of the front hall. Her canvas sneakers were not in the boot rack.

"She's gone gadding about," Alfred concluded. She sometimes did disappear for an hour in the early evening to smoke and gab with her friend on Evanson Street, leaving them to clean up the supper dishes and Alfred to see to it that Joe bathed before going to bed.

Hours later Joe awoke in his airless small room at the back of the house to the heat, heavy, like a cat had settled on his chest. And to an electric guitar screaming to a crescendo. It broke off, and the roar of the crowd at the arena became a solid wall of sound.

He hadn't put the fan in the window because he'd wanted to hear the rock concert, but he had fallen asleep before it started. We never go anywhere, he thought. When he went to move now, he found his legs were tightly intertwined in the sheet. The more he fought to free himself, the more tangled he became. He thrashed against what seemed to be the thwarting of even the smallest of his desires, and suddenly he was free, and panting in the heat. The roar of the crowd had lessened and was overtaken by the rising tide of traffic along Portage Avenue, and the honking of horns.

He heard Alfred speak and turned toward the light in the hall. Since the heat wave, Alfred had moved the nightly cribbage game to the upstairs veranda and he was out there now, stripped to the waist, rivulets of perspiration running along his crooked spine and into the indentation on one side of it, where Joe had once been able to fit his fist. Alfred used to play checkers every night with his war buddy, Earl, when they were imprisoned in Japan. A wood crate had been the board, the stones they'd gathered from the prison yard, the checker pieces. Earl thought to darken some of them with lamp black. Every night they buried the stones for safekeeping. Alfred slept on a shelf near the roof of the prison barracks, and sometimes he saw the stars through a crack and tried to count them. What he hadn't said was that his nose was inches from the roof and that he was unable to stretch out fully, which was why his

head jutted from his shoulders, as though he was perpetu-
ally belligerent.

Alfred began counting his cribbage points now, slapping
the cards down on the table. When he was done, the other
card player counted his cards, and Joe realized it was the
boarder, Cecil, and not his mother, playing with his father
tonight. Her unusual prolonged absence made him want
to go out onto the veranda, crawl beneath the card table
and slide up between his father's knees.

There was the clink of pop bottles being gathered up,
and then Cecil's heavy step along the hall as he went to
his room. Joe heard water run in the bathroom, his father
showering in preparation for work. He'd soon go off down
the street to the Baghdad carrying his army rucksack with
a Thermos of tea, sandwiches and the pills he had to take
at certain times of the day and night. Toothpicks rolled in
cigarette paper.

Usually the night breezes would have risen by now,
bringing the odour of dust and grass, smoke from the fires
burning up north near the town where Verna and Alfred
had grown up, unaware of each other until Alfred returned
from Japan. Since the forest fires had started, Verna called
her friend and her sisters often, wanting to know if they
and their families were safe, and had learned about the
herd of caribou in the schoolyard, and how a cougar had
come into one of her sisters' gardens to drink from the
fish pond.

Usually, by the time Alfred left for work, the house
would have begun to cool. Not long after, the television
would go silent and his mother would set the table for
breakfast. Then he'd hear her quick-footed tread on the

stairs and along the hall, her bedroom door closing and shutting out the sporadic sound of traffic rising from Arlington Street.

Living near the centre of the city had made Joe aware of how loud quiet could be. At the end of a day when the downtown emptied quickly and the ongoing rumble of the city ceased, the sudden quiet was unsettling. It sometimes sent him indoors to perch on a stool and watch while his mother prepared dinner. The hollow tick of her family clock in the dining room became a hard and determined click of sound, the muted voices from the kitchen radio, a hissing and spitting quarrel. The sudden workday quieting of the city, the quiet that had descended after the rock concert, was like a withheld breath.

A moment later Alfred paused in Joe's doorway. "You're not sleeping," he said.

"I was. You woke me up."

"I've got to go to work now. Cecil's not going anywhere. You need anything, he's here."

"Okay."

Cecil liked to think he was boss. He likes to throw his weight around, Verna sometimes joked at the sound of the accountant dropping his dumbbells on the floor. Cecil trimmed his beard to make himself look like Mad Dog Vachon, the wrestler.

"If you're still awake when your mother comes home, be sure to tell her good night. And don't get out of bed."

"But what if I have to go to the bathroom?"

"Except for that."

As Alfred went downstairs, Joe spread his fingers against the light shining from the hall. The scab on his knuckle looked like a thick black beetle. Maryanne Lewis sounded like Betty on *The Flintstones*. Friendly, nice.

A dog began to bark, and then another, and Joe scrambled across the bed to the window. He was relieved to see his bicycle leaning against the clothesline pole where he'd chained it before coming to bed. Since the Pan American Games had begun, a lawn chair and a sprinkler had grown legs and wandered out of the yard. The accountant's Pontiac was parked beside the garage. A moment later Joe saw what had alerted the dogs—Steve, bare-chested, emerging from the darkness of the lane into the pool of light cast by the street lamp towering above the garage. He had brought his newspaper bag with him.

Joe dressed quickly and then, in the event that Cecil might look in on him, rolled up a blanket and made the shape of a body crooked in sleep and covered it with a sheet. But when he went past Cecil's door, the crack under it was already dark. He held his breath as he went downstairs.

The boys hurried along the lane, going toward the river and the meandering street that followed the river's course, a street whose traffic was light at most times of the day and night. There was less chance they'd be stopped and asked what they were doing out at that hour. They followed the dampness and odour of fish for minutes, and then reached the place where the creek emptied into the river and where the train trestle bridge spanned its breadth, a geometric puzzle set against the city-lit sky.

There they cut away from the river to go through a neighbourhood of newer and large houses, their destination the arena at Polo Park where the rock concert had been, and where they would scavenge for bottles beneath the end zone bleachers. They'd often done this after an afternoon football game, but this was the first time they'd gone at night. Joe felt a wind blowing inside him as he hop-skipped across Portage Avenue, a blazing corridor of lights, and he denied the urge to run while the traffic hurtled toward him.

As they went along the sidewalk Joe was unaware of the car coming up behind them in the parking lane, slowing and inching along at their pace. He only noticed it when it pulled away in a burst of speed, the ice-white lights fleeing across the trunk. Half a block away it veered sharply into the curb and parked, its engine idling as they came near.

"Don't worry, it's not the fuzz," Steve said, sounding older.

When they were abreast of the car the driver leaned across the seat, the passenger door opened and he called out, his voice rising in a question. Do you know? The last of what he said was lost to Joe as he remembered his father's warning earlier in the day about the man in the yellow shirt. As Steve went over to the car door, Joe took off running.

His feet skimmed the pavement, and the curlicues of lights across Portage Avenue became a blur. When he saw the Hot Spot Café, he knew he'd reached Arlington Street, and then he was soon racing along it, dashing through the halos of yellow light shed by the old street lamps, the chasms of darkness between the lamps where his childhood nightmares nested.

When he saw the police car parked in front of his house he slowed to a walk. As he came nearer he saw his father, sitting on the veranda steps between two policemen, leaning forward and holding his head as though to shut out whatever the police were saying. Joe feared they'd come to arrest him for breaking into the church and his urgent need to tell someone about the man in the car was gone. Perhaps Cecil had discovered him missing and called his father at work, and his father had called the police.

Joe entered the yard and Alfred looked up at him, bleary-eyed, as though for a moment he didn't know who Joe was. Joe was surprised and vaguely disappointed that Alfred hadn't asked why he was outside, clothed, and not upstairs in bed.

"Dad?" he said and the policemen looked up at him, unsmiling.

"Is this your son?" one of them asked, and when Alfred nodded, he muttered, "Christ."

"Joe, you haven't seen this before, have you?" Alfred plucked a piece of paper from his thigh and laid it carefully across his palm as though it was something alive and not a rectangle of lined paper, wet and almost transparent.

"It's a receipt from Quinton Cleaners," Alfred explained.

Joe shook his head, without even looking, he knew he hadn't seen it.

"It has this address on it. The name, Beaudry," one of the policemen explained to Joe, then stared down at his hands hanging between his knees.

"I told you, that doesn't make it Verna's," Alfred protested. "She wouldn't go for a swim in the river."

"Wading, Mr. Beaudry. That's what the witnesses said. They were out in their backyard and saw a woman wading along the shore. This receipt was found in her pocket."

"There's got to be an explanation. It is not my wife,"

Alfred said, and transferred the receipt to the policeman's thigh.

"Wait here," Alfred said to Joe and went into the house to call Verna's friend on Evanson Street, while one of the policemen got up and went to the patrol car. He returned a moment later carrying a plastic bag.

Soon after Alfred came out of the house, the screen door slapping shut behind him as he stood rigid, his arms tight at his sides. Older, suddenly feeble looking. "She might have gone to a movie, to a double feature." He sagged against the veranda railing.

The policemen went over to him and helped him to one of the veranda chairs, and he fell back into it. Then the officer picked the bag up from the step where he'd set it, opened it, and took out Verna's blue canvas sneaker. Alfred grabbed hold of the arms of the chair and looked away, over Joe's head and down the street as though he thought he might see Verna coming along it. And then he seemed to shrink as he said, "That's her shoe."

Joe rushed up the steps and one of the policemen made a grab for him, saying, "Son." But Joe pushed on past him into the house, and went pounding upstairs to his room, thinking, if only Alfred hadn't called her friend on Evanson Street. If only they hadn't left the house. Already blaming himself that his mother had not come home.

Throughout the following days he looked for Steve. He expected him to show up somewhere, to be across the street when they emerged from the funeral home after the service for Verna, her family bunched up around them, moving slowly as though wading through deep snow.

It was not Steve, but his mother, the youngest baby on her hip as she waited at one side of the door, as stricken looking as everyone else around Joe. She stepped toward him and he expected her to say, *Sorry for your loss*. But when she hesitated, Alfred nudged him to keep moving, and the moment to ask her about Steve was gone.

While he waited for his father and the others to return from the cemetery Joe played Scrabble with his cousins on the back stoop, all the while hoping that Steve would come by in the lane. *My mother drowned*. He had not yet been able to say it out loud. A cousin shouted and pointed at a jet stream that arced across the northern sky, and when the others resumed the game Joe watched as the vapour stream grew wide and gradually faded into the blue. She's not there, one of Joe's aunts had said when the coffin was being carried to the hearse for the trip to the Pine View cemetery. Your mother's spirit has flown away. And he wondered now, could she see him?

That night he filled the bathtub and then slid down under the water and held his breath, listened to his pulse, like a knuckle flicking against the side of his skull. Was he really here? He went on to ponder that universal question, although he could feel the water buoy up his arms, the bob of his penis. Or was he dreaming? Sometimes when he was younger he'd dreamed of being in the bathtub and awoke to the hot sensation of himself peeing. Even now he might wake up and find himself tangled in the bedsheet and hear his mother counting out cribbage points. He pushed up to the surface, gasping, gouging the water from his eyes. As he dried himself, he saw his face in the mirror, and although he looked the same, he knew he was not. He was about to turn away when he noticed that Verna's toothbrush was not in its holder.

He suspected Steve might be watching the house for signs that his aunts and cousins had left. They had arrived days before the funeral to help with the arrangements and would stay for several more days to fill the freezer with meals, occupy Alfred with cribbage, ease Joe into his loss as though it was a body of cold water he would eventually grow used to.

The moment their car pulled away from the curb the house was too suddenly quiet and large with their absence. Alfred went to his room and shut the door. Joe sat out on the veranda steps, thinking that Steve might appear from behind a tree across the street. Finally he got up, determined to find him.

Steve lived in a small crumbling cottage-style house at the edge of the downtown neighbourhood where it gave way to used car lots and pawnshops. Its picket fence leaned out to the street and the lawn was trampled to hard earth. You and me should get to know one another, Steve's mother had said to Verna one day when she'd gone by, and had invited her in for a cup of tea so strong you had to chew before swallowing. Steve's mother had lost her Indian status when she'd left the reservation to live with a white man, something Verna had seen happen often up north. In the town where she grew up, she'd gone to school with Indian kids and she had no qualms about Steve and Joe being friends.

Joe began to hear a wailing as he went along the lane toward Steve's house, and it grew louder the closer he got, like cats were yowling, and under it was the rhythmic boom of a skin drum. When he reached the house he stopped, the hair on his arms tingling. Although the yard was strewn with toys, there was no one in sight and the window curtains were drawn. Indian singing, he thought as the voices suddenly grew louder and rose higher. It came from the basement. He knew Steve was part Indian, his mum had said, but except for the time when Steve's grandmother, his kokum, had come for a visit, Joe had never thought about Steve being Indian. He was darker-skinned, but so were lots of kids in a neighbourhood that was made up mostly of immigrants.

He turned round and walked away quickly, the reverberation of the drumbeat quivering in his breastbone. He began to run, his feet pounding hard against the pavement. He knew then that he wasn't dreaming, that his mother had opened her mouth to breathe air and had breathed in water.

Days later Steve appeared at Joe's door, his hair cut short and slicked back from his forehead. He wore what looked like a new T-shirt, and cradled a stationery box in his arm.

"Do you want to help deliver flyers?" he asked, his dark eyes flicking to Joe's face, and then away. The camp was going to start at the church within days. "It's free. You get gumballs for attendance. I'm going." Steve said this in such a way that implied that even if Joe didn't, he would. For the remainder of the day, their eyes didn't meet again.

"I want to go to the day camp at church," Joe told Alfred through the bedroom door that evening and was surprised when it opened and Alfred stood blinking down at him. He hadn't shaved, and tufts of silver whiskers hung from his chin. Joe stepped back from the billow of sour air. A plate with a half-eaten sandwich rested on the floor beside the unmade bed.

"What's it about?" Alfred asked.

"There'll be games and things."

Alfred's shoulders sagged beneath his undershirt as he went over to the bureau and returned with his wallet, his hands trembling as he opened it.

"It doesn't cost anything," Joe said.

"Buy some groceries." Alfred held out several bills and when Joe took them, he asked, "You doing okay?"

"I'm okay."

As Joe went toward the stairs, Alfred's door closed again. He stood at the top of the staircase looking down, remembering having sat beside his mother on the bottom step. And that he hadn't wanted to kiss her. He crunched the money in his fist and shoved it deep into his jeans pocket, then sat down on the top step, thinking that likely he wouldn't ever slide down the banister again.

The following week Joe leaned over the railing of the church balcony and looked down at Steve. It was Steve's idea that they jump from the balcony, the small cramped space near the ceiling, the paint on the plaster walls blistered and mottled with mildew. At its centre stood the silver Come to Jesus Chair. Joe had wanted to be the first to jump, but he regretted that now as he looked over the railing. Spread about Steve on the floor were the sofa cushions they'd arranged in a hurry, and the gaps between them seemed larger than they had been when Joe was down there among them. He wished that he was outside with the others, playing a game of dodge ball.

"You're chicken," Steve said. In the silence, flies trapped between the window blinds and the glass buzzed loudly. He hugged his chest then, as though he was suddenly cold. "Didn't you tell *anyone* about the man?"

For a moment Joe didn't understand. Then he remembered the man in the car calling out to him and Steve, and Steve going over to see what he wanted. And although he didn't recall a white baseball cap, the man might have been wearing a yellow shirt. But he wasn't sure, as after that terrible night one day had flowed into another in a continuous stream of ache. When he'd gone house to house with Steve stuffing flyers in mailboxes, at last he'd been able to say, my mother drowned. I know, Steve had said and they continued on as though nothing had changed.

"Why didn't you tell my mother about that man in the car?" Steve asked now, his voice full, as though he was near to crying.

"I forgot," Joe said.

"There you are," Maryanne Lewis called out to Steve, her head and shoulders emerging into view below the balcony. Joe hung onto the railing as the walls suddenly began to move. His legs felt like they were melting.

"I wondered where you got to." Maryanne followed Steve's upward gaze to the balcony, and Joe.

The heat, the paint fumes from the silver chair were a force dragging him down to the floor. He pressed his forehead to his knees and wrapped his arms about them.

He was unaware of Maryanne as she climbed the stairs to the balcony and crouched beside him. Then he felt her hand on the small of his back.

"We're so sorry, Joe. All of us. We know what happened

and we've been praying for you. You're not alone. We're here. And Jesus is here. Jesus promised that he'd never leave us or forsake us," Maryanne said.

Soon Joe found himself kneeling at the chair on the balcony of the Salt & Light Company and admitting that he was like everyone else in the world. He had sinned and was lost. Like everyone who'd ever lived, he had fallen short of the glory of God. He hunched over on one side of the chair, while Maryanne knelt at the other, reading aloud from a small booklet she had taken from her skirt pocket. He was oblivious to her breath pouring over him.

"Listen to your heart, Joe. It will tell you your sins."

The traffic streaming by on Portage Avenue was a dull rumble in the church balcony as Joe searched for something to own up to that would prove that, like all the people in the world, he needed to be saved.

He had often argued with his mother. He'd told her he had brushed his hair, when he hadn't. He was sometimes mean. Only this morning, when he saw that Cecil had left the cap off his toothpaste, he'd squirted out some paste and written *Slob* on the bathroom mirror.

"I tell lies sometimes," Joe said, his voice sounding shaky and high.

"Yes," Maryanne whispered.

He confessed that he had once taken a bag of marshmallow puffs his mother had been saving for a special treat. He'd hid behind the TV console and stuffed his mouth with as many marshmallow puffs as he possibly could. He'd almost choked and had leapt out from his hiding place, his mouth foaming.

"Adam and Eve hid too, Joe. They tried to hide from God when they ate the forbidden fruit, after God had told them not to. They hid because they were afraid," Maryanne said.

Because they didn't want to get caught.

Maryanne rested her elbows on the chair as she knelt across from Joe on the balcony, clasped her forehead and closed her eyes. "God has a wonderful plan for your life," she said.

"I hate Karen Rasmussen." He realized it was true. It was Karen's fault his mother had drowned. When the police came to the house, no one knew Karen was also gone. It wasn't until the next day that Cecil heard on the radio that she'd been found dead after having given birth to a baby, and that a neighbour told Alfred he'd seen Karen leave the house looking angry and then Verna chasing after her. Joe's aunts and Alfred had figured it out: Verna must have seen Karen jump from the bridge and had gone into the river to try and save her.

"I don't need to know who Karen is, or why you think you hate her. But I do know *hate* is a pretty strong word," Maryanne said. "I'm going to keep my eyes closed, but you open yours now."

He saw her hand turned, palm up, on the edge of the chair. "Put how you feel about Karen, in my hand. And Jesus will take it away."

The blinds rattled in the sanctuary below and Joe realized Steve was still down there, listening. But he didn't care. The other kids had come into the church and gone to the basement classrooms and he heard them begin to sing. *Deep and wide, deep and wide, there's a fountain flowing deep and wide.*

"Okay," Joe said and he lifted his hand and dropped

Karen Rasmussen into her palm. His body began to hum, as though he was a wire that had just been plucked.

"Now close your eyes and repeat after me," Maryanne said. "Dear God. Thank you for sending Jesus to take away my sins. Come into my heart, Lord Jesus."

He heard himself repeat the words. And when he opened his eyes he saw the water stains on the ceiling, like cirrus clouds of iodine. He was lying near the balcony railing on his back without knowing how he'd got there, legs and arms spread wide, his palms turned up and buzzing. He felt a light growing around him, the colour of liquid honey, and his body swelled with it. He wanted to laugh. A fountain spurted up, and water gushed from his nose and eyes. When he turned his head he saw Maryanne Lewis, head bowed, kneeling by the chair.

As Joe nears Medicine Hat, the highway gives way to a corridor of fast-food restaurants, motels and gas stations, the light-trimmed facades and signs washed out by the setting sun. Keith spots a particular gas station and tells Joe to turn onto the service road.

He pulls up at the pumps, then turns off the engine and hands the keys to Keith. "This is where I leave you. Thanks for the ride." Joe is relieved to be parting company.

"You betcha, take care, now," Keith says.

Bryce gets out of the van and heads off toward the garage and Joe follows, leaving Keith at the gas pump. Bryce's stride is long and energetic; he has the physique of a runner, Joe thinks, and he must hurry to catch the door before it closes behind him. He follows Bryce along an aisle toward the sign indicating the presence of washrooms.

He waits off to one side of the door in a corridor made even narrower by the stack of boxes along one wall. The gas station with its overstocked shelves and carousels of junk food and road trash, is an assault of colour after the hours spent staring at the beige horizon. Joe spots a rack of phone cards at the counter. He'll buy time for his cell there, then he'll grab something to eat and call Deere Lodge and talk to the supervisor before he talks to Alfred, and if he's still awake around midnight, he'll call Steve again.

He hears water running in the washroom and then a towel roller being unwound. The washroom door opens. "Wait," Joe says as Bryce is about to go past him. The boy stops abruptly and takes him in, looking blue-faced cold in the harsh fluorescent lights. "I likely won't be seeing you again," Joe says, wanting to say more, but he doesn't know what.

Bryce ducks his head, looks embarrassed, not knowing what Joe expects of him, while Joe feels a light pressure of warmth, like hands, come to rest on his shoulders.

"You be safe." Joe goes still inside, listens for what to say now. *His light is shining all around you.* "Do you need anything?" he asks. The skin across his cheekbones feels drawn and tight.

"What?" Bryce asks. His Adam's apple bobs as he swallows.

"Are you all right? Why don't I give you my cellphone number? If something's not right, call me," Joe says.

Bryce backs away as though Joe's threatened him, his face turning red with confusion. "Take off," he mutters and pushes past Joe in the aisle, rushes over to the counter where Keith is now paying for the fuel.

Joe leaves the gas station and strikes out along the service road toward what looks to be a village of fast-food restaurants, their facades like sheets of polished bronze as the
sunset reaches its apex. The western sky is layered with
burning colours, like liquid glass spilling out from the
corona. *In the twinkling of an eye,* Joe thinks. Some small
part of him still hopes to be rescued.

Behind him, the eastern sky is a dark bruise, night
already enclosing the land. He thinks of Laurie, and it
occurs to him that perhaps he's not so much leaving her
as he's being drawn away. He pushes aside the thought,
feeling that he's in danger of making a fool of himself. As
he already had with the boy. Be safe, he should have only
said that.

Nearly an hour later, the hot meal and the heated air
pouring from a vent above the booth bring on weariness
and the desire for four walls, a space he can enter, close
the door and sleep. He doesn't want to land on Steve's
doorstep flat broke, but if he gets a motel room, he'll be
close to it. He's made a point of not borrowing money
from anyone except those in the business of lending it, and
he can't imagine borrowing money from Steve. He pushes
aside his empty plate, thinking that he could have eaten
more. As the waitress passes by the booth he calls her over
to refill his coffee. Then he wraps his hands about the mug,
its heat steadying; reminds himself that he'll need to call
Deere Lodge soon.

The sound of the television above the bar rises, gaining
his attention and that of the people around him. A newscast is in progress, an account of a police stakeout earlier
in the day. The journalist's voice is brittle with urgency as

she reports from a country road that the pedophile had been holed up in an abandoned farmhouse and surrendered when the boys with him broke free and fled. In the background is the green van. Joe senses the collective relief round him, and as the volume is turned down and the newscast continues, he recalls Bryce, slope-shouldered, already looking defeated.

As he calls Deere Lodge, beyond the window nightfall is almost complete, and the headlights of vehicles are pinpoints of light moving steadily along the highway and across his distorted reflection. A woman answers abruptly, identifying herself as Debbie Laurence, the supervisor. When she learns it's Joe, her voice lightens.

"Your father says that you're out of town right now. Will you be away for long?" she asks.

"Several weeks," Joe replies although he's no longer certain what, if anything, he might accomplish in such a short time.

"I was hoping we'd have a chance to talk face to face," she says.

"About what?" Joe fears she wants to talk about money. Alfred's pension doesn't cover anything more than basic care, a haircut now and then, and his private phone line.

"Your father is ninety-five years old," she says and Joe wants to laugh. He thinks, my father has always been ninety-five years old.

"I understand that you're his only living relative."

"Yes," Joe replies.

"So you'll need to let us know what your wishes are regarding your father's health care."

"I'm not sure what you mean."

The line goes quiet, and for a moment Joe thinks they've been cut off, until she says, "What I mean to say is, the X-rays your father had this morning show that he's developed pneumonia. We see this happen all the time with the residents. He *is* ninety-five," she says again, as though Joe must face up to that fact. "Once this happens, it's usually only a matter of time."

When Joe doesn't reply, she continues. "Our facilities are more than adequate to keep your father comfortable. We can do the usual things, such as suction him, for example. But if you want more proactive care he'll have to be hospitalized."

Joe is unable to breathe. The waitress approaches his booth with the carafe of coffee, and he shakes his head. "How soon do you need to know?"

"The sooner the better. Now would be best."

"Let me talk to him," Joe says, not knowing what else to say.

"I believe he's already tucked in for the night," she says.

"At eight o'clock?" Joe says.

"It's half-past. We kept him up as long as we could, but I'm afraid he ran out of steam. Let me go and see if he's still awake."

A minute later she's on the line again. "He's here. I've given him a phone."

"Dad?" Joe says.

"It's me, Joe."

"I understand you're under the weather."

"Who told you that?" Alfred's words come out half formed, sounding wet.

"The supervisor," Joe says.

"Just what did she say?"

"You're not wearing your chompers, are you?"

"They make us take them out for the night."

Alfred has seldom gone without his dentures; it's a matter of pride for him not to be seen without them. Joe winces inwardly as he recalls his father's suitcase falling open during their struggle, the hollow clatter of those flesh-coloured wedges when they skittered across the floor.

"The supervisor says you've got something on your chest," Joe says.

"That's true. I do have something on my chest."

Joe hears a hollow sound, voices, a click, and then Alfred is back. "She's gone," he says. "We can talk now. So you're in Regina then, and not Vancouver."

"What makes you think that?" Joe asks, startled.

"Didn't Laurie tell you she called?" Alfred says. "It was good to hear her voice."

Joe holds his breath waiting for Alfred to continue. He both dreads and wants to know what she might have said, what she's feeling. Headlights sweep across the window of the restaurant as a car pulls into the parking lot, the glare stinging his eyes.

"Laurie tells me you've got this temporary job. She sounded worried. When your man, Clayton, was here the other day, he said you've been bleeding money for years."

"Things have been tough." Joe is relieved that Laurie hasn't said anything about him not being with her.

"Tough? I put two and two together. It's not hard to figure that you've gone belly up," Alfred interrupts.

Belly up, like a gutted fish, fingers slick with slime and blood. Belly up, an expression from the Depression era.

That's Alfred. Way back there. Crude. Blunt as a hammer. His father.

When Joe doesn't reply, Alfred says, "Let's not talk about this, Joe. It's no one's business but ours. There are too many ears around here. Don't go through the desk when you call tomorrow. Call me directly."

In the moment of silence between them Joe hears the flutter of phlegm. "Dad? You still there? Everything okay?" he asks.

"Everything is not okay, Joe, and we both know it. What are you doing in Regina, there's nothing there." And then, with vehemence, he adds, "For God's sake come back, Joe. I need to go home."

"I know," Joe says. "I know you do, Dad. I know. I'll call you tomorrow."

Five

THE LITTLE SHITHEAD, Alfred thinks as he hangs up the telephone. His private term of endearment for Joe fails to defuse his exasperation at having stayed awake waiting for his call. He expects he'll do the same tomorrow, wait for Joe. Waiting is not something he does very well. Not since he came to understand that people who kept him waiting were often telling him he was no more worthy of consideration than a coop of brainless chickens.

He gropes for the lever on the side of the La-Z-Boy, a nuisance of a contraption if there ever was one. It's designed to keep him put, but he surprised them and himself when he proved to have enough strength to tilt it back. It's an easy thing to pull the lever and send himself flying upright, which he does now. Clear across the room one of these days.

For a moment he's gripped by a spasm of coughing that leaves his chest feeling squeezed. The young fellas in this place who stay up half the night playing cards in the solarium aren't happy unless they've got something to gripe about. The yelling man has stopped yelling; either that means he's shipped out, or been given something to keep his head down. The card players will be complaining about me, the coughing man, next.

Okay, then, up and at it, he tells himself. He sees his reflection in the dark windowpane across the room, a knuckle of a man slowly and cautiously uncurling as he rises from the La-Z-Boy. After a moment he ventures off to his first stop, the metal chair, and reaches it. The Eagle has landed. Twice now, he's had to tell the girl not to move the chair, which has become his way station to all parts of the room. He looks down at his hands clamped round the chair back, topographical maps, shrink-wrapped by skin the colour of brackish water.

He sets off again and arrives at the window, its marble sill a jolt of cold against his palms. "One small step for man," he says without the self-deprecating humour that usually accompanies his mutterings. In the window his eyes are startled and tufts of wiry hair shoot out from the sides of his head as though he's shocked to have travelled the long dark distance between the earth and the moon, a ninety-five-year crossing. There's only one in Deere Lodge who's older than him, and like himself, he looks like a raisin with eyes. But while Alfred can't remain still, that man is confined to a wheelchair and usually parked.

The lamp on the bureau is a spot of light in the window, its metal shade the shape of an infantry helmet. He won the lamp at cards while working in the lumber camp before the war, and it's the only relic he has from his bachelor days. Joe won't want it. The lamp will likely wind up in a stranger's house, or as landfill. Verna kept Joe's baby teeth in an old face powder box thinking that one day she would show them to his children. Joe won't want those either, but maybe Laurie will.

He thinks of the plastic bag of dentures stowed among the socks and underwear in the bureau drawer; he should do something about them before he can't. If he doesn't, Laurie will have to deal with them and he doesn't want that. He would chuck them in the bathroom garbage if it weren't for the fact that he would likely be asked why he'd done so, and any answer he might give would be written down somewhere and added to the sum of his senility.

If the house was on fire and you could only save one thing, what would it be? He'd once heard Laurie ask her friend this question, and it got him thinking. He'd saved four things. The lamp, Joe's baby teeth, his dentures and the family portrait, which was Verna's Centennial project. Saved her pennies and saw to the spit and polish one Saturday afternoon for the trip down to Simpson's Photo Studio. Everyone in the country had a Centennial project, why not them? Joe will want the photograph.

The photo sits on the bureau lit by the lamp. Verna, alive as spring in a dress the colour of green apples. Joe's young pale blue eyes shine into the future. He never let you get inside. Even now, when he's got trouble, he's too conceited to admit it, never mind ask for help. He might not want the lamp, or his baby teeth, but he's sure to want the portfolio. The money from Verna's life insurance policy is worth nearly a million bucks now. All Joe knows about is the twenty-some thousand locked in a GIC. The government had waited as long as they could for most of the

Hong Kong vets to expire before coughing up compensation, but Alfred had outlasted them.

The money, the house. Both will be handed to Joe on a platter. He'll have the life of Riley. No kids to keep him awake, to fret over, to wind up with nothing to show for it but a kick in the pants. Why don't you dig my grave and get it over with, he hears himself say to Joe. He still doesn't know what got into him, the rage that had him by the throat. When it came time for him to go to Deere Lodge, he'd intended to speak his mind. I'm your father, and this is my house. I plan on leaving it feet first. He guesses that's what got into him. A sudden and brief flare of anger that made him all arms and legs, pushing, pulling, swiping at Joe, when what he really set out to do was speak his mind. Instead, he'd foolishly tried to take Joe down.

The city lights blur as though the window is running with rain, or Alfred is seeing them through cellular debris, the swamp that floats across his corneas. He's heard that near to 80 percent of dust in a house is dead cells sloughed off by a person's body throughout the years, and if that's so, then there's still a lot of him back home. Although the city is dark with night, and the vitreous scum clouds his vision, he imagines he sees the fringe of greenery above the rooftops, the forest of old elms in his neighbourhood that came from a single tree. That first one is gone now. Cut down by the city, no matter that a woman chained herself to it in protest.

He sees himself wheeling Joe in the carriage along Arlington Street beneath the elms. In winter, he'd swaddled him in blankets and scarves, like a mummy, and pulled him on the sleigh. Wherever they went, people couldn't help but notice Joe. *Isn't he perfect.* A woman had said this when she looked at Joe, her eyes rising to Alfred's face then, and he knew she'd decided he was too old and hardbitten to have produced such a beautiful, large and clear-skinned child, whose wide eyes took in everything and everyone as though he already knew who they were and nothing surprised him. Joe might well be a genius, Alfred had sometimes thought. There was no accounting for Joe and Verna's presence in his life, other than Lady Luck. The kind of luck that turned up the exact card you needed to win a hand at cribbage.

He feels Verna watching from the veranda as she usually did, as she had on the last day of her life, her fingers set against her mouth to keep from calling out. *Don't be too hard on him.* A joke, that. Until recently, he'd never thought to raise a hand against Joe.

In his lifetime he'd seen too much brutality to want to become a bookkeeper father tallying up the misdemeanours of a young boy. The neglect of his own parents had left him misshapen, like a tree that had grown in nothing but rock. The things he'd witnessed during the seven-hour suicidal battle to defend Hong Kong against the Japanese had made sleep a torture. He never knew when the nightmares might ambush him, just that they would, triggered sometimes by nothing more than going into a butcher shop and smelling freshly cut meat.

He'd spent more than a thousand days and nights as a prisoner, first in Sham Shui Po, and then in Japan. In the greyness of dawn he was roused to go down into the pitch darkness of the mine shaft, and he emerged some twelve hours later when the sun had already set. On a clear night he could see stars, and sometimes the moon, through the cracks in the roof above his sleeping pallet. He'd come to the conclusion that there was no one out there, no God who was remotely interested in whether he lived or died. He didn't tempt fate by claiming there was, as others had, only to be struck down by dysentery and diphtheria, or a rifle butt. He'd succeeded in going unnoticed, and he survived.

None of this had made him indifferent to the suffering of others. Rather, it grieved him to see it. He'd been determined to spare Joe the indignity of injustice and injury—physical, or otherwise. It never once occurred to him that Joe might one day prove to be the source of both.

He senses Verna's thoughts flying down the street toward him, smacking him on what was, in those days, only a spot of baldness on the back of his head. He thinks to wave, but Verna is already turning away, already rising from the steps to go into the house and get a cold drink for Karen Rasmussen. Verna is already gone.

And when he saw Verna's lifeless face in the morgue he fell headlong into a well where he was swarmed by his thoughts, daylight being a lid across that well about the size of a dime, while at night the bottom grew deeper.

Verna had rescued the man from the child he'd been, wretched with neglect. Once Joe came, he knew that to be true. Back when he was a kid, he'd thought his life was like any other, as he stuck his nose through the wire fence into the farmyard, hoping to catch a breath of fresh air when it passed by. When he got too big for his mother to carry on her back, his father penned him in the coop to keep him safe, to keep him clear of mischief while he, Alfred's mother and his brothers went into town or to work out in the fields. As the half-assed chickens went at each others' backsides, pecking one another featherless, he would think of his brothers, the way they pecked at one another until a scuffle broke out and they used their fists. Sometimes his father was right there in the middle of it. He'd been a child filled with hope and not despair, as he wished upon the face of the moon for the sight of the horses bringing the wagon and his family into the yard at the end of the day.

Despair set in later when he occupied a desk at the back of a schoolroom and tried to hide the fact that he'd been hurt, that his ignorance was deep and abiding, that he was not like the others around him. Verna was only a pigtailed chit of a girl then, sitting at the front of the classroom, just one among all the other town kids he sought to avoid. He'd gone out to the farm for the last time when it was being sold. He'd wanted to see his brothers, who had come from across the country to shut down the house, but more than that, he wanted them to look at him and for once see him. He'd felt like a stranger as they sat around the kitchen table and recalled their youth as though he hadn't been there. As though their young lives had been one long game of hockey they had survived, and they didn't mind showing their scars.

He hadn't recognized Verna when he passed her on the street, it was only in the restaurant, when Ivy introduced herself and Verna, that he remembered her. She was taller than him, her dark hair already streaked with grey at the age of thirty-five. A quick-witted beanpole of a woman with a sense of humour a mile wide. Being with her was like being in a warm current of water while swimming in a cold northern lake. He stayed on in town after his brothers left, told himself it was as good a place as any to be haunted by the dead, especially the women, the nurses he'd come upon in the wards in the hospital in Hong Kong, raped and then bayonetted from stem to stern.

Within months Verna gave her sisters notice. It was their turn to care for their aging parents, as she'd taken up with a man whose three toes were missing from frostbite, and who had an infection in his back that refused to heal. She planned on marrying him. When they returned from the Justice of the Peace, Verna took Alfred straight to the Indian woman's shack outside of town. The woman had once made a paste that had healed the infected sores on Verna's mother's diabetic feet. The woman sniffed at the infection eating away at his back, then prepared a concoction that smelled like spruce gum. He and Verna went south to Winnipeg then, where she took him from doctor to doctor until they found one who put him on the thiamine treatment that kept his mind and heart steady. A year later when she was pregnant with Joe, he cashed in his share of the farm and what he'd saved while working in the lumber camps, and bought the house on Arlington Street.

When she died, it took months for him to find himself. He came out of the darkness one morning when the telephone wouldn't stop ringing. It was like a pesky fly, divebombing his head in the way it would stop and start up again minutes later. He went downstairs, wondering why Joe wasn't answering it. It was Earl calling, saying, "So my friend. What's up? Are we still on, or not?" Earl had surprised him once by coming by the house soon after Verna died. Tell him I'm not up for a visit yet, Alfred had said to Joe. Earl was calling now to remind Alfred that since Verna's passing he'd gone without his weekly ration of ale, and he wanted Alfred to make a run to the liquor store.

"Grease those wheels and go and get it yourself," Alfred said, as he looked about the kitchen and saw the dishes stacked, unwashed, in the sink, the cupboard doors gaping open, the floor littered with garbage.

"I'll be in the park, at the usual place," Earl said and hung up.

Earl's call was a blunt reminder of how quickly the living went on doing just that, while the dead were just as quickly being discounted. Alfred took in the cluttered counter, the almost empty shelves in the cupboard. And as he passed through the living room, he saw Joe's half-built Ferris wheel on the coffee table, the pile of clothes on the floor. The boy had left a glass of milk and a box of saltines on the TV.

He realized that for too long, Joe had only been a sound moving about in the rooms below him. He'd been aware of the television being on far into the night. The times when hunger drew him downstairs, he sometimes came across a piece of paper with an arrow on it pointing to the sandwich Joe had prepared and left out on the arm of the easy chair. He was aware of Joe in the bedroom wanting money for school supplies, his weekly allowance; of the telephone messages he slid under the door, the paper that required a signature for him to participate in a project at school. At some point, Cecil, the boarder, had moved out. No more of Verna's home cooking, and a house falling to rack and ruin.

When Alfred went past the park he wasn't surprised to

see Earl already seated at a picnic table, a newspaper spread across it, his wheelchair parked off to one side. But he was surprised to find that the sidewalk was slippery underfoot with a compost of leaves, and the trees were already bare. There was a work party going on at the church, men up on ladders cleaning windows, others, among them several children, raking leaves. Alfred didn't recognize any of them. He'd once thought to ask Joe what he did over there in the weeks after Verna died. Lots, Joe said, his face flickering with annoyance.

He searched for Joe among the people in the church-yard as he passed by, but failed to see him. He would have been satisfied with a glimpse of what was left of Verna, her dark hair, the way her mouth pulled to one side when she was thinking, long legs carrying her about with such swift resolution.

Joe's bike was chained to the step railing along with several others, and so Alfred knew he was at the Saturday club, where he'd said he would be in the note he'd left beside the telephone. Exposure to religion of any kind would be an antidote against it later on, Alfred had told himself when Joe asked if he could attend services at the Salt & Light Company. The truth was, he was relieved Joe was occupied and supervised; it meant he required less of Alfred's thinking time.

He reached the intersection at Portage Avenue and waited for the traffic light to change, thinking that Joe was likely in the basement. Carving a squirrel or cat from a bar of soap, or filling in the blanks on one of the worksheets he was forever bringing home. Blessed are—*the poor in spirit*. Blessed are—*they that mourn*, Joe's handwriting, tight and careful. Alfred didn't know that at that moment Joe was with a church deacon who scanned the lines of scripture with his finger for Joe to follow as Joe read aloud, falteringly, stumbling over the archaic arrangement of sentences in the King James Bible, beginning to commit scripture to memory that would eventually sound like poetry coming from the boy's mouth.

The liquor store and the Fuel and Supply hardware store shared the same building, its bright green exterior dominating the city block. Just beyond it was Weston's Bakery whose red brick chimney stack towered over the store, and today the odour of bread baking was almost overpowering. Why were the bakery windows bricked in? Alfred had often paused to wonder, and concluded that if there was something called sin to be counted against a man, then it was a sin to shut out daylight. Nor was it right for the smell of baking bread to turn a person's stomach.

He came out of the liquor store with the box of beer clenched under his arm. Beyond the entrance of the Fuel and Supply store the yellow canoe still hung on wires from the ceiling. He had planned on working it into the sphere of Verna's toleration gradually. To put the canoe on the river a couple of times before it got too cold, give Joe a bit of experience before next summer when he'd license Earl's old Jeep and take Joe camping. The idea of taking Joe out on the water seemed like a betrayal of Verna now.

Earl saw him coming and took a haversack from the seat of his wheelchair, readying it to receive the carton. Alfred wedged the box down inside, and Earl tore open the lid and took out a bottle and offered it to him. When he refused, Earl uncapped it and drank deeply before pushing it out of sight between his thighs. Alfred sat down at the table across from him, cold suddenly.

"It's supposed to snow," Earl said.

Alfred nodded, seeing the cover of blue-grey clouds hanging above the city in the north. He thought of Verna in the ground, wearing a light dress one of her sisters had chosen, a lace shawl, no protection against winter.

They sat in silence for a long moment, watching the activities at the church. A car arrived and several women, who appeared to have been waiting for it, got in. At a time like this, religion might give a person something to shake a fist at. A good woman had been taken too soon, and there was nothing to blame but chance.

And then Earl expressed his disgust over the number of draft dodgers being given refuge in the country, the anti–Vietnam War protests going on south of the border, and when that failed to gain a response from Alfred, he read aloud from the newspaper, beginning with the front page story of the killing of Che Guevara in the Bolivian jungle, while Alfred listened, but did not take in the words, and the remainder of the morning passed.

Around noon, Earl barked, "Here comes trouble," and seemed relieved at the sight of Joe running across Arlington Street into the park, Pastor Ken and Maryanne crossing the street behind him.

Joe suddenly grew shy as he neared Alfred, and he stopped to stand looking at the ground. Pastor Ken and Maryanne Lewis moved in to flank him.

"I'll be going now," Earl said and lifted his stumps as he swung round on the bench. He raised his hands and scowled to fend off Pastor Ken when it appeared he would come to his assistance. He pulled his wheelchair close, lifted the haversack of ale, and then slid off the picnic bench into the chair and set the haversack onto his lap. "Be seeing you around, tiger," he said with a wink to Joe.

Pastor Ken came over to Alfred, gripped his hand, the handshake becoming a kind of embrace as he enclosed Alfred's hand in both of his and held on, until Alfred drew his own away.

"It is good to see you again," the pastor said, and his steady gaze flickered. Likely he was remembering why they'd met in the first place, Alfred saying to them as they were about to leave the house, *It would seem to me that you folks would have your hands full preaching to people in your own country*.

"We want you to know that we've all been praying for you," Pastor Ken said.

"What for?"

The pastor seemed startled and his wife broke in to say, "These past months must have been very difficult for you. And for Joe." She put her hand on Joe's shoulder and he looked up at her as she nudged him toward Alfred. "He's such a fine boy, Mr. Beaudry. It's been a blessing for us to get to know him."

Alfred could only nod. The little shithead. He saw Joe turn and scan the park, pretend he was not part of what was happening. He was still wearing the Spiderman T-shirt Verna had bought at the beginning of summer. It had stretched and hung like a skirt beneath his windbreaker. His hair had grown thick and long, and was coppery from having been bleached by the sun during summer.

"We want to thank you for allowing Joe to be part of our worship family," Pastor Ken said.

"Yes, well," Alfred replied. He hadn't realized this was what he'd done.

Joe looked at his father then, his pale eyes clouded and swimming.

You've left him in the chicken coop and he's been waiting for you all this time, Alfred heard Verna's voice say, and it was like a rock dropped on his foot.

Moments later when Joe and Alfred went toward home they were caught in a downpour of snow pellets that bounced before their feet and in the street beyond, the air a swirl of white around them, suddenly, and filled with the sound of crackling.

"I need a new parka," Joe said, his shoulders shrugged up to his ears against the cold.

"We'll get you one." Alfred's bank account was scraping bottom, as the pension didn't stretch far enough. Tomorrow he would call the club and let them know he was ready to come back to work. He went to brush the ice pellets from Joe's hair, but let his hand fall to his side. Pay off what's owing on the canoe, he told himself. Store it in the garage rafters until spring, start a layaway for a tent and a couple of sleeping bags.

"Sorry," he muttered to Verna under his breath as they went along the walk to the house, covered now in a layer of snow that had begun to melt, their footprints slurred and quickly filled with water. Joe pushed on ahead, wanting to be the first to the door, Alfred realized, as the boy held it open wide enough for him to pass through.

Alfred entered the hall and was confronted by the odours of furniture polish, cleansers and bleach, of Verna's cleaning day. Even before he ventured farther, he knew that the house had been transformed in his absence. The clutter was gone and the floors shone, freshly laundered clothes had been ironed and folded and lined up on the couch in several piles. The kitchen sparkled with cleanliness and order; there was a lasagna on the stove and a note saying what temperature to set the oven, and for how long he should cook it.

Alfred followed Joe from room to room, feeling that he'd been accused and found wanting, then feeling that, no, he'd been invaded. Likely by the women he'd seen getting into the car in front of the church earlier. Strangers had rummaged about the shelves and drawers, disturbed Verna's arrangement of things. The smudges of her hands on the cupboard doors had been wiped away, her ashtrays emptied and washed and lined up on a windowsill.

Alfred remained silent as he took in Joe's room, the bed made up with fresh linen, the pillows plumped, toys arranged on the shelves, as though Verna had only just straightened them. Christ, he thought. Even Earl was in on this. Alfred had sat there, shivering with cold the whole time, thinking he was keeping the man company.

He left the inspection of his own room for the last, and realized as he went along the hall toward it that he was clenching his fists. The worst of it was that these women had breathed in Verna's house. The do-gooders had taken in particles of Verna and left something of themselves behind. He pushed open his door and was relieved to find that they had sense enough to leave his and Verna's room as it was. He stood for a moment taking in Verna's rubber thongs on the floor beside the bed, when he felt Joe watching him from the door.

"The house looks great, eh, Dad?"

"Some people should mind their own business," Alfred said. Then he picked up Verna's thongs, held them for a moment before putting them in the closet. Your intentions were good, he thought to say to Joe, but when he looked up, Joe had gone.

The traffic along Portage Avenue flows past Alfred's window at Deere Lodge, currents of lights streaming both north and south, and through it he sees his own face reflected in the windowpane. When he'd been a prisoner of war in Japan he'd seen enough men die to be able to recognize his own end coming for him a mile away. His legs are shaking now, made unpredictable by his fever, and he has to bear the brunt of his weight on his arms.

He thought death was coming for him when he'd been sent to work in the coal mine in Japan, in the shaft that had been dug out under the sea. In places it was chest-deep with water that stunk of sulfur. By then his feet had become like clubs, swollen three times their size, and he couldn't gain purchase with his toes to feel his way along the shaft that was scattered with rocks, the ground uneven with hollows and sudden risings. He told himself that if he was going to survive, he had to remain upright. He had to keep moving, to concentrate while he chipped away at the scant splinters of coal to be found in the mined-out seam.

But now, his life is behind him. It's across the room on the bureau. Joe and Verna: Alfred's second birth coming in a sudden burst of noise and light when he was forty-four years old.

"Mr. Beaudry?" an attendant calls from the door, startling him, and his knees cave in. She grasps Alfred tightly about his chest, preventing him from doing serious damage to the floor. He says this aloud but she doesn't appear to have heard and calls out to someone, and seemingly within an instant another woman is lifting his arms and putting them around her neck. "Lock your fingers, Mr. Beaudry," she says and as Alfred hangs on to her, he feels the heat emanating from her body.

He reflects on the effort it takes, the number of people, the amount of time to keep someone like him from toppling over and becoming a danger to himself and others. The women guide him across the room, and he says, "Not the bed. I need to sit up," and is relieved when they steer him over to the La-Z-Boy.

When they leave he struggles upright, trying and failing to reach the clock radio on the side table and turn its face away. The effort brings on a convulsion of shallow coughing that hurts, and he lies back and pushes against his ribs to hold it in. From down the hall the yeller calls out suddenly, the sound large and hollow, as though he's inside a barrel. So the yeller is still with us. Still standing between him and the great scythe about to mow them both down. The yeller calls for a nurse, but it sounds more like a grunt, like he's saying, hearse, hearse. Why don't you give the poor man what he wants, Alfred will say to the women when they return.

He closes his eyes against the irritation of the glowing digital numbers of the clock and immediately sinks toward sleep. But within moments his legs below the knee grow clammy and cool. It's like he's calf-deep in water, in the mine shaft and heading deeper into the blackness under the sea. And then he sees himself guide the yellow canoe among large rocks and away from the shore. He hears Joe call out, his voice deep now and strong. "It's okay, Dad. I've got it." Joe moves slowly, for his benefit, his broad back bent over the canoe as he steadies it and waits for him to climb inside.

Joe pushes off a rock shelf with the paddle and they shoot out from the shallows into the sudden depth of the lake and into sunlight, the water smooth and as solid-looking as sheet metal. And the next moment they're coming near the cabin set back in among cottonwood and pine, where people crowd about the shore waiting for them. They wave, call out for Joe, anxiously rush forward when the canoe bites into the red sand, as though they intend to lift it with him and Joe inside and carry it on their shoulders up the rocky slope.

People emerge from the cabin and across its broad cedar deck and along a narrow footpath winding through dark spruce, Joe among them, all of them wearing what look to be white robes made of bedsheets fastened at the waist with hemp rope. They file down to the shore, wait there for the pastor and the deacon to call them out into the lake to be dipped backward beneath the surface, one by one, held there for a moment before being brought up, gasping, water streaming across their faces.

Alfred hears sobbing, and laughter, then a song rise from the congregation gathered along the beach, the singing giving way and becoming the sound of ringing bells, the tinkle of glass chimes, the cry of the bird falling toward the water. Look, someone shouts. Look, the bird, the Holy

Spirit descending on Joe. A gull, fishing in the shallows, despite the hullabaloo. Joe cries out, *Hallelujah!* again and again, his hands raised, his features lit with what might be joy, the word Verna had superimposed on the photograph of Joe taking his first baby steps; the word he used to think was the spelling of his name.

Alfred digs too deeply with the paddle, mining the water and bringing it up in splashes, a stroke that soon has his back in stitches. It's not like the simple efficient J stroke Joe had learned years ago at church camp, but it's his. Early in life he'd learned that if he only waited and watched long enough he'd find the answers to any questions he might have, and he'd learned his paddle stroke from watching the canoeists going along on the river. As the shoreline recedes he knows the congregation is gathering around the tables spread with food, Joe and Crystal among them, their hands entwined. It's a love feast, Dad. Stay, join us, Mr. Beaudry. Joe's and Crystal's beatific smiles and voices like balloons sailing right on over his head.

When he'd seen that arm of rocks reaching far out from the shore he knew it was a good place to fish, and he'd tucked into the bay on the other side of it, fished there until the baptism party was over. He should have been able to figure that one out. Crystal, coming round to the house with Joe more and more often. He might have guessed there was something behind Joe's willingness to make the outing a weekend camping trip, and not the usual rushed affair to put the canoe in the water for half a day.

In the evening Joe poked at the campfire hard, and sparks flew up all around him.

Alfred waited until the sparks had arced out over the

lake, and disappeared on the surface of the water. "So why did you want to be dunked?"

"Because," Joe said, which was what he said when he didn't want to answer. And then he heaved the stick into the fire and turned to him. "Because I wanted to rededicate my life to God."

"With a public spectacle."

"Dad, Dad, Dad." Joe shook his head and surprised Alfred by laughing, as though Alfred was both incorrigible and lovable at the same time. As though he was a child.

"My baptism is a public declaration that I intend to serve the Lord. You may as well know, Dad. Crystal and I are engaged." Then he looked straight at him, his pale eyes steady. "We plan on going to a Bible college in the States. We'll be away four years, at least."

The words were a cement truck hurtling toward Alfred. "But I thought you wanted to be a teacher. That's what you said when you went to university." Joe's eyes slid away, but not before Alfred had seen what he took to be regret. Joe, Joe, Joe, he thought. Someone's got you by the short hairs.

"The time hasn't been wasted. I can get credit for most of my courses. But I'm not sure yet where my studies at the Bible college will take me. Crystal and I want to be open to whatever God has planned. Who knows, maybe I'll go into the ministry."

"Become a preacher?"

When Joe nodded, Alfred thought, Crystal, the church mouse. She was bright-eyed enough, and the daughter of the deacon. A man who had taken a special interest in Joe. The times she'd come to the house Alfred hadn't been able to hear most of what she had to say, as her voice was so soft. He'd stopped asking her to repeat herself when he saw that it took a considerable amount of courage for her to speak in the first place. But he was certain Crystal was behind the plan for Joe to leave the country and study the Bible.

"When is this going to happen?" he asked.

"As soon as we've both got enough money to cover the first year. Maybe sooner. Crystal's father wants to help us out. And there are others who want to support us too," Joe said, and Alfred had thought, well, don't expect the same from me.

Voices grow louder along the hall now, and he hears the squeak of shoes when someone hurries past his room. It's the hearse, going to attend to the yeller. When he opens his eyes they come to rest on the picture above the bed. A buck and doe step out from a forest at sunset, the sky a pink wash of colour, as it was when he and Joe returned to camp after the baptism party. He'd been lucky fishing that day. Three walleyes in half a dozen casts and then nothing after that. He'd fried the fish in butter, toasted bread over the fire. "There may not be enough here to feed a crowd of thousands, but there's enough for a baptism supper," he remembers saying.

"Let's just say there is a God. And let's say God wants you to do this. How do you know?" he'd asked Joe. "Did you hear him say so?"

"I don't need to hear, or see anything. I just know," Joe replied. Then he went walking along the shore in search of flat stones that he sent skipping out across the lake, and Alfred thought his heart would stop beating.

* * *

Joe's likely downstairs now, watching hockey, Alfred tells himself, forgetting that Joe is away and had just called. Laurie is watching one of her TV programs in the bedroom, or she's at the dining room table with her laptop, her eyes fixed on the screen, her periodic tapping at the keyboard telling him she's playing a game, or researching vitamins and minerals, something to put more zip in his step. Or she's talking to people—sometimes when he goes across the room, a person will peer at him from the computer screen, looking like they've just seen a ghost. Laurie laughing then, saying, they can see you, Dad. She tells the startled person on the screen, "That's just my father."

And he'd come to think of himself as being her father, too. Although the first time he'd seen her, he'd wanted to shut the door in her face. Verna's sisters had said they often saw the girl going about town with her grandmother. Unfortunate, they said. A bit rough around the edges. But they held no grudge against Laurie who'd been an innocent bystander. Alfred came to agree, but it was another thing to see the girl on his veranda. He'd known immediately who she was, all that reddish-blonde curly hair, like her grandmother, Ivy, and his impulse had been to slam the door.

"Mr. Beaudry?" Laurie asked as though she suspected she'd got the wrong house.

Yes, he was that. He was Mr. Beaudry. Her jade green eyelids fluttered. Where had she got her height? he wondered, her grandmother and mother were half-pints. "And you must be the Rasmussen girl."

"I'm Laurie," she said nodding. "I'd like to talk to you about my mother. But I'll understand if you don't want to."

"There isn't much to say," Alfred replied, his apprehension somewhat eased by her hesitance. Your silly chit of a mother couldn't decide what to do with you. Whether to give you away to a good home, or to keep you. And so she tried to take you with her. And Verna went after her down to the river, to the nest of trampled grass she'd come across during one of her walks. Likely she thought that's where your mother had gone and went down there, only to see her go flying off the bridge.

"That's okay," Laurie said in a way that suggested she didn't expect anything more from him.

She turned to leave, and Alfred found himself calling out. "We have a picture of her, taken on the day she died."

But when he went inside the house and looked in all the usual places, he couldn't find it.

"Joe should be home soon, he'll know where it is," he told her and invited her to wait.

Laurie perched on a veranda step and Alfred sat in one of the Adirondack chairs, listening while she talked. She was like a cecropia moth in the way she was folded up into herself, her body covered in layers of clothes the colours of rust and earth, the peasant skirt meeting the toes of her crinkled suede boots. The frayed cuffs of her brown sweater were darned with what looked like white string and the child-like mending took away his remaining antipathy toward her.

She went on to talk about how much cooler it had been earlier in the morning when she'd got on the bus for the trip to Winnipeg. She'd spent half the day registering at a college, where, in September, she would take courses and become a dental assistant. And before she caught the bus home, she had to check out several more rooms for rent, as so far, she'd had no luck. Her earlier hesitance vanished and was replaced by a look of tragedy as she described the rooms she'd seen, about the size of a closet. "I wouldn't let my dog stay in some of them," she said.

"You have a dog?" Alfred asked. Joe was allergic to dogs, he did not say, but studied the thought for a fleeting moment, the fact that he was considering the consequences on Joe of her having a dog.

"It's my grandmother's," Laurie said. "Our house would not be a house without a dog—one time we had three. Three rooms in the house, and we've got three dogs, can you imagine?"

No, he couldn't, Alfred said.

"You'd never guess how much people are asking for a room," she went on to say, and then described at length the bathroom amenities of that place where she would not leave a dog.

"That's Joe coming now," Alfred said. With him was Crystal, her arm linked through his, her spring plaid coat open and flaring with her spirited walk. Since their engagement, she'd become less of a mouse in the way she took over at the supper table, rising to go to the kitchen to get something Joe had forgotten, sending him and Alfred to the living room while she cleared away dishes and washed up.

Laurie raised her head, and Alfred thought Joe must feel her wavering smile half a block away, her exuberant mouth wide and bright with orange lipstick. Joe stood still, then came toward them, leaving Crystal hurrying to catch up.

"This is Laurie Rasmussen. The daughter of Karen," Alfred said quickly to get it over with.

"Rasmussen," Joe repeated, recognition dawning, and yet there was nothing in his face that said he was anything but curious.

Laurie got up from the step and went down to him, and Alfred noted they were almost the same height. "And you're Joe. My grandmother has an album full of pictures of you."

When Joe extended his hand, she hesitated before taking it, her mouth twisting with uncertainty when she did. "I've always wanted to meet you," Joe said, surprising Alfred.

"And I've always wondered about you."

Joe almost tripped over his feet as he turned to Crystal to introduce them. "My fiancée," he said before saying Crystal's name, as though he needed to establish that fact right off the top.

"Gosh, you two are engaged," Laurie said, and Alfred thought she was like a bonfire suddenly flaring up, and Crystal looked as though she wanted to put some distance between them. Laurie *was* rough around the edges, like she was flying apart the way her hair was a pile of kinky wool on her head, about to come tumbling down. Her sweater hung low at the back and held the shape of her behind; the hem of her peasant skirt dipped lower on one side. She had dressed for the cold morning, likely, and it would be cold again by the time she left. But it had turned out to be a warm enough day. And it was still warm, yet she kept on the heavy sweater. Perhaps she felt she needed protection.

"So when are you getting married?" Laurie asked Crystal, making what she thought was small talk, Alfred knew, but he saw the pained look Crystal gave Joe.

"We haven't set a date yet, but we're planning on a year from now—next spring," Joe said, and Alfred was surprised, thinking, so they must be getting their money together. Joe worked full-time now at the small tool repair depot where he'd worked every summer for years, and Crystal at the insurance company that employed her father.

The photograph Alfred hadn't been able to find was up in his room, Joe said and he went inside to get it.

In his absence Crystal seemed not to know where to look, taking Laurie in with quick glances, while chewing on her bottom lip. Laurie sat back down on the top veranda step and tucked her skirt in tightly around her long legs, once again the cecropia, her wings folded. Alfred invited Crystal to sit in the other veranda chair, but she chose to perch on the bottom step instead.

When Joe returned with the picture, he sat down beside Laurie, holding it between them. Alfred listened as Joe told her about the film having been in the camera almost a year before they'd thought to have it developed. He went on to tell her that in the picture her mother was sitting on these very steps.

"My grandmother has never wanted to talk about what happened," Laurie said. "I guess that's because she not only lost her daughter, but her best friend, too." She turned and glanced up at Alfred, measuring how he'd received what she'd just said.

"That's true," Alfred said.

Then Joe told her all that he knew about what had happened that day, Laurie taking it in, their faces intent on each other, while Crystal looked up at them, spots of colour rising in her cheeks.

"You keep the picture," Joe said to Laurie when he'd finished speaking.

"Are you sure?" she asked, saying, "Gosh," when Joe assured her that he was. Then she cupped the picture in both hands and gazed at it for a moment before tucking it into her oversize bag on the step beside her.

And what had brought her to Winnipeg? Joe asked and Alfred heard the story of her long day, once again. That the college had proven to be on the outskirts of the city and she'd had to wait at least forty-five minutes for the right bus. And then by the time she'd found building C, where she was supposed to register, she'd almost been flattened by the wind. When she came to the point in the story where she'd seen the rooming house that was not fit for a dog, Alfred interrupted. There was an empty and good-size room upstairs, he said. Maybe she would like to see it. However, there would be no dogs, as neither he nor Joe was fit enough for a dog. She laughed then, her mouth wide open and head tipped back on her shoulders, and Alfred thought it had been too long a time since he'd heard someone laugh from their belly.

By the time summer and autumn had passed and winter set in, Joe and Crystal had gone their separate ways. And in the new year, after Laurie returned from holidays with her grandmother, Joe bought her a tube of red lipstick. And the following spring, he bought her a dark red pop-top that bared her midriff whenever she raised her arms. Laurie graduated from college, and by the time she'd moved out of the house and into her own apartment, she'd already been working a year. Instead of returning to university as Alfred had hoped, Joe continued to work at the small tool repair depot. Then he went into debt to open the Happy Traveler.

And now that business is belly up. Alfred would like to see the look on Joe's face when he finds out about the money from Verna's life insurance policy. When he learns that the cash from the policy his mother was able to pay for by cooking for and cleaning up after boarders had been invested wisely and now amounts to a million dollars. And it's his. To do with as he sees fit.

After the nurses had settled him into the chair, they'd left him in peace to doze. But he knows they'll be back, this time with a pole and drip. With a pad for his bed that will let them know if he's up and roaming about, or if he's thrown himself overboard. There's no two ways about it, he's old. Deficient and decrepit. And like the old, not to be taken seriously.

He looks for the metal chair, his way station to the room. When he doesn't see it anywhere, he realizes the nurses have figured out how he managed to get as far as the window and have taken it away. He's surprised to find that its absence makes his eyes grow wet. He recalls that when he was in the prisoner of war camp he sometimes saw the faces of men about to die suddenly stream with tears, as though a dam had given way inside. He sometimes saw them turn and look at something that wasn't there.

Six

Late in the evening Laurie enters the shopping mall foyer, intent on using a pay phone. When she sees the metal barrier closing off access to the stores beyond she feels affronted, as though the mesh curtain is a hand raised in her face.

A man using the instant teller glances at her when she goes over to the bank of phones. He keys in a transaction and the electronic burps are inordinately loud in the enclosed glass space; without the doors opening and closing with the constant traffic of people, the air has become overheated and stale. She anticipates Joe's voice, while at the same time doubts that he'll answer. More than likely, he's got the cell turned off to conserve the battery. She hesitates, wanting to know that he's all right, but dreading that he'll tell her why he left. A second trip to Canadian Tire after she ran into Pete only confirmed that Joe wasn't there, nor was he welcome to return. She calls his cell, feeling as though she's caught in a patch of turbulence, not knowing when the ground might suddenly give way. He doesn't answer.

She scoops up her change, drops what's left of it into the sock. She went through a lot of money while talking to Alfred. She called him thinking to learn, without coming right out and asking, if he'd heard from Joe. Then she'd almost spilled the beans. Why was Joe working if they were on a vacation, he'd asked, and he hadn't bought her lame answer. All she'd accomplished by calling was to alarm him, and she regrets that now.

Across Gibson Road the stark whiteness of the apartment buildings has faded to grey with the setting of the sun, and shadows darken the windows of the basement suites as though night is working its way up from the ground. Here and there, the anemic lights in windows brighten. It's the time of day when she would go into Joe's office and watch the cloud of gulls above the city dump, bright gold pieces flashing against the northern sky. During the time Steve was stationed in Germany she would think of him, that the sun had already set where he was. And as if he knew, he would sometimes call just as she and Joe were sitting down to dinner. When Joe had finished talking and passed the phone across the table to her it was a struggle not to react when Steve went on about how much he wanted her. Although they hadn't seen each other for years, she'd always thought of him whenever she came upon the bustier, the crumple of butterfly thongs pushed to the back of her lingerie drawer. She wonders if the attraction will still be there, and what will she do about it if it is.

The instant teller whirrs and she turns toward the sound just as the man retrieves his money, folds it and jams it into his jean pocket. The doors swing open as he leaves, striding off toward a black 4x4 parked in the fire lane with its engine running. She realizes again that it's Friday. People are going out and doing things, as she hoped she and Joe would do. She realizes she is hungry.

Although she knows it's futile she goes over to the instant teller, takes the credit card from the sock and feeds it into the slot. The card came to Joe in the mail unsolicited, with a pre-approved ten-thousand-dollar line of credit. Within months that limit was increased to fifteen thousand and then twenty. As the machine tugs the card from her grasp she holds her breath, and when it's ejected she's surprised by bitterness, a seed bursting open on her tongue.

She's about to turn away when she sees a transaction slip lying on one side of the shelf. Either the man forgot to take it, or, as she so often did, only glanced at it to reassure himself he wasn't overdrawn and left it. His bank balance, she discovers, is half of what she and Joe would usually go through in a month. The thought makes her nauseous. She scrunches up the receipt and drops it into the waste receptacle. How little they had to show in the end for a hundred and twenty-five thousand dollars a year, just the tables set up on the veranda and down the walk heaped with household goods. Boxes and boxes, crates and an assortment of laundry baskets covered the lawn, filled with pictures and books, cosmetics and sets of bathroom soaps, lotions and scrubs, still unopened. She'd priced CDs and DVDs at a dollar apiece, and some people had complained, and wanted to bargain. There were beautifully designed boxes of stationery, which, although she hardly ever wrote letters, she could never resist. But people at the garage sale had resisted, and in the end she'd foisted as much stationery as she possibly could on her friend Sandra.

Sandra had helped arrange the crystal on a special table spread with a dark cloth to better display it, including several pieces of Waterford alongside the hand-painted Japanese tea set, the wedding gift from Joe's aunts, so appealingly colourful that for years Laurie had kept it out on the buffet. Laurie had set her Noritake dinnerware on the special table; the pottery she'd bought at various craft shows throughout the years; wood inlaid boxes and hand-carved bowls, and the blown glass pieces that leapt off the shelves and bit her while she toured a glassworks in Victoria.

She'd placed her marble chessboard at the centre, which for years had been set with the keepsakes she'd found in various shops across the country while travelling with Joe. She'd bought the chess set for the board so long ago she couldn't recall what she'd done with the actual pieces. You're not going to part with that, Sandra objected and offered to keep it for her, as she would the photo albums. A tiny clear glass moose marked the occasion of Laurie's first orgasm with Joe. It had happened while they were on a canoe trip. Her moaning, he'd said, sounded like the mating call of a moose and he expected their campsite to be stampeded. A pewter rowboat and its tiny sailor marked the passing of Earl, Alfred's long-time friend; the small amber egg, Steve's gift when he returned from Germany, and when he'd dropped it down the front of her dress it felt like silk between her breasts. Yes, that, she'd said to Sandra. She was tired of dusting it.

The garage sale was an opportunity to be more discriminating, she told herself when she and Sandra hauled things out of the house. It was a chance to start over as she sometimes had with her wardrobe, emptying the closets and bureaus in one fell swoop, packing the clothing into garbage bags that she left at the various charity drop boxes. Then she'd go shopping. Only to discover a year later that discrimination had flown out the window and that she'd replaced her wardrobe with one that was almost identical.

In the past she'd sometimes happened upon the dismal displays of goods set out on yard-sale tables and the people perusing them, only steps away but a world apart, she'd imagined. She'd scrunched up her nose, thinking of the many times when, as a child, she went to church rummage sales with her grandmother, poking through the broken toys and smudged storybooks, the malodorous jumble cast off from other people's lives. She refused to recall the excruciating anxiety of knowing there was a limit to the amount of money her grandmother would give her to spend, whereas the allure of objects proved to be unending. Invariably she wound up wanting what she hadn't bought. Soon after she got her first job, she spent most of her paycheque on two pairs of shoes when she couldn't decide between them, just because she could.

On the day of her own yard sale, Laurie was still in her bathrobe having a first cup of coffee when people began to arrive in cars and trucks, parking in front of the house and in the back lane, people coming on foot and bicycles almost two hours earlier than the advertised start time for the sale. She dressed quickly and went out onto the veranda and shouted at them to keep their distance, relieved when at last Sandra arrived and they dismantled the barrier they'd erected across the steps and took the sheets off the tables, dragged out from under them the boxes and baskets. The chessboard and its symbolic pieces sold immediately, as did most of the other items on her special table, dealers, Sandra said, knowing exactly what they wanted. Laurie realized with a pang of regret that she'd underpriced them, but consoled herself with the thought that she'd never really liked crystal, china, or Japanese tea sets.

By midday the people were gone and the lawn was trampled, boxes upended and the remains of the contents strewn about. A lampshade was wedged into the branches of the lilac bush. When Laurie went to free it, she found a mat rolled up and shoved in among the branches. Someone had stashed it there thinking to come back later and get it. She unrolled it, a soft pleasant-looking handmade cotton mat she had bought in the Cascade Mountains in a craft shop. Made by a native woman, its colours like the earth, moss and birchbark. She'd paid a hundred and twenty dollars for it and its price tag of ten dollars was so high, apparently, that someone had wanted to steal it.

That afternoon she piled the remainder of the garage sale items, including the mat, against the backyard fence where the usual garbage pickers going by could rummage through the boxes and take what they wanted. The garbage cans were filled to overflowing, and what Joe couldn't fit into them he'd thrown into boxes along with the remains of the small appliances he had smashed days ago with the sledgehammer.

She was surprised when she saw one of her angels, and then all of them, scattered among the battered pieces of metal and spikes of plastic as sharp as daggers. She had intended to leave the angels in the house, had positioned them where they might surprise a person who happened to glance upward. She'd hoped that this gesture of goodwill to the next inhabitants would in some way be returned to her and Joe. But he'd thrown them out.

As he had the flint stone. She scooped it up from among the rubble and cupped its chalky mantle as though to shield it from the rain. In spring, while readying the upstairs veranda for the summer months, she took the stone from the windowsill and washed it free of dust. And she sometimes recalled the moment when Joe had given it to her, the day she lay beside him on the beach still feeling the thrum and shudder of waves in her body. She'd been waiting for calm, when she could speak without her voice trembling. She wanted to tell him it was over. She wanted time to be on her own, to grow into her work as a dental assistant, the apartment she had rented. Sandra was moving to the city, and they were going to live together, going to go to Cuba in the winter.

She and Steve wanted each other, she did not tell Joe. They'd come so near to having sex at the Glass Spider concert. When their hands first touched she knew it would happen, and they soon found themselves in a corridor, their bodies pressed together hard, their mouths and hips grinding. Where's a cold shower when you need one, Steve had said laughing, shaking, when they came up for air. She took him by the hand and led him to a nearby coffee shop, her face hot and her breath coming quick. Joe, she said. They'd left him in the blue section of the arena when David Bowie had appeared, the crowd going wild as he descended on stage in the glass spider. She'd scrambled over the seats to get to the floor, Steve coming after her, but Joe had stayed behind. In the coffee shop Steve reached for her hands, covered them, pressed them hard against the table. It's always about Joe, he'd said. And although she knew she should pull her hands away, she hadn't.

When she lay beside Joe on the beach the next day, about to tell him that she wanted to end their relationship, he turned to her. While she'd been out on the lake windsurfing he'd gone for a long walk and found this, he said and put the flint stone in her hand. And then, suddenly, ardently, he asked her to marry him.

Verna, God rest her soul, would have been so tickled, Laurie's grandmother had said when Laurie broke the news, and raised a glass of sparkling wine in celebration of her announcement. *God rest her soul.* The words were a bookmark on each of Laurie's birthdays, marking the page of Verna's sacrifice. Are you sure about this? Sandra kept asking in the days leading to the wedding. Yes, she was sure she wanted to marry Joe. And what about Steve? Sandra finally asked, and Laurie listened to herself explain that she'd only wanted to break it off with Joe because after three years it wasn't going anywhere. Steve had just happened to come along. Joe's aunts and uncles, her grandmother, all of them had already made plans to come to Winnipeg for the wedding. They'd reserved several rooms in a nearby hotel when Alfred insisted the wedding be held in Winnipeg. He didn't care who married them, whether it was Pastor Ken, or not. As long as they were married in the backyard. And although Pastor Ken had declined to marry them, Laurie was relieved, for Joe's sake, when at the last moment, he and Maryanne decided to attend.

She's reluctant to leave the stale, heated space of the shopping centre foyer and return to the Meridian. Its batteries are low and she'll need to run the generator for a time if she's going to have enough light to read, or to watch TV. If she'd known they were going to be boondocking for a time, she would have kept several candles, the down-filled duvet, the picnic hamper, complete and compact in its wicker case. She'd thought, three days at the most; she hadn't counted on this stopover. Or that they would live in the Meridian once they got to Fort McMurray. When they'd started out Joe had said he would drop the motorhome off at an RV place in Edmonton, where the owner would come to get it. They'd rent a townhouse in McMurray. And buy a house soon after in whatever city they settled in. Where she would upgrade her dental assistant skills, and find work.

The parking lot is almost empty now, except for the scattering of vehicles parked along the east and west ends of it, Safeway and Walmart still being open. She could buy a can of soup. When she was a kid, she'd lived on canned soup and hotdogs. The thought makes her shiver. She decides to conserve what money she has in the event Joe doesn't return tonight, use it to call Steve in the morning, see if he's heard from him.

The chilly air bites through her sweater as she hurries across the parking lot hugging herself. There are several people sitting out on the apartment balconies wearing toques and heavy clothing. One of them looks to be swaddled in a blanket, like at a football game. She recalls the young men she saw earlier, dressed for summer while racing to Walmart to beat the cold. During her periods of self-help she read somewhere that you should focus on what you want and then act as though you've got it. Perhaps the people in Regina are trying to bring on warmer weather. *You'd love the people here, they're just so laid back and cheerful,* she will write on one of the postcards to Sandra. *So unfashionably positive. So far I haven't met a single scary person.* A toy city, toy people. She pictures the perfectly round-headed and brightly painted Fisher Price people, the lower half of their benign bodies being pegs designed to fit into the passenger holes in buses, cars and trains.

When she gets near the motorhome she notices something set against the rear of it and hurries over, thinking Joe has returned. A folded-up lawn chair, she discovers, and her euphoria collapses when she realizes the Meridian remains in darkness.

She steps inside it calling for Joe, though she knows he's not there, then sinks down into the lounger, its leather cushions a cold jolt of reality. Just then the parking lot lights come on, flooding the dinette table and the postcards scattered across it. There's enough light for her to see her way into the cab of the Meridian, where her fleece jacket lies on the passenger seat. She puts it on and goes back outside.

Only feet away from the Meridian at the base of a light standard is the garbage barrel she had used earlier, and she concludes someone intended to discard the lawn chair, and instead, decided to bring it to her attention. She opens it and discovers that it's a type of lawn chair she hasn't seen in ages. The seat has been stretched in the shape of a bowl, but the green and white plastic tubes are intact and look clean.

She sets up the chair on one side of the Meridian steps and when she sits down in it, she fits nicely into the bowl-shaped seat. This is where Joe will find her, should he return during the night. She'll be here watching as he comes toward her in the dark, and something inside her will fly across the space to meet him. And come up against a wall.

For almost an hour she watches the last of the late-night shoppers straggle from Safeway, laden with bags or push-ing carts of groceries they unload into trunks. Headlights sweep across her as one by one the shoppers drive away, turn onto Gibson Road and pass from sight. At her back, the traffic along Albert Street becomes sporadic, and she wonders if the nightlife of the city happens elsewhere.

There's a Jeep at the curb in front of an apartment on Gibson Road with a couch on its roof. She notices, too, that there are fewer people out on the balconies, and many of the apartment windows pulse with television images. She imagines herself in the bedroom of their house on Arlington Street, feet up on a towel as she exfoliates, then clips and paints her toenails, a glass of wine at her elbow while she watches *Desperate Housewives, Big Love,* faintly hearing the roar of the crowd when a goal is scored in the hockey game Joe and Alfred are watching on the big screen in the base-ment family room.

Her routines had become life as she knew and expected it to be. The future was a distant land where there were no pension funds or savings; the meagre amount they'd set aside had been plowed back into the house to live up to the gentrification of the neighbourhood. Do not go there, Laurie cautions. She crams the future into a jar, screws the lid down tight and sets it up on her imaginary shelf near the ceiling.

Curtains slide open on a balcony door where, earlier in the day, she saw the woman and the potted plant. A man emerges, the husband she decides, and she recalls how the woman's dark head scarf intensified her pallid complexion. The man seems darker-skinned, and even from the distance he appears more lively and bright-faced. He squats, lifts the plant, what could be a Norfolk pine, and she notes how his white shirt glows in the shadow cast by the overhang of the balcony a floor above as he carries the plant inside.

A jetliner rises from the airport suddenly, filling the sky just beyond Laurie where it seems to hesitate, and then, its engines screaming, ascends swiftly out of sight. The little girl in the pink gym suit comes onto the balcony and the man behind her. She points skyward and he hikes her up into his arms to give her a last glimpse of the airplane as it soars beyond the city into the eastern sky.

Laurie recalls the dark-eyed Pakistani girl who used to live near them. How she would slip in the front door when Laurie was out in the backyard, or in the back door when she was out in the front, and leave evidence that she'd been there. An ornament had been moved from one shelf to another, a single dandelion flower set on the stairs, a skipping rope twined round the newel post halfway up to the second floor.

It occurs to Laurie that all the while the girl lived next door, she'd never seen her in the arms of an adult. She couldn't figure out who, among the many people living in the house, might be her parents. She may well have been a neglected child, given the way she planted evidence around Laurie's house as proof she'd been there. Especially the flesh-coloured ball, leaving it in the bowl of a serving spoon in the cutlery drawer where Laurie would be sure to find it. The ball looked malleable, like a piece of play-dough, but it proved to be hard and rebounded high and swiftly off the sidewalk when Laurie threw it over the fence into the girl's yard.

Days later, Laurie was surprised to come across the ball again while uprooting the spent petunias in the veranda window boxes where it was tucked in among the leaves. It was wet and a brighter pink, as though it had just been washed. She rolled the ball between her palms, debating what to do, laughter breaking in her throat. Although the girl's bicycle was lying on the lawn, she was nowhere to be seen.

Laurie turned at the sound of Alfred at the door. "Over there," he said and gestured to the girl's running shoe on the boulevard, and she understood. With exaggerated stealth she crept up on the shoe, and much to Alfred's amusement, tucked the ball into its toe.

Several days later she was preparing a casserole before going to work, looked up, and there was the ball on the sill of the bay window. The angels on it had been rear-ranged into a circle, and at the centre was the pink ball. Nearest to it was the tallest of the angels, this being a wooden Polish angel in a flowered robe, its scalloped gold wings narrow and rising straight above its head. It was one of few angels she'd come upon that hadn't been childlike, or a prepubescent female.

Enough, she told herself and dried her hands, determined to go next door and ring the doorbell and make a point of returning the ball to one of the adults. She would tell them about the child prowling about the house and put a stop to it. The neighbourhood wasn't one where doors needed to be locked when someone was home. Alfred had never caught sight of the girl in the house, had never heard her come and go. Her stealth was unsettling.

She wasn't sure which of the adults she should speak to, but they were all smiling people, from the distance of their yard, friendly in a way that suggested they believed it was required of them and they were making the necessary effort. Friendly enough that one of the oldest of several women who appeared to live there, once suggested to Laurie that she might want to water their outdoor planters for two weeks while they were away. The fact that the flowers were healthy and blooming briskly when they returned wasn't mentioned, nor had she been thanked.

Nip it in the bud, Laurie told herself but was stopped by the ringing of the telephone.

"Do you have the television turned on?" Joe asked, his voice sharp with tension. "Don't ask, just turn it on. And get Dad. Watch it with him." What channel? It didn't matter, he said, and hung up. Moments later she and Alfred watched in disbelief as the second of the World Trade Center towers collapsed. When she called Joe back, Clayton said he'd already left for home. Hours later he still hadn't got there, and they ate dinner without him.

That night she lay awake listening for the Explorer in the front street and hearing Alfred moving about in his room at the end of the hall. He was going over to the window, she knew, to look out into the yard to see if the Explorer was parked on the pad. Sometime later she felt his brief presence in her doorway. "Is that you, Dad?" "It's not like Joe to be away without calling," Alfred said, telling her what she already knew.

With each hour Verna's clock in the dining room seemed to tick louder, as though her ghost was telling Laurie to pay attention to the time passing. She went downstairs thinking to silence it and when she turned on the light, there was Alfred, fully clothed, sitting at the dining room table. Spread about him on the table were several boxes of chocolates he'd received from the Legion at various holidays and birthdays, which he kept locked in a cabinet only to be taken out on Sundays after dinner or as a consolation prize to whomever he defeated at cribbage. Or on the occasions when Verna's family remembered he was still alive and paid a visit. Alfred remained silent, blinking rapidly in the sudden onslaught of light. Laurie guessed that he was regretting his miserliness with chocolates. Perhaps, in some disjointed way, he hoped to lure Joe home with them.

Late on the second night, Joe telephoned to tell them he was in Vancouver and would return in a couple of days. He'd driven to the coast to think things through, he said. And didn't care to say what those things might be. "I'm okay, honey. Don't worry." He was going to see the Lewises, Laurie had concluded. But he returned home sooner than she'd expected, unshaven, his shirt spotted with coffee, clothes rumpled from having slept in the car, and he said he hadn't been to see them. Still, that was the beginning of Joe's unexplained hours of absence, his need to spend time alone, in a bar sometimes, he said, which accounted for the odour of smoke on his clothes.

Soon after 9/11, the Pakistani family left the neighbour-hood. Sometimes when Laurie went about the house she half expected to come across the flesh-coloured ball, which, ultimately, she had put in their mailbox. She wonders now where the child is, and how tall she is, and whether or not she continues to infiltrate other people's spaces. It's what she herself had done. She'd come to think that she'd infil-trated her young mother's body. Her grandmother's three-room house, and her messy life with her on-again, off-again boyfriend, a trapper she'd known for years, who expected her full attention whenever he got to town. And then Laurie had taken over Joe and Alfred's house, arranging and rearranging the rooms to leave her mark.

The little girl in the pink sweatsuit and the man have gone inside and the curtain is now drawn across the slid-ing door. Then she sees him come out of the building at the main entrance below, carrying a coil of rope. He walks over to the Jeep that has the couch on the roof. He snakes a length of the rope over the couch, and with the agility of a gymnast, begins to lash it down. When he's done, he gets in the Jeep and drives away.

The city seems to hunker down into quiet now, and the air grows still. Although it is not as cold as it was last night, there will likely be frost again. At Safeway the lights have been dimmed and all around her the parking lot spreads out, empty of vehicles, the people vanished. She thinks of Joe and can't imagine that he would have hitched a ride somewhere or set out on foot, can't imagine that he would have gone to a bar and met someone, a woman, and gone home with her.

She stifles a rising panic as she gets up and hurries toward the mall entrance and the pay phones to call Steve, or Sandra, thinking that because the instant teller is open twenty-four hours she'll be able to get into the foyer. But the door is locked and when she inserts her card in the slot, it doesn't activate.

She returns to the Meridian, shivering at the thought of cold bedsheets. She plunges her hands into her jacket pockets to warm them, and feels something stiff and crumpled. A twenty-dollar bill, she discovers. Breakfast. She often came across coins and bills in the pockets of garments and she views this find as a good omen. She'll run the generator and charge the batteries, turn on the lights, watch television, as if this were any other night when Joe is later than expected.

Hours later she awakens on the lounger to the sound of voices coming from the television. For a moment she imagines she's on the fold-out couch in her grandmother's living room, the voices coming from the bedroom, her grandmother and her boyfriend talking after having made love, which is sometimes only a gentle rocking of the bedsprings, other times a wrestling match. At which point Laurie would turn up the television, signalling that she's pissed off. She wants to yell at them to grow up. Now, suddenly, her grandmother is present in the smoky sweet smell of cigarettes and perfume, leaning over her. *You must have won the sweepstakes, TV, lights left on all over the house.*

Laurie gets up and turns off the television, then feels her way toward the greenish light in the bedroom doorway. She lowers the blind, the light a laser thin line along the edges of the window. She goes to the closet and pages through the garments until she finds the fur jacket, and beside it, the leather parka. Tomorrow she'll take them to Clara's Boutique, tonight they'll keep her warm.

She puts herself to bed fully clothed, arranges the jacket and coat over her body. Yes, I've won the sweepstakes, she repeats, and curls up beneath the weight of the garments, recalling her grandmother's sudden spurts of extravagant affection, her largesse, after Laurie had left town for Winnipeg. Laurie had made a point then to call her grandmother weekly, and knew that when she sounded vague and distracted she was going through her usual boyfriend challenges. Talking to her grandmother during those times was like throwing jelly at a wall. Nothing Laurie said stuck.

Then, in the midst of one of those periods, a parcel would arrive at the bus depot without warning, filled with puzzling objects: a loop of ribbed rubber that was meant to unscrew stubborn lids from jars, economy packs of flashlights and batteries of various sizes, plastic mousetraps that looked like overgrown clothespins and were touted to be a gentler way to kill a rodent. So gentle, in fact, she never caught anything. The loud clattering in the cupboard kept her awake most of a night as the mouse pushed the trap about, turned it upside down and sideways to get the last bit of peanut butter.

Her grandmother had sent her and Joe boat-sized fuzzy rabbit and basset hound slippers, a Holly Hobbie doll she'd found at a rummage sale, still in its original packaging, and always there would be a tin of licorice allsorts, the candy Laurie wasn't able to live without as a child.

The gifts were compensation for the fact that even when her grandmother was present she was away, preoccupied with untangling the snarls in her heart. She had loved her daughter, given the number of pictures of Karen in the box under her bed, along with the crayon drawings, the school yearbooks, the caption under the picture of Karen in the last yearbook saying she had wanted to be a nurse. And Laurie's grandmother had also loved Verna.

Where were you when I was born? Laurie had once asked when she was still a child, but old enough to have wondered for a time, before she worked up the courage to ask.

"I was right here," her grandmother said and pointed to the floor in the kitchen. "There were forest fires burning. Verna, God rest her soul, phoned me the day she died. There was this helicopter going over the house and I couldn't always hear what she was saying. It was Parks Canada, keeping a watch for wild animals. All kinds of animals came out of the forest into town that year, deer, even a moose, as big as a truck, that got into the church."

"And what did she say?" Laurie asked.

"Who?" her grandmother said.

"Verna Beaudry, what did she say?"

"Not much that I could hear. She said Karen was as big as a house, and it looked like she was going to pop soon. She wanted to know if I planned on coming, or should she sit with Karen, once labour started. I'd just got Laddie, and he wouldn't trust anyone but me around him," her grandmother said, referring to the stray dog she'd rescued when it came limping out of the bush one day as she was driving home from work.

"So you couldn't go," Laurie said, old enough to realize that her grandmother thought more about caring for a stray dog than she had her own child.

"Karen didn't want me there anyway," her grandmother said. "Your mother took to Verna, right from the start. She would have wanted Verna to sit with her." The start, being when Laurie's grandfather had been killed in a logging accident and her grandmother became a widow with a young child to raise. She'd needed to find work then, and Verna, who was already taking care of elderly parents, took care of Karen, more often than not.

"Who's your daddy? I haven't a clue," Laurie's grandmother had said then.

From the height of the train trestle bridge, the island she'd been born on looked like a bristly porcupine. Years and years ago when the neighbourhood had been sparsely populated with market gardeners and an ice harvesting company, one spring, during high flooding, a shed became lodged in the riverbed. And gradually debris snagged onto it, a rowboat, branches and lumber, straw; silt had collected and seeds sprouted. The small shed mired in the mud became an island. Just as she had, she'd thought when she saw all the goods that had become attached to her, spread about the yard at the garage sale.

I've won the sweepstakes, Laurie thinks again, this time wryly as she takes the twenty-dollar bill out of the pocket of her fleece and smooths it flat against her breastbone before setting it on the bedside table. Smitty's, for breakfast, early, to beat the crowd.

An hour later she's awake, sweating and clammy, angered by a dream. She and Joe were in a department store and about to enter a crowded elevator. Thinking he was behind her, she pushed her way through the people to the back of it, where she was pressed on all sides by strangers who

157

suddenly seemed menacing. She discovered that Joe hadn't got on the elevator. He stood beyond the doors, shoulders scrunched up and grinning like a boy about to play a trick. He would take the adjacent elevator and meet her on the next floor, he mimed as the doors began to close. The elevator rose, stopped, the doors opened and the people quickly went away. Instead of finding herself on another floor of merchandise, she was in the countryside, and beyond her stretched a seemingly endless and barren field. Joe was nowhere to be seen.

The feeling of betrayal fades as she listens to the night, expecting to hear the skateboarders, but except for the sound of a vehicle going by on Albert Street, it's quiet. She gets up, pushes the blind aside to bare a crack of window and notices a small truck parked beyond the gardening compound, near the far perimeter of the lot that borders Albert Street. A blue light sputters on the ground, disappears and reappears, as though someone's crouched and moving around it. She notices the cabana on the truck and realizes that it's Pete. Hurriedly she jams her feet into running shoes and goes outside.

When she draws near she sees the frying pan on the camp cookstove. Pete sits on the edge of the lowered tailgate, his body curled, hands at his mouth as though playing a harmonica. He starts when he sees her, gets up from the tailgate, his body rigid with wariness. As she moves out of the shadow of the truck, his eyes widen.

"You," he says. He lowers his hands and she sees the hotdog in one of them. He looks across the parking lot at the Meridian, the swirls sweeping across its side suggesting speed and flight.

"That your RV?"

"Yes," she says. Yes, but. It is and it isn't, she wants to explain. Always feeling the need to do so, to give away too much. Steam rises from a saucepan on the tailgate, hot chocolate, she concludes from the sweet smell that instantly draws attention to her hunger. It's hunger that's awakened her.

"Isn't that something," Pete says, and for a moment he looks as though he wants to say more. Then he says, "I see you found a use for the chair."

Him? The surprise is not an entirely pleasant one. "So I have you to thank."

"I guess that guy of yours hasn't showed up yet."

Laurie hears an accusation, and it stings.

The faint sound of a siren rises from far across the sprawling city. Something's happening out there. Something is going on, while here there's an eerie quietness in the absence of traffic, the amber lights at the intersection flashing caution, the street beyond the lights dropping off into darkness.

"There was this man at Robin's Donuts. I take it he's your friend. He said you and Joe were away on a job. What happened?" Laurie asks.

"Yah, well, one of us was on the job. I guess Joe wasn't interested in making some pretty good money." He goes over to the tailgate and takes a long drink from the saucepan, then bites into the hotdog, his cheek bulging with bun and wiener as he chews.

"Excuse me, I only just finished work, and this here is my supper," he says speaking around the food. "I've got to get it into me. This is what happens when I don't eat in time." He holds out his hand to show her its pronounced tremor. His puffy fingers are dark red and sore-looking.

"Do you know where Joe might have gone?"

He shrugs. "He made a phone call, and took off. You and him have a fight?"

She doesn't reply, thinking that the telephone call Joe made was to the Lewises. And that he knows now that she didn't relay Maryanne's message. She's about to return to the Meridian when Pete suddenly starts to curse. She sees what he sees, two burly security men hurrying toward them from Walmart, one of them breaking into a trot.

Pete stuffs the remainder of the hotdog into his mouth, then quickly folds up the camp stove and takes it and the fry pan to the truck where he loads them into the cabana. He flings the contents of the saucepan across the parking lot, the splash of hot chocolate steaming as it meets the asphalt. He throws the pot into the cabana where it clanks noisily as it hits something inside. The two men part to skirt the puddle of chocolate; slow down now and advance with caution.

"Okay, okay, I get the message," Pete calls out. He shuts the cabana door and slams the tailgate into place. Then he comes round the side of the truck and instead of getting into it, he crosses his arms and leans against the door. His narrow face, the way the tip of his tongue worries the space between his front teeth make him look like a desert lizard.

"Move that piece of junk," the largest of the two men calls out, his voice is a smoker's voice, dull and raspy.

"Don't sweat it, I'm leaving," Pete says. "But not before you guys tell me, how come it's okay for her to park here, but it's not okay for me?" He motions in the direction of the Meridian.

The two men turn to look beyond Laurie at the motorhome. Walmart encourages boondocking, Joe said. The presence of RVs meant that should anyone be intent on theft and vandalism, there were extra pairs of eyes watching.

"Look, all I know is that we're given the licence numbers of vehicles that are allowed to be here overnight. And yours isn't one of them. It's not our job to decide who gets to park," the smoker says.

Laurie turns and heads back to the Meridian, feeling their eyes on her. As she goes up the steps she hears Pete's truck start up. Once inside she kneels on the lounger, raises the window blind in time to see him drive past the recycling bins toward the back of the parking lot and the exit there. The two security men watch for a moment, and then they both turn at once and look in her direction. She thinks they're about to come over, but they return to the office.

Until the adrenalin rush subsides she won't be able to sleep. When she switches on the light above the dinette, her eyes come to rest on the postcards, glossy and bright with primary colours. The collage, she reminds herself, and goes to the bedroom and returns with the manicure scissors and wearing the silver fox jacket, telling herself, yes, as she feels instantly warmer.

Within moments curled hard bits of images are scattered across the table. She looks about for something more, the label on the wine bottle, the newspaper spread open on the lounger. Then she remembers the bathroom garbage she'd emptied in the can outside, the embossed packaging, tissue paper, the various manufacturer's tags on strings.

It's as though the short distance between the Meridian and the garbage can is a stage—she feels watched as she crosses it. Grasping the rim to brace herself, she leans deep inside. Although it's near to being empty and lined with a plastic bag, the stink of decay and rust is almost overpowering and she holds her breath as she quickly plucks up the packaging and flings it over the side. There are crumpled serviettes, several plastic store hangers, McDonald's hamburger wrappers, the gloves she used to colour her hair. Then she snags onto something that feels alive. She tries to shake it off and it flaps against her hand, flaccid and clammy. A tape worm. She bolts up from the can and when she sees the condom hooked about her fingers she swears, and frantically flicks it loose.

She goes back to collapse into the lawn chair, leans over her knees, forehead pressed against them, gasping with the effort to keep the imaginary jars on the shelf from toppling and crashing down on her head, to suppress the large cracking sobs she won't be able to crawl out from under. This is what she's left with. Herself. In a Walmart parking lot, waiting for Joe who, she knows, has long since stopped loving her. She's stranded on a raft that's been swept out to sea. "Oh my God," she says, the words a spasm heaved up from her stomach.

There's a sudden clash of noise and she looks up to see a small hooded figure going across the Safeway lot, collecting stray carts. What would a kid be doing working this late at night? she can't help but wonder, and as she watches his dogged, almost robotic movements, her breathing steadies.

The garbage lies scattered about on the tarmac, metallic

blue and white embossed flattened boxes, like seashells. She thinks of a night on the beach near Varadero, the sun already set. She recalls the eerie phosphorescence of the pounding surf; seeing the shapes of overturned boats, like large beached fish, and drawing Joe over to one. Taking his hand to show him she wasn't wearing panties. She remembers the air being humid and thick with the smell of the ocean and humus in the wild growth near the fishing boat, Joe's groan of desire. It was the last time he'd made love to her with any passion.

She collects the packaging and is about to return to the Meridian when she realizes she forgot the tissue paper. She dumps the material onto the lawn chair and returns to the garbage can where she plucks it up, and when she sees the pizza box at the bottom of the can, she hesitates. They always order a larger pizza than they need to, and usually there's some left over, and usually they pitch it out, as neither of them care for reheated pizza.

The weather has been cool most of the day. Feta and spinach, there was no meat that might have gone rancid. She looks about. Except for a single lit window near the top floor of one of the apartments, all the windows are dark. She rises on her tiptoes, the rim of the garbage can cutting deep beneath her ribcage as she retrieves the box and comes up with it, gratified by a heaviness sliding to one side. The cardboard is soft and stained by moisture, but the box is tightly closed.

It's as though she's on stage, and in the audience at the same time, seeing herself, a forty-one-year-old woman heavy around the waist and wide in the hips. That fact made more pronounced by the snug-fitting jeans hugging her thighs and flaring out across her running shoes, the scroll of embroidery and sequins running down the sides of her long legs failing to reduce the swell of her stomach. An overweight woman in a silver fox jacket, diving for food.

Seven

IN THE FAR DISTANCE a vehicle approaches, its headlight a single white beam that wavers and pokes at the darkness, as though testing it for depth. It grows near, and the beam becomes two lights steadily and swiftly bearing down on Joe where he stands on the shoulder with his arm raised. When the vehicle rockets past he's submerged in the sudden dark that follows and it takes time for his eyes to adjust, for the land to emerge, the colour of ashes.

The traffic is light now and his chances of being picked up are slim. He should have tried for a lift at one of the gas stations along the service road in Medicine Hat, found someone who was going straight through to Calgary. As it is, the first ride took him only as far as a hamlet, a half hour away.

A dog barks, a large one from the sound of it. He turns and looks at the house he just walked past, its lights glancing through tree branches stirred by the wind. The animal has only caught scent of him now. Just what he needs, an angry dog challenging his right to be here. He scans the edge of the ditch for a stick, or a good-size stone, and is relieved a moment later when the barking stops.

According to the young man he talked to when he paid for his meal at the restaurant in Medicine Hat, Calgary is less than three hours away. If he got an early start from there first thing in the morning, he could be in Fort McMurray by the end of the day. He turns to look at the shimmer of Medicine Hat on the horizon, a long walk back, but the alternative is getting off the highway to find someplace sheltered to sleep. He's in a barren and exposed stretch of country, and his face feels scoured and hot from the wind that rose shortly after he set out. He doesn't relish more of this.

After talking to Alfred he had another coffee, and considered returning to Winnipeg, finding temporary work in one of the box stores in the south city limits, living in a cheap motel on the Pembina strip that would give him anonymity, freedom from telephone calls and mail. He could work nights, spend the days with his father. But he couldn't take him home. And while Alfred understands that a business might go belly up, he wouldn't understand how it was possible for him to lose the house.

Still, in the south end of Winnipeg there would be little chance of coming upon people he knew, except for Pauline. People such as the deacon who surprised him by calling last winter. When he and Crystal were engaged, Joe had shared many meals with the family, and been a frequent weekend guest at the lakeside cottage. The deacon began calling him son. After he and Crystal split up, the man had found ingenious ways to look straight through him.

The deacon explained that when he'd heard Joe's business was suffering, he'd put him on his prayer list. "It's been some time since we've seen you, Joe. But you're never far from our thoughts. The Lord laid it on me to call. Why don't we get together over lunch and talk."

Joe thought to say that until the Lord laid it on him to accept, he'd have to decline. After he and Crystal parted she went to live with relatives in Toronto where she eventually married a stockbroker and had several children. Her happiness and Joe's failure had eased the way for the deacon to call. Joe feared he'd be asked to pray over the meal. And he would hear himself come up with something that sounded shallow and rehearsed. And so he'd turned down the invitation.

A light shudders on the horizon, a semi-trailer, given the height of the beams. As it approaches, he turns his back, his body buffeted by the current of wind as it barrels past. Three more semis follow, passing him like a sudden storm. They round a curve in the highway, their running lights like one long and continuous string.

At the Juba Industrial Park there was a garage that serviced such rigs, and when the drivers came into Pauline's diner he noticed how they sought one another out, truckers of all ages, gathered at tables talking the lingo of the road. He'd once belonged to a group of people who'd had their own language. *The Lord laid it on me to call.* Catchphrases that seemed to stop conversation, rather than encourage it.

As he walks, the sky seems to grow darker, the stars white and brittle. He senses the Rocky Mountains in the dryness of the wind blowing in his face and imagines the undulation and thrust of stone, the long and gradual ascent of the high-way, straight and rising for miles into the mountains. He walks faster and then breaks into a jog, and feels the jolt in his knees, his clumsy heaviness.

He counts the seconds, hoping that soon he'll be aware of nothing but his feet moving across the ground. The mantra of his youth comes to mind, what he told himself while facing a difficult exam, or his fear of heights, or running cross-country with Steve whose endurance seemed endless, even though he was a smoker. The recitation of *I can do all things through Christ who strengthens me* turned him into a warrior armed with the sword of the Word, marching to do battle with himself.

Although he'd played varsity basketball and was on the track team, he had mostly chosen to remain on the side-lines of high school life. Except for Steve, his friends were kids in the church youth group, and they often went bowl-ing, or to a movie, or for pizza, with Pastor Ken and Maryanne, or one of the parents. When they were older they sometimes drove out in several cars to the gravel pits on a hot summer night and leapt from the cliffs into the deep pools of turquoise water, or to the Big Whiteshell Lake in winter where they cross-country skied, ending up at the cottage of Crystal's parents for chili and games of charades.

It wasn't difficult for Joe to decline soft drugs or to avoid the girls willing to make out at the parties he sometimes went to after a basketball game. *Stuck up. Beaudry thinks he's something.* He'd learned to keep quiet about his convic-tions in high school and especially university. Open-mindedness only went so far. Had he confessed to serving prison time, or to being gay, he knew acceptance would have been more forthcoming than if he'd professed that Jesus Christ was his personal saviour.

Steve stopped coming to church when he and Joe reached their teens, although he still showed up for youth night once in a while. Half the time he didn't get what the pastor talked about and the other half he felt he was being pressured by Joe and others to make a decision for Christ, as though he wasn't good enough the way he was. Pastor Ken had advised Joe that of course they could still be friends, but best friends? He doubted Steve was the wisest choice. *We all love him, he's a great guy. But being nice, being a great person, just doesn't cut it. I am the way, Jesus said. No man gets to God, except by me.*

The reality of being human sometimes clashed with Joe's youthful zeal, and Steve had been witness to some of his struggles. Steve brought him home, dead drunk, from his first and only experiment with hard liquor. There had been other lapses, like the time they'd gone to the beach and Joe, seeing a Walkman left unattended on a blanket, picked it up. Hours later the owner, a woman, came upon him and Steve at the concession stand and Steve was listening to the Walkman. Joe was forever shamed by his own silence while Steve endured the woman's string of racial invectives. "Screw you," Steve said to Joe when he tried to apologize later, and his lips had gone blue with anger. He took off, and Joe waited for him until the last bus, and then returned to the city alone. Steve had hitched a ride into town, and the next day his father had driven him up to the reserve. Steve did sometimes go to Sandy Lake to stay with his grandmother, but this time he was away for the rest of the summer.

* * *

In the last year of high school, Steve and Joe took the Bushy sisters with them to an abandoned farm. All that spring, and then into the final month before the track meet, they'd been parking the car at the farm site and going out cross-country running along the ridge bordering the nearby coulee, a deep bowl scooped out of the earth that had a stream running through it. Sometimes deer rose from whorls of flattened grass near the stream, looked at them a moment before skipping off into the thickets of chokecherry. Janice and Helen Bushy. When they'd landed at the bus depot they'd called, Steve said, taking Joe to the nearby rooming house where they were staying. He'd met them years ago at a powwow.

"They couldn't make a living fishing up there," Steve said without explaining how it could be that the two girls had been employed catching fish. When they entered the sisters' room near a staircase on the main floor of the rooming house, Joe was surprised to discover that the older girl, Helen, who was seventeen, had a baby.

"This is my friend, Joe," Steve said, and Joe felt something in the broad-faced girl's leap forward to welcome him, although she only nodded with the barest hint of a smile. Her dark hair lay across her forehead in heavy bangs, the style of the Indian residential school kids, like a bowl had been set on her head and someone had cut around it.

Her eyes pooled with worry as she looked past Joe to the fussing baby, clad only in a diaper, who was hauling himself up to his feet in the crib in a corner of the room. She went to him, lifted him over the side, and as he straddled her hip, Joe laughed at the sight of his huge thighs, ringed with rolls of fat.

"He's a midget sumo wrestler," Joe said and when Helen didn't react, it occurred to him that she might not know what a sumo wrestler was. Or a midget.

"Jordan's got a rash, eh," Helen said above his fussing. "Look." She turned his arm to show Joe the inside of it, then the back of his leg, both having patches of rough looking skin that oozed.

It was as though she expected he could do something about it. Jordan took notice of Joe then, and began to cry, grabbed at his mother's neck and pressed his cheek against hers, as though trying to get inside. Joe wanted to wipe away the rivulet of clear mucus glazing his top lip.

Steve, who'd been straddling the only chair in the room, got up and motioned for Helen to give Jordan to him, and Joe was surprised when Steve did what he'd wanted to do, lifted the hem of his T-shirt and wiped away the snot. Steve jostled the boy in his arms while speaking to him in Cree, and gradually Jordan grew quiet.

There was only enough space in the room for the sagging double bed, a chest of drawers whose veneer was partly stripped away, the single straight-back chair. A thin rope was strung diagonally across the space, and moments later, the younger sister, Janice, a taller, slender version of Helen, came in, having rinsed out several diapers in the bathroom down the hall, and began slinging them over the line to dry. She too dipped her head in obvious embarrassment when Steve introduced her.

Their eyes, like Steve's, darted away from Joe's whenever he looked at them directly. Where did they eat? He found the answer when he saw the garbage can at the foot of the bureau, crammed with fast-food wrappers.

"At night Jordan cries. It's hot in here, eh, and the rash gets bad," Helen said. She perched on the side of the bed and stared at her sandals, her thick toes looking dusty, though the nails seemed wet with red polish.

"They bang on the door. Tell us to keep him quiet. I take him into bed with us, but it gets hot, and then he gets more itchy."

Steve said something to her in Cree and she laughed, her face a plum blush of embarrassment.

"Helen usually doesn't talk much. It must be love at first sight," Steve said and she snatched up a pillow and pretended to throw it at him.

Later they went for a walk and wound up at Vimy Ridge Park where they came upon Alfred and his friend Earl at a picnic table and stopped to talk for a moment. Joe looked on, thinking that Steve seemed looser-jointed, relaxed and full of teasing with the sisters present. He'd never heard him speak Cree until now.

On the weekend after Steve had taken Joe to meet the Bushy sisters they picked them up at the boarding house for the drive into the country, Steve at the wheel of his father's car, a rust bucket he kept licensed for the times when Steve's mother grew lonely for her family.

That the sisters had been watching for them became apparent when they pulled up in front of the rooming house and the door opened immediately. They hurried down the steps, looking summery, Helen in a pale blue cotton dress belted at the waist, Janice in a flared skirt and blouse, both of them carrying white clutch purses.

Dressed as though going to church, Joe thought with a start. Thinking of the girls at church finding each other and disappearing into the washroom and then sweeping into the sanctuary, Crystal among them, trailing sweet-smelling hairspray and perfume. Even Jordan appeared to be dressed up for the occasion in a pair of stiff-looking jeans and a T-shirt that looked new, and a miniature version of Kodiak workboots that must be uncomfortable given the way he sat on Helen's lap in the back seat, his legs straight out as though he was afraid to move them.

"Hey, big guy, how's life?" Joe said once they were under-way, reaching back to grab Jordan's hand, startling him. Jordan pulled it free and stuffed it into his mouth while staring at Joe. Jordan Bushy. Right on. Joe smiled as he thought of the teasing the boy would face down the road, given his bushy hair.

"Those are great boots," he said to Helen.

Her smile was filled with gratitude. "They're cute, eh. I got them at the Army and Navy." Joe realized that she had wanted him to notice. Her voice was low, like Steve's, but smoother in the way one sound glided into another. Like jazz.

The sisters hardly spoke during the drive through the city, but Joe sensed their anticipation and Helen's watch-ful eyes on the back of his head. When he turned and pointed out the fighter jet at the entrance of Assiniboine Park, she looked at him and not the airplane, her face lit up with such intensity as she smiled, that he forgot what he wanted to say.

It must be love at first sight. His thoughts careened about as he made small talk with Steve.

At school Joe had learned about the use of condoms in the event he was going to have sex; the classes he attended at the Salt & Light Company focused on how to avoid having it. The special series for teenaged boys, Frank Talks About Sex, were conducted by Pastor Ken, and whenever he entered the room at the start of the class inevitably someone would say, "Hey, where's Frank?" or "Heeere's Frank!" in the way Ed McMahon introduced Johnny Carson. Then they all laughed too loudly, and Joe along with them. Let's face it, guys, I've been your age. Believe me, I know how hard it is, Pastor Ken said, which caused an uproar of giddiness that took several moments for him to rein in. And then he talked about masturbation and Joe barely listened, thinking how he couldn't look at Maryanne Lewis without imagining the size and shape of her nipples. He wondered if they were light or dark, remembering what he had seen in the magazines Alfred sometimes left lying open on his bed. Joe had seen the slash of a woman's sex, the puff of hair around it, and whenever he awakened from an erotic dream painfully stiff, he masturbated while imagining that Maryanne's nipples and hair were silver, and her slit was a pearly pinkness like the inside of a conch shell.

As they drove toward the city limits Joe pondered how he might get rid of Steve and Janice at some point in the day. And when they were about to pass through the neighbourhood straddling the edge of the city, he saw the drugstore and asked Steve to pull over.

"Just what did we forget?" Steve asked, referring to the full trunk.

"Rubbers," Joe said under his breath, and for a moment

Steve didn't understand. And when he did, he got out of the car, and Joe followed.

Steve leaned against the hood, his arms crossed against his chest, the muscles in his thick neck working. "You're kidding," he said. And when Joe didn't answer, he said, "What, you plan on losing your virginity sometime soon?"

Joe looked over his shoulder at the Bushy sisters in the car, and Steve swore. "You know what? You're something else." Then he snapped his fingers in Joe's face and said, "Where's the money."

Joe jogs along the shoulder of the highway remembering how eager Steve had been for him to meet Helen and Janice Bushy, to introduce Joe to his people, and Joe's Christ warrior mantra seems a mockery. He recalls Helen looking up at him as he stretched out beside her on the blanket he'd spread under a tree. The string of saliva at the corner of her mouth breaking when she laughed, her dark eyes turning in the direction Steve and Janice had gone for firewood.

"You like me," she said, and Joe knew it was a question. "Yes, I do," he replied.

He could see the edge of her white bra at the V neckline of her dress, how it pressed into the curve of her breast and he was about to reach out, his fingers stiff and shaking, and undo a button. Then his eyes came to rest on Jordan lying on the other side of her, staring at him as though trying to memorize his face.

Joe got up then, and went over to the car, unnerved when Helen unfastened her dress and Jordan crawled into her lap and clamped onto her nipple. He took the rifle and targets from the trunk, set one against a pile of boards near the abandoned farmhouse and started to shoot, the sound bringing Steve and Janice back to the clearing around the homestead, Steve with an armful of firewood. He saw Helen on the blanket, fussing with the front of her dress, and threw the wood to the ground.

"Targets, fucking boring," he said to Joe. "Come on, let's shoot at something that moves." He indicated with a jerk of his head that Joe should follow him.

They crossed a rectangle of earth, bordered on one side by a row of apple trees, that must once have been a garden and was now thigh deep in weeds. Joe puzzled over Steve's apparent anger as he stooped to avoid branches and followed him over to a large and sagging tin shed.

The spirited chirps of the sparrows echoed loudly as they approached, but when they stepped into the dim interior, the chirping stopped. The sudden silence was eerie and Joe felt watched, smelled heat and feathers, and as he grew accustomed to the semi-darkness his eyes were drawn upward. "Holy." There must be dozens of birds, perched on the rafters.

The sound of his voice and Steve's sudden movement as he motioned for the rifle brought about the flutter of wings as several birds took off and flew to the far end of the shed. Steve began to shoot, and the birds tumbled from the rafters, while the others lifted up at once and swarmed toward them where they stood, daylight at their backs, the doors hanging askew on the hinges. Joe felt the air move as the birds veered away, flew to either side of the shed, their wings backpedalling when they met the walls, their chirps piercing as they flitted above them, looking clumsy now, and heavy.

Steve kept shooting, the bullets pinging as they met the tin siding. He hadn't picked off more than a single bird in flight, and the clip was spent now. He lowered the rifle. "They'll come back," he said and ejected the clip, and when Joe gave him another, he turned away and went closer to the open doors, while Joe stood still, craning his neck as he looked up. There was a hole in the roof, the size of a stovepipe, through which he could see daylight.

Within moments a bird fluttered down onto the rafters and soon after the others followed. He expected Steve would shoot now, and when he didn't, Joe was about to turn to him when Steve said, "You know what, Joe? I was with that man three days. With that freak. By the time my mother could convince the cops I was missing I was gone three days. If that had been you missing, how long do you think the cops would have waited to start looking for you?"

Joe's scalp tightened as he imagined the impact, the bullet boring into his shoulder blade.

"You think you and me, there's no difference between us. But there is. Big differences," Steve said. Joe heard a noise, and then Steve was at his side and shot another round, the rifle rebounding in quick small jerks, while several birds dropped to the floor.

"Thanks," Joe said when Steve gave him the gun, feeling stupid for having said, *thanks*, his arms shaking. The gun was warm, and felt heavier than he knew it to be.

"You think Helen is an easy lay because she's Indian."

Joe didn't reply, but raised the gun and without aiming, shot at the rafters. Not because of that, he thought. She'd had a baby, and so she'd been around. He turned to see that Steve had left, could see his back through the fruit trees.

In the days that followed Helen began calling Joe from a pay phone on a corner near the rooming house, asking, so what are you doing? Asking, do you want to do something? Go for a walk? One night she called him from the Children's Hospital where Jordan had been admitted with croup and was having trouble breathing.

Joe could hardly see for the milky cold mist when he entered the steam room, Helen a dark shape leaning over the crib at the centre of it where the mist seemed to be the heaviest. He made his way among the cribs, most of them empty, and when he reached her, his shirt was damp. She didn't see him coming and when he stepped up to her side, she grabbed his arm and then threw her arms about his neck, her body shaking as she began to cry.

"Okay, it's okay," Joe said. He wanted to embrace her with love. In the way the elders and deacons embraced one another following communion, in the way the people around Joe in church reached for him, and for each other in an exchange of agape love, but his penis had raised its head. He stepped away and went over to the crib and looked down at Jordan, curled on the mattress, relieved to see his chest rising and falling.

"I didn't know who to call," Helen said. Steve's mother wasn't home. "And I don't know where Janice is." She ground at her eyes with the heels of her palms. "Sometimes she comes back late at night and she won't say where she's been."

Joe felt as though he was suddenly treading water in a deep lake. He'd seen Janice once, downtown near the repair depot where he worked during the summer, her features vivid with cosmetics, looking older than sixteen. She was going past the Albert Arms Hotel with someone who was old enough to be her father. He had to make a phone call, he told Helen, but he would come right back.

He found a pay phone at the end of the corridor beside a waiting room. He called Pastor Ken, and when he hung up he went into the room and picked through a pile of magazines on the coffee table. Then he sat down with a *National Geographic*, settling for an article on the Apollo 17 mission. He looked at the purplish-grey landscape and the black sky beyond the Lunar Rover, the astronaut raking up rock samples, while the earth appeared to sit on the curvature of the moon. He thought to take the magazine home to Alfred, who was sometimes skeptical about whether or not there had been a moon landing. The wall clock hummed as the time passed, and when he heard a noise down the hall he set the magazine aside, thinking Helen might come looking for him.

When he came into the steam room he was surprised to see a man and woman who stared at him when he went over to Helen, likely assuming that like them, he and Helen were parents of a croupy child. He stood at the end of the crib, while Helen hung onto the side railing as though it was saving her life.

"His face is hot, now," Helen said. "He's worse."

"Do you want me to get a nurse?" Joe asked, worried. Jordan's breathing did sound more raspy now.

As though in answer, a nurse entered the room, her shoes squeaking noisily on the wet tile floor. Helen quickly stepped back when she came over and reached into the crib to take Jordan's pulse, then shook a thermometer and put it under his arm.

"It sounds like he's having real trouble breathing," Joe said, knowing Helen wouldn't speak up.

"It always sounds worse than it is," the nurse said and then looked at him. "Are you a relative?"

He was a friend, Joe explained and she raised her eyebrows, then turned away to retrieve the thermometer. Just then Maryanne Lewis hurried into the room, Crystal behind her.

"More friends?" the nurse asked Helen, who looked at Joe to explain their presence.

"Well, all of you can't be in here," the nurse said and went over to greet the other couple waiting for her at their child's crib. When she greeted them, Joe noted the friendliness of her tone as she spoke to them.

"We left as soon as you called," Maryanne said, her attention turning to Helen as he introduced her. Then she swooped down and gathered Helen into a hug. Helen shrugged free angrily, and turned to Joe, wanting him to answer the question in her eyes. "We're friends of Joe's," Maryanne explained. "We thought you might be able to use a break."

Joe couldn't help but notice the contrast, Maryanne's springy platinum hair, her crisp candy-striped blouse and capri pants, against the man's white shirt Helen wore, damp and clinging to her chest, the shirt-tails hanging at her hips. He couldn't help but notice the shapelessness of her thick, strong body. *You like me.* It wasn't a question, but an appeal. He heard the callousness in his reply.

"Why not come and have a cup of coffee. We'll go down to the cafeteria. Joe and Crystal will stay," Maryanne said.

At the mention of her name Crystal stepped forward.

"He'll be okay with us," she said to Helen, and Joe was surprised when Helen allowed Maryanne to lead her away.

"Hi," Crystal said when they were alone. She turned her luminous flat eyes up to his face and her Adam's apple bobbed as she swallowed. Sometimes when she entered the sanctuary with the other girls he noticed that she would look for him. In a room full of people he'd feel watched, and see her turn away. Her family had been visiting the Lewises when he'd called, she explained. Maryanne had asked her to come along.

Then she glanced down at Jordan and her nervousness was gone. "Oh, is he ever cute," she whispered.

Jordan opened his eyes then, and seeing her, he began to whimper.

Crystal leaned into the crib. "Hey, don't worry. Mommy's coming back soon," she said, her voice startling Jordan into silence.

She drew the flannel blanket over his shoulders and began to hum, a song Joe recognized as "Jacob's Ladder," the children's hymn he'd learned when he'd first gone to the Salt & Light Company and thought he was beyond the age to sing and mime the action of climbing a ladder. But he remembered the words, the line ending with *children of the cross*. And he thought, that's what he was. He was a child of the cross. That was the real difference between him and Steve.

Days later Pastor Ken bounced a pencil against his desk while Joe talked. His eyes bored straight through Joe when he confessed to having bought milk, the makings of sandwiches, fruit and breakfast cereal, for the Bushy sisters. He'd gone with Helen to a clinic to see about Jordan's rash, which had turned out to be eczema, and bought the ointment the doctor had prescribed. He didn't say that they'd had sex one afternoon when Janice took Jordan out to the park, a quick event that was over in a sudden push and flare of pleasure. Instead, he said that he had a deep concern for the welfare of the Bushy sisters.

"You may mean well, Joe, but believe me, this is not for you," Pastor Ken said.

"This?" Joe asked.

"She's not the kind of person you would want to be involved with, is she?" Pastor Ken asked and Joe sensed he was holding his breath. They locked eyes for a moment before Joe turned away. "No, she's not," he said.

"All right then," Pastor Ken said. "I'll let some of the women know about the Bushy sisters. It's not up to you to do this."

Helen, Janice and Jordan arrived at church the following Sunday and were escorted by the deacon to the front of the sanctuary with an older couple who had volunteered to take the sisters under their wing. They were seated on an overstuffed couch, the man and his wife on either side trying not to look pleased to have been asked to dedicate themselves to the Bushy project. Crystal and her friends claimed Jordan, taking him downstairs each Sunday where they entertained him in the baby room, released him to Helen's arms at the end of the service, sometimes clutching a new toy, or a box of animal crackers, his stubborn bushy hair wet and brushed flat at his crown. When Helen called, Joe made excuses why he couldn't meet her, and on Sundays he avoided the bewildered puzzlement in her eyes, and then her anger.

One Sunday, the elderly couple arrived without the Bushy sisters and the baby, quietly concerned about their whereabouts. When they had gone to pick them up, they'd been told the girls had moved out. There had been others like the Bushy sisters, who suddenly appeared at the church one morning, stayed for a time and left, and there would likely be more. If they were meant to stay they would have stayed, the deacon explained. Sometimes the winnower would come to the threshing room floor and separate the chaff from the wheat.

After Joe and Steve graduated from high school, Steve left Winnipeg to take up full-time what had been his summer job, roughnecking for a drilling company in Brooks. Joe went on to university. Now and then throughout the years Joe would suddenly hear from Steve after months of silence. He would call from a pay phone in a small town near the drilling site, and from a gas station in Sandy Lake when he went to the reserve. He'd called once from Venice Beach, drunk, shouting above the noise in a bar that he was going to get married, and the next time Joe talked to him he couldn't remember having said that, or who the woman had been. For a time Steve worked in Texas, and he had his own apartment then, and Joe was able to call him frequently. When Joe opened the Happy Traveler, Steve sent a bottle of Bollinger champagne, his card saying, *Still playing with toys, Joey, only big time now. Way to go.* And then he enlisted with the Princess Patricia Canadian Light Infantry, and was stationed in Shilo. On his first leave he came home, wanting to connect with his family, wanting to meet Joe's skirt, Laurie, whom Joe had been going on about for some time now. He had tickets for David Bowie's Glass Spider concert.

* * *

When Steve came up the walk to the house, Joe hesitated at the door, not recognizing him immediately. He was twice the size, his forearms beefy and pectorals straining against his T-shirt, while his thighs threatened to split his jeans. He'd been working out, Steve explained, an understatement given the bulk of his sculpted body. His greeting was stiff, his voice tight. But when Joe was in the kitchen fixing coffee he heard the old Steve, the smoky huskiness, the cracks of laughter, as he visited with Alfred.

Steve arranged to meet Joe and Laurie later, at the entrance of the stadium, and as he came toward them he seemed unaware of the effect he had on the people milling about, awed by the hugeness of his muscled body, how they grew quiet and gave way to let him pass through.

"Holy mackerel, Joe, how in hell did you manage this? Ugly mug like you," Steve said as Joe introduced him to Laurie. Joe saw the sudden shyness in her eyes, her smile go sideways.

They went to claim their seats and there was a moment of awkwardness as Laurie chose not to sit between them. And then, as though to cover for it, she became animated, touching Joe's thigh, grabbing at his arm when she talked past him to Steve. He saw her as Steve must, her sexual energy in the impatient shifting of her body, the way her breasts came forward when she raised her arms to refasten the clips in her hair. When Bowie at last descended on stage in the glass spider, the roar of the crowd was instantaneous and deafening. "You're not going to let her go alone?" Steve yelled when Laurie pushed past them to get down to the floor, and before Joe could respond, he went after her.

Laurie and Steve were at least a head taller than most of the people, but Joe quickly lost sight of them, and when after a few moments he too fought his way down to the floor he was unable to spot them among the crowd, which had gone instantly wild at the moment Bowie appeared. Joe took refuge at the side to watch the spotlights, the dancers, Bowie, everything an undulation of colour and movement that made no sense; nor did the music, distorted, and ultimately drowned out by the howl of the crowd.

He made his way to an exit and burst through the doors feeling as though, like Jonah, he'd just been regurgitated. He went to the parking lot to wait for the concert to end, leaned against the car and turned his face up to the night coming down over the city, the warm autumn air tinged with the onset of decaying vegetation and the smoke of stubble fires in outlying fields. He was grateful for Clayton, his assistant, who would keep things running without a hitch at the Happy Traveler tomorrow when he and Laurie went to the lake for what would likely be the last of windsurfing, before it got too cold.

The music reverberated in the buildings around the stadium, and he got into the car to escape it, turned on the radio and thought of Laurie and her appealing uncertainty. When are you going to make an honest woman out of that girl, Alfred kept asking, his way of letting Joe know he wanted to keep Laurie in their lives.

He rolled up the window to better hear Grappelli playing "Limehouse Blues" and watched two boys going along the railway tracks, one of them whacking at weeds with a golf club. It was the same freight line that skirted the edge of his neighbourhood, crossing the Assiniboine River on the train trestle bridge.

And he thought about how he and Steve had hitched rides on that slow-moving train, how they rode it across the bridge and out to the sugar beet factory. Then they hiked across country to where a stand of burr oak sheltered the ghost town. He remembered the eerie quiet as they went through yards, feeling there were people at the windows watching. Mouse dirt, broken glass, rotting linoleum, the musty smell of abandonment and ruin. He remembers a cupboard in a yard, small drawers holding pieces of metal. He and Steve, sitting on a bench in grass that was as tall as their shoulders, Steve saying he wanted to be a policeman, but he couldn't do the math. He'd go away and stay with his grandmother on the reserve and then had to struggle to catch up at school when he got back. Joe had lent him his notes, taken him home for a bowl of Alfred's barley soup and a quiet place to study, had tried to tutor him. But it was true. Steve couldn't get math, no matter what way Joe tried to come at it. "Why aren't you guys out setting cars on fire," Alfred said to them from the doorway when they studied, which is what he would say to Joe when he came upon him in his room on a Saturday night, boning up for Sunday school. Boning up on God.

Those times when he and Steve were young teenagers going out into the country, he had sometimes turned to watch that train moving across the horizon and thought that heaven was a freight train, and he was the man riding on top a car, his forehead resting on his knees, on a journey away from, and toward something; heaven was that movement of being carried along, being held between the beginning and the end.

He listened to the music playing on the car radio and watched those two boys disappear into a culvert beneath a street, and he thought if he ever had a child, he'd need to make time to take him places, as he and Steve used to do. During a drive down the coast to California he'd seen the large number of streamliners on the road, the parks filled with motorhomes, and came back to discover there were only two RV dealers in the entire city of Winnipeg. Once people got to know where he was, after a slow first half year of business, he hadn't looked back. And now two years later, although he could sometimes steal a day or two to go canoeing or windsurfing with Laurie, he seldom got out into the country.

He must have fallen asleep, as it seemed the next moment people were swarming from the exits of the stadium into the parking lot. He waited another quarter of an hour, and was about to go into the stadium to look for Laurie and Steve when they emerged at the far end of the lot, coming quickly when they saw him, expressing relief and surprise that he'd waited. Steve's arm dropped from Laurie's waist and she stumbled toward him, her eyes too bright when she hauled him into a prolonged kiss. He smelled coffee.

He released her, and looked at Steve, expected the usual wisecrack to deflect the tension between them. Steve's eyes held his, hard and unswerving. "What kept you guys?" Joe asked.

It was Laurie who answered. They'd taken the wrong exit and wound up way the hell and gone on the opposite side of the arena, she said, while Steve turned away and lit a cigarette.

The following day when Joe arrived at Laurie's apartment, he was surprised to find her waiting at the lobby door, subdued and dark around the eyes. Of course, he thought. Steve had been to see her after they'd parted last night. And she'd let him in. He imagined Steve's dark hands on Laurie's body, and he reached for her, thinking they would go upstairs, but when he tried to kiss her, she turned away.

When they were out on the lake she didn't follow when he began tacking toward the shore. Instead, she went out farther and faster than she had in the past, without him being there to signal or shout instructions. He beached his board, then stood watching, noting the straightness of her back, her obvious strength, her hair like a banner streaming.

He went walking along the dunes until they gave way and the shoreline rose in a blunt cliff carved out by the wash of water and wind, which had exposed a stratum of shale, gravel and soil. A glint of light caught his eye and he went over to it and pried loose a chunk of flint, but which he took to be obsidian, black glass. He jostled it from hand to hand and felt it grow warm. It was a stone that had come out of fire. On its smooth dark surface were minute ripples and whorls, and as he ran his finger across them he imagined he was feeling God's breath. Even before the stone had been magma, before the world had been made—whether that had happened in seven days, or seven trillion years, didn't matter—God knew all the ripples and whorls inscribing his life. Did that mean then, that his mother's death, the way she'd died, had been predestined?

He had often wondered, and throughout the years, Pastor Ken never came right out and said, *yes*. Only, that the end result of his mother's tragic death had brought Joe into the kingdom of heaven. Joe went over to the water's edge and dropped to his haunches, the stone dimpling the sand between his feet. And his mother's death had brought Laurie to the house that day. The stone, he thought, was an object lesson, a reminder that nothing happened in his life without there being a reason.

He'd been like the ancient Greeks, viewing his own dark and hazy reflection in a piece of burnished brass and thinking he had a clear picture. His notion that the events of other people's lives had been arranged by God for his benefit, was like the ancients believing that light emanated from their eyes.

On the day the Twin Towers came down, he'd been flipping through channels at the office and happened upon Pastor Ken and Maryanne's weekly TV program, the two of them, stricken, seated at a table and clutching each other's hands while they tried to make sense of what had happened. He'd taken off for Vancouver then, feeling threatened the whole time. He met up with a blizzard around Golden. Driving in near zero visibility, he'd hit a patch of black ice and almost slid into a guardrail and the ravine hundreds of feet below. He kept seeing the trapped people at the windows on the top floors of one of the towers, and hearing Pastor Ken say that 9/11 was a wake-up call, that he didn't believe the people had died for nothing. God would use their deaths to shake up the world. Joe pulled over into a rest stop, shivering with fatigue, got out and walked along the railing overlooking a canyon. Water plummeted down the face of it and into a rock-filled stream, far below. He stared into the canyon, and it came to him that saying their deaths were a wake-up call was taking ownership of their tragedy.

By the time he'd reached the outer limits of Vancouver his need to talk to Pastor Ken had dissipated. He pulled off the road and got a room at a motel, slept around the clock, then headed back. And during the drive home, he thought of Crystal, and how sure he'd been that they were meant to go to Bible college. And then how certain he'd been that Laurie had come into his life for a reason. But Crystal had always been there. And once people realized she had claimed him, suddenly they were a couple and found themselves being seated together, given the opportunity to be alone more often. And when Laurie came to live with him and Alfred, the smell of her shampoo stung his nostrils and followed him down the hall to his bedroom. He couldn't sleep for hearing her move about on the other side of his wall.

During the drive back to Winnipeg he realized that he'd grown weary of the winter trips to hot climates, the dinner parties that wound up with everyone drinking too much, himself included. Of the house, whose rooms had become busy and exaggerated, *eclectic*, Laurie's friend Sandra had said. *How she pulls it all together is beyond me. But it works.* Which meant that everywhere he looked, there was something else to see, like a furniture showroom he had to fight his way through. Perhaps if they'd had a child, he'd thought. That might have been reason enough for them to be together.

His feet are hot and tender now, and he feels the stones of the shoulder through the soles of his running shoes. But when he's on the asphalt he keeps looking behind him, although he knows he would hear a vehicle coming. There's more traffic going east than west now, the lights steadily boring through the darkness across the broad median of rolling land.

A moment later a dark shape comes toward him in the field beyond the ditch, an animal, he realizes, when he sees the white bars on its chest shining in the dark. The prong-horn antelope stands just inside the fence now, taking him in, its ears pricked forward, its curiosity stronger than its fear. He imagines the air quivering between them with the intensity of the animal's awareness. This is something he can tell Steve about when he calls him later. A buck, given the black cheek patches, a big sucker. Suddenly the antelope turns and is gone, the solid thud of its hooves giving way to the sound of an approaching vehicle.

One of the headlights is brighter than the other, and the car travels slower than most. Come on, come on, Joe urges through clenched teeth, raises his arm and is shot through with hope as the driver begins to brake. The car, an old Chrysler New Yorker, pulls onto the shoulder and stops about a hundred feet ahead of him.

He resists the urge to sprint when the driver gets out of the car and comes round the back of it, watching as Joe walks toward him. A black man, and tall. Looking even taller for the mustard-coloured garb he wears, a robe of some kind, the hem rippling around his ankles in the wind. As Joe draws near, the man's smile is sudden and broad as he extends his hand in a greeting.

"Good evening my friend, my name is Lino. May I ask, what is yours?" His handshake is a brush of warmth against Joe's palm.

"Joe," Joe says. He suspects this is an inspection, and he must pass it if he's going to be given a ride.

"Joe," Lino repeats. "Is that like Joseph, then?" His voice is the boom of a kettle drum, reverberating and deep.

"Yes." He hasn't often been called by his full name and he finds himself straining toward it, as though *Joseph* is a shining sphere suspended in the air just beyond his reach.

Joseph Alfred Beaudry. Joseph after Verna's father, whom he never met. The man died without having witnessed the miracle of Joe, born to Verna and Alfred Beaudry despite their advanced ages, and the possibility that her eggs and his milk had soured. Joe, a breech, the umbilical cord snaked twice around his neck, a miracle delivery. The Dalai Lama, the Christ Child, Prince Joe, Verna's sisters used to refer to him among themselves. The boy with eyes that were far too pretty for his own good. His long, dark and curling eyelashes would wear thin on a grown man. You could see men with eyes like that, who'd been doted on as kids because of their looks, and were left holding the bag when they'd gone bald, not realizing that their pretty eyes looked ridiculous now in the scheme of things.

Those blue incandescent eyes that Alfred hadn't been able to look into without getting a knot in his throat, are now sore and half shut against the wind-driven grit.

Joe follows Lino to the passenger side of the car where a woman has rolled down the window in anticipation of their approach.

"Amina, this man is Joseph," Lino says and she sticks

her long thin arm through the window and takes Joe's hand in her own and shakes it. He stoops to greet her, and is met by a blast of hot air and a spicy scent.

"Welcome to you, Joseph," she says. Her mouth takes up half of her face, and her smile is a flash of light.

"Amina is my sister," Lino says.

"Where are you going to go?" Amina asks, her eyes gone serious with the question.

When he tells her Calgary, Lino says, "Aha. We are going to Brooks. If you like, we can take you that far."

Joe agrees and waits while Lino arranges boxes on the back seat to make room for him.

Within moments of being on the road, Lino begins to talk loudly above the sound of the heater. He and his sister work at a meat processing plant in Brooks. They're returning from a day in Medicine Hat where they and several friends rent a small space outside a clothing store in a shopping mall. Where they set up tables and display their crafts. This day was his and his sister's turn to sell, Lino says. That is why they're dressed the way they are, he explains, people around here need to see some colour. "It makes them happy. And when they're happy, they're more apt to buy something." He laughs. "You see, I'm not in this country very long, but I know something."

"I will show you what we have," Amina says and releases her seat belt, turns and tugs the headrest free and drops it on the floor behind her. She leans across the seat to rummage through one of the boxes, her thin arms wiry, and gleaming as though with oil. The red cloth she wears is knotted at one shoulder, the other being bare, and at its base there's a jagged Y-shaped scar.

A moment later, she sets on Joe's knees, in turn, several small framed pictures of giraffes grazing in trees, elephants bathing in a stream; flowers in vases, of which there are only just a few left, she says, as they had sold very quickly. "Sittina will have to make more flowers," she says to Lino.

"Aha," Lino says in agreement.

She rests her elbows on the back of the passenger seat, cups her chin and watches intently as Joe looks at the pictures, the images cut from bits of fabric and glued in place, the scenes finished with fine line drawings of a grass hut, a bird in a tree, scribbles of clouds, a small naked child holding a long stick. She is waiting for his appraisal, he knows.

"They're great," he tells her, and adds that he hasn't seen anything quite like them.

"So, do you like them?" she asks with concern.

When he assures her that he does, she digs into another box and comes up with a pair of salad servers which she hands to him, urging him to feel the smoothness of the pecan-coloured wood, the geometric pattern notched into the ivory material banding the handles.

"They are carved by hand," she says, and reaches over to tap one of the handles, saying, "That is not plastic, Joseph. It is bone. You only need to rub them with a little bit of oil, that's all. You don't have to use soap to clean them."

At a loss as to what to say, Joe asks if she made them, and her smile fades. She half closes her eyes and looks away from him as she says, "No, they're from Kenya. From our mother and our half-sisters. They make them. They are twenty dollars," she says turning to look at him again.

Joe laughs to cover his discomfort, realizing that she

means for him to buy something. When he tells her that he doesn't have a need for salad servers, she looks puzzled. "For your wife, your family. For your mother," she adds in a way that suggests it's preposterous he hasn't thought of that.

"No wife, no family." Joe is caught by her brief startled glance, her "hmn" as though she is weighing what he's said. She takes the salad servers from him, then dives into another box. Her long narrow body is halfway in the back seat, and he realizes that she's the source of the spicy scent, and that it comes from her hair.

She gives him a small box filled with bracelets made of polished black stones, interspersed with red beads. The black stones are magnetic, she tells him and demonstrates how they cling together. "It is good for your pain," she says and taps her wrist. "Lino makes them. He is very quick. He can make one while he takes his supper." She picks up a bracelet and smells it. "I think he was eating peanut butter."

Lino's deep laughter fills the car. "Amina is going to do well in university, wouldn't you say, Joseph?" His large head swivels on his neck as he turns to look at Joe, and then he goes on to explain that in autumn she will begin to study at the University of Alberta. "She is going to be a doctor," he says. "And when she is finished, I will become an engineer. She is first, because she is more intelligent than I, and if I can't do the engineering, then my little sister can look after me. Yes?" Once again his laughter fills the car. She says something to him in an African language and raps his shoulder with her knuckles in mock annoyance.

She takes the box of bracelets from Joe and puts them away. "Now I will show you what I make," she says, with the eagerness of a child. From a shopping bag on the floor she carefully takes out a bundle wrapped in tissue.

"Mats," she says as she unwraps it and holds out to Joe what proves to be layers of cloth.

"Amina, say, placemats," Lino shouts.

"Yes, for the table," Amina says, with a bashful grin.

She peels one off and gives it to Joe.

The placemat has been pieced together from beige, brown and blue swatches of cloth that look like bark, burlap, and the shimmer of water. The fabric is interwoven with twists of hemp, frayed and knotted coloured yarn, and strands of copper wire.

"Trees, flowers, that is lightning," she says pointing out the copper wire to Joe.

"A river?" he says, and runs his finger across a patch of blue silk.

She smiles in appreciation and nods. He notes that the mat is lined with the same mustard-coloured fabric as the robe Lino wears. This is something Laurie would go for, he thinks, and then complain later that it couldn't be cleaned. "Awesome," he says, having picked out the abstract pattern of a landscape.

"It is fifty dollars," Amina says.

"They're beautiful, but I'm afraid not."

"Why do you say, *afraid*?" she asks, puzzled.

"I'm afraid of the price," Joe says with a grin, and as he goes to return the placemat to her, she shakes her head and holds up four fingers.

"Fifty dollars for four of them." She looks at him, long and hard.

"I'm sorry, I'd like to, but I can't buy anything," Joe says.

She studies him a moment longer and then says, "That's okay."

She takes the mat from him, rewraps them and puts them and the pictures away. Then she slides down into the passenger seat and for a moment looks straight ahead into the highway rushing toward them, the lights of approaching vehicles like multi-faceted beads rolling across the land.

She's thinking, Joe assumes, judging from the stillness of her profile, and he regrets that he cannot buy anything. Lino speaks to her twice before she hears him, and then she says, "Okay," and fastens her seat belt.

A moment later she says something to Lino, what sounds like a question, and Lino replies. There's another short exchange between them, and then Lino calls to Joe, "Amina and I, just now we are together after not seeing each other for five years. So we sometimes like to speak our language. It is necessary."

Joe is about to ask Lino about the circumstances of their reunion, when Lino goes on to say, "Amina says she thinks that you are poor. Is that true? Are you a poor man, Joseph?"

He's startled by the question, objects to it in his head, and then is surprised to hear himself reply, "Right now, I am, that's for sure."

"I don't understand this," Lino says. "How is this possible? How is it possible for a person in a country such as this one, to be poor?"

"It's a long story," Joe says and he tries to explain how he came to lose his business. Lino listens carefully, his ear turned toward Joe, nodding and saying, "Aha," while Joe runs through the litany of factors that caused business to drop off at the Happy Traveler, hearing himself speak as Pauline would have, feeling injured, a victim of fate.

"This is very unusual for me," Lino says after a moment of silence, the tires humming and thumping as they come upon a section of the highway where the potholes have been recently patched. "I cannot say that I understand it. You have no family. No wife. We were told that here, in this country, there are more women than there are men. Me, I am now waiting. But when I finish my education, I will marry. I think this is the reason why you are poor, Joseph. Excuse me if I say so. You are poor because you have no family."

He is poor because he has a family, Joe wants to say but he would need to explain the irony. The maxed-out credit cards, the trips they couldn't afford, the two leased vehicles, a house full of overpriced crap. We threw our money away.

They soon arrive at Brooks and Lino drives on past the exits for about a mile, and lets Joe out near a rest stop beyond the highway, a piece of land enclosed by trees.

"There's a picnic shelter, and if you can't get a ride you could stay there for the night," Lino tells Joe. "Do you have matches, Joseph?"

When he says he doesn't, Lino reaches across Amina to the glovebox and comes up with a packet. "You can pull some grass," he says as he presses the matches into his palm. "It is dry enough to get a fire going, and then you can put on some wood," he says as though Joe might not think to do that.

"Goodbye, Joseph," Lino and Amina say and in turn they shake his hand. He senses that their farewell is not as embracing as their greeting was.

Later the flames of the bonfire in the firepit have subsided, and Joe stares into the glow of embers, his chest and
face warmed by the intense heat. It is like the coals are
breathing as they flare and recede with the rise and fall of
the wind flowing through the screens of the picnic shelter.
He imagines words emerging in the embers still holding
the shape of the log, the black letters faint and thread-like,
a line of script on the side of a fiery cliff in a mountainous
landscape of heat. *What person, when his child asks for bread,
would give him a stone.* He thinks of the flint stone, of his
blindness, his need to see himself in everything and everywhere. His self-delusion, vanity, that he would come to
believe that even his mother's death had been predestined
for his benefit.

He thinks of his father's anger: the feeble pummelling
of his fists against his chest was like a club smashing open
his ribs. When he hefted Alfred up from the floor in the
foyer at Deere Lodge, he was amazed at how heavy he was.
A meteorite. A chunk of iron. His body, shrunken and
compacted by age.

The unyielding hardness of Alfred's body made Joe
aware that he'd seldom had reason to touch his father.
Laurie had taken on the tasks of elder-proofing the house;
installing the bathroom aids that ensured his safety. She
took on the toenail clipping and scrubbing of Alfred's head.
Once when Joe chanced upon Laurie helping Alfred out
of the bathtub, he'd caught a glimpse of his father's buttocks, two brown and creased leather bags hanging from
his rear. The sight had nauseated him.

But that day at Deere Lodge, when those dentures fell
and scattered about on the floor, he wanted to gather his

father in his arms and carry him to the Explorer parked at the entrance where Laurie waited, hugging the steering wheel, her face hidden.

A car passes by on the highway, its sound blending with the sound of the wind sweeping across grass in the fields beyond the rest stop, and he wishes he had persevered a bit longer on the chance he would have got a ride. He doesn't want to sleep on a bench, whether it's sheltered or not.

The crunch of gravel under his feet is inordinately loud as he walks along the road circling through the rest area, toward a row of trees at the far end of it. He's aware of the vastness of the fields beyond, the absence of lit windows. He begins to smell damp earth, and hears water running. There must be a stream below. He peers down the slope of land, which drops into a stand of small trees and underbrush. As his eyes grow accustomed to the shadows he sees three antelope, their faces turned toward him, frozen, as they take him in. When he prepares to relieve himself, they move several steps down the slope, and stop. Moments later he sees the white bars on their chests emerge in the dark.

"You're not going to believe this, but I'm in your neck of the woods, near Brooks, in the middle of nowhere, surrounded by antelope. Bucks, three of them, from what I can tell," Joe tells Steve in reply to his question of where he's calling from. "I wish I had my rifle."

"Yeah, sure," Steve says and laughs. "Maybe you could get close enough to club one of them with it."

"Thanks a lot," Joe says. The one time they'd been deer hunting, they'd gone out to the abandoned farm site. From the rim of the coulee, Joe had been the first to see the deer below, five of them going along the frozen creek. He'd succeeded in wounding the largest of them, and they'd followed the trail of blood into the bush where they came upon the buck, which tried to rise to its feet at their approach, and failed. Steve finished the animal off, when Joe couldn't.

"Brooks is nowhere near my neck of the woods. What're you doing in the armpit of Alberta, for Christ's sake?"

"Just passing through," Joe says while he returns to the picnic shelter and the light glowing in the firepit, aware of an edge in Steve's voice. "I talked to your boy earlier, did he tell you I called?"

"Yeah, that was Dakota. He left me a note. Space Raider, eh? You noticed the baseball caps. I thought you'd get a kick out of that. These days I'm Space Raider 1, the big chief," Steve says.

"So, are you and Snow together again?" Snow being the woman Steve lived with for a time after they had a child.

"Snow's out of the picture. This time for good. I didn't like what was going down with the boy, and so he's living with me now. Has been for a couple of years. Dakota's a great kid. When I look at him, I can't believe I was ever his age. He's right up there in school, Joe, figure that one out, eh? Are you coming to see us, then?"

"I'm hitchhiking. If I get lucky, I could be there by tomorrow night. Listen, Steve, I need to find some work. A job. I was thinking maybe you would have some leads." Joe gets it out quickly before he won't, and cringes at what sounds like desperation, but there is no other way for him to say it.

After a moment Steve says, "I take it things are not going great. So what's up?"

"I had to shut down the place. There was nothing happening," Joe says knowing that Steve will likely guess the truth. "I'll fill you in when I see you."

"And Laurie? Is she back in Winnipeg?"

"Regina," Joe says. "We have this RV. I left her there with it. I think we've split. It's complicated, but it's been coming for some time." As he speaks, he knows it's true.

"I guess it happens, eh. That's tough," Steve says. "Sure, come on up. Dakota and I share this place with two other guys, but he can bunk in with me for a bit. Things aren't as hot and heavy around here as they used to be, Joe. Places like Tim Horton's are still begging for help, but I can't see you doing that, eh?"

"I can see myself doing whatever it takes," Joe says, irritated by the suggestion that he would think himself too good. He turns toward a sound on the highway, and sees the far-off headlights of an approaching vehicle.

Steve breaks the silence as he says, "Look, Joe, likely this could wait until you get here. But what the hell, maybe it's easier on the phone. I've been wanting to talk to you about this for ages."

Joe holds his breath. Steve and Laurie. The few times the three of them had been together he'd noticed the teasing way they had with each other. That they knew things about one another. Now that he's said he and Laurie have split, Steve wants to come clean. Let me tell you what you don't know about Laurie.

"There's not much I can do about what's happened in the past, Joe, except live with it. But I can let go of some parts of it. Let bygones be bygones. I've been thinking, especially since Dakota's come to live with me. That night you and me took off for Polo Park, we were eleven years old. I don't let Dakota out of my sight after dark and there we were, must have been close to midnight. Going after drink bottles." And then he says, "Christ, you and me, two little kids. That was the same night you lost your mother."

Years ago. Like a dream. And yet his throat goes tight. "Yeah, when I got home the police had already found her." He sees the car on the highway slowing down, and its turn signal blinking. "That's about all I remember. The police being there, and my dad, freaked out."

"No kidding," Steve says. "I always liked your mother. I'll bet you don't know that she once paid for my swimming lessons when my mother was short."

The car turns off the highway to the rest stop and comes along the winding drive leading to the picnic site. A lumbering Chrysler New Yorker, one of its headlights brighter than the other. "No, I didn't know. Let's talk, then. When I get there. You're not going to believe this, but I've just got company. These people who gave me a ride earlier, they're back," Joe says, his voice steadier now.

"Is that okay?"

"Yeah, sure, they're okay," Joe says as the car doors open simultaneously and Joe and Amina, wearing jeans and matching fleece jackets, come toward him.

Eight

"I sure hope that's a single malt," Alfred says to the nurse as she fiddles with the bag on the pole and the clear liquid drips more rapidly down the tube on its way into his arm.

She laughs. "Don't you wish. No such luck, this is plain old Johnny Walker." You've got good veins, you're lucky, she'd said. Otherwise you might wind up looking like a pincushion.

"Just a little something to put a tiger in your tank," she adds, and pats him on the shoulder, then takes a blanket from the foot of his bed and wraps his legs in it before leaving. Swaddled like a baby. Her footsteps recede along the hall, her voice rises suddenly and then it's gone as though a door has closed behind her.

He'd meant to look for the moon, and now that the chair is gone it's likely he won't see it again. In his lifetime the moon had gone from being made of cheese, to a man's face watching over him when he'd been left on his own, to a pale luminous sphere whose predictable waxing and waning, whose remoteness, had somehow been reassuring. He's heard that the moon might one day be colonized by seniors. People of an age when the pull of gravity on earth has become a danger. Good thing he won't be around to see that happen. The moon, littered with canes, walkers and adult Pampers.

His old neighbourhood, he imagines, lies at the bottom of a pool of darkness, hugging the river. Laurie and Joe are working late tonight, and he'll need to wrap their supper in newspaper and stick it under the couch cushions to keep warm. Or they're going out to eat, he can't remember if Laurie called to tell him, or not.

Or there might be something on at the church, and that's where Joe is now, he thinks, forgetting that it's been years since Joe's attended. If this is Wednesday, then he's at the prayer cell. Alfred had always imagined the prayer cell would be a small room, windowless, with hard wooden benches—not what it was, Crystal's family room, large and cushy with velvet curtains and rose-coloured furniture. They'd plunked him down in one of those tub chairs at the engagement party. People of all ages coming up to him and sticking their faces in his, shouting to make themselves heard, plying him with glasses of the sickly sweet punch that eventually did him in. When he went to go to the bathroom, he'd had to fight to free himself from that deep velvet chair, and had sent a table of food and glassware flying. He knew some of them thought he was drunk.

It could be that Joe's down at the public TV station, taping another program that Alfred will happen upon one afternoon while looking for something to watch. He forgets that it's been many years since Joe's been on television, that the Salt & Light Company had stopped broadcasting when the Lewis couple left Winnipeg.

He'll see Joe talking about the valley of the shadow, about victory, as though his life is a war that needs to be fought each day, the pastor and his wife looking on and nodding, agreeing with what their protegé has to say. Alfred hears their little moans of recognition when Joe talks about failure, the ordinary circumstances of his everyday life being dissected and put under the microscope to detect which parts might be good enough, and which are rotten, as though it is a sin to be wholly human.

He'd once tuned in just as Joe was telling the viewing audience that after the drowning death of his mother he had thought, for a time, that she lived in the television. He saw her. He saw his dead mother at a garden party. There were tables heaped with cakes and sugared fruit, and his mother came toward him across the screen carrying a parasol, looking like Vivien Leigh in *Gone with the Wind,* smiling at something beyond him. He truly believed, Joe said, that his mother had been saved. Before she died she had uttered the necessary words.

Yes, well, Alfred thinks. As a child it would make sense that a password might be necessary to get into heaven. Just as heaven being an ongoing garden party would make sense. But Joe's grown-up version that Verna was upstairs, that she was living beyond the universe in a house Jesus Christ had built for her, sounded like wishful thinking. "You have made yourself God," Alfred had once heard Joe say. He'd looked straight at him from the TV screen, his pale eyes shining. "You've become the centre of your life. You love yourself more than you love God."

Not true, Alfred thinks. What he loved more than anything, was Verna, and Joe, and now Laurie.

But he has to admit, Joe sounded good. He'd had to listen. And during the times, too, when Joe was a kid and Alfred let himself be talked into going to his Christmas concerts, he saw Joe's confidence with his own eyes. He heard the authority in his son's voice when he read from the scriptures, noticed that people went quiet and listened. Maybe Joe had been born for the pulpit, in the same way some were born for medicine, or politics, or to go to the moon. But Joe had not been born for business, Alfred had seen that failure coming a mile away. He wasn't hungry enough for money to do without, in order to get it.

If Joe were here now, in a collar, carrying the Good Book, what words would he give to a man who was about to head out under the sea, back into the darkness from which he came. Would Joe's words make a difference, in the way that even a lit match had made a difference in that absolute darkness. The light from even a match had kept him steady and made another hour possible.

If faith *was* a gift, as Joe had kept harping, then why hadn't it been given to him? If he'd been given faith, become a believer, he would now ask God for a favour. He would like to have a visitation. There were people, like Verna, like some of the men who'd died in the camps, who'd heard and seen invisible things. But he never had, and he doesn't expect that he will. Although he wouldn't mind. He wouldn't mind seeing Verna one last time, just as Verna had seen her own mother on the day of her death.

Verna, at the sink, peeling potatoes, turning and seeing her mother in the doorway, seeing her smile, her nod of assurance that she'd forgiven Verna for leaving her to go off and marry the likes of Alfred. Now, *there* was a gift, if there ever was one.

He wonders now if Joe's *I just know* came from practice, in the same way he himself had memorized the images in the Centennial photograph across the room on the bureau, so that now, even when he can't see them, he sees them more clearly than ever.

Nine

THE URGE TO SLEEP IS LIKE a hood that keeps slipping down over Joe's head as they tunnel through the dark, the land only existing as far as the sweep of the headlights. He must struggle to follow what Lino says and opens the window a crack to combat the hot air pouring from the heater. Moments later Lino explains that he owns the car with another man, a co-worker at the meat rendering plant in Brooks, and he hadn't been able to take Joe to Calgary without first speaking to him.

"But I might have been gone," Joe says.

"It only took a few minutes to find out. And you see, you are here. I thought, this is a chance for us to get to know one another." He speaks to Amina now and she reaches over to silence the music playing from the radio.

"Amina and I have two older brothers. We haven't seen either of them in many years. Maybe you will be our Canadian brother."

Joe laughs. There's something appealingly boyish about

Lino. "Maybe I will. Where are you and Amina from?"

Amina turns to look at him, her large mouth gleaming with lip gloss. "We're Sudanese, but we came from Kenya, the same refugee camp as our mother. In Kukuma," she adds again as though hoping Joe will recognize the name.

A grocery clerk once said to Joe when he asked, "I come from Eritrea, have you ever heard of it?" From the look in her eyes he knew she needed reassurance that it existed beyond the realm of her memory. He senses the same hope in Amina, but the truth is he'd not heard of Eritrea and would need to look at a map to know where Kenya and Sudan are.

"Lino has been here already three years, but I came only six months ago," Amina says.

"You must have arrived in winter, then. I'll bet the cold was a shock." It is the only thing he can think to say.

"Phfft," she replies with a wave of her hand. "Yes, at first it was cold. But I quickly got used to wearing more clothes." She plucks at the neck of her fleece jacket. "It is not a problem," she says almost scornfully.

Earlier when she had wanted to show him the handicrafts she had taken the headrest out of the seat back and now when she turns to face forward, her long neck, her head pebbly with tight curls, are a complete and precise silhouette against the glow of the dashboard lights. Joe thinks of the young woman on the Wildcats field hockey team who came from Trinidad. She was larger-boned than Amina and ran with great loping strides, while Amina is thin and long-limbed, which likely means she's light on her feet, and fast. The Trinidadian wasn't nearly as black as Lino and Amina, whose skin shines as though polished, and is the blackest Joe has ever seen.

"When Amina was only a baby and I was seven years old, we were separated," Lino says taking up where Amina left off.

"It happened one night when the raiders came—the Murahiliin. They burned our village. They took the girls and killed the adults and boys. My two older brothers were away at university, and so we don't know what happened to them. We don't know what happened to our father, either," he says, his voice vibrating with regret.

"I, along with some other boys from my village ran into the bush that night. Even though I was only seven years old, I was used to looking after the goats, and I knew what cowards the hyena could be. The lion, the python, that is another matter, Joseph. I was afraid I would be devoured. But my parents had told me, should there be a raid, I was to run into the bush and not to come back, you see."

Not knowing what to say, Joe remains silent, watches the white lines rush toward them, the miles being eaten up. He recalls a movie, an African child threatened by a hyena, holding a branch up over his head to make himself appear taller.

"I could see the fires burning, and so I stayed hidden," Lino continues. "Maybe you know what happened, Joseph. I was never able to return to my home. Instead I had to run away, and soon there were other boys from other villages, all of us not having anywhere to go. Eventually there were over twenty thousand of us, boys, like me, walking, looking for a safe place to stay. Looking for our families. Going where there was food and water. Some were as young as three years old, and sometimes they had to be carried on the backs of the older ones. Twenty thousand boys, can you imagine? We walked for five years, over a thousand miles," he says again as though he can't believe it.

He swivels his large head to glance back at Joe. "Do you believe miracles can happen?" he asks.

"I haven't given it much thought," Joe says. But the truth is, during the last years of his church life there had been a sudden interest in miracles. Where once a miracle meant that a person's life had been turned round for the good, the destitute were being clothed and fed, suddenly a miracle meant that a stunted leg would grow longer, arthritic fingers uncurled, herniated discs disappeared, miracles such as being able to find a convenient parking spot. Maryanne had wanted healing for a toothache, and the deacon had laid his hand on her face. Days later she showed anyone who asked, the chalky yellowish splotch on her molar. God had filled the tooth, she said, and Joe wanted to ask why God hadn't given her a new one. Why were the miracles always patch-up jobs, he'd wondered. And they came with strings attached, such as being contingent upon the degree of a person's faith.

"Aha," Lino says. "Well, I am proof that they do." He taps his own shoulder. "And there is another." His graceful long hand rises from the wheel and gestures at Amina.

"Amina was only a baby when they burned our village. She was taken from our mother's arms. Twelve years later, she found us. At first when she arrived at the camp, I didn't recognize her. But our mother did, that's for sure," he says. "For sure," he repeats and swipes at his eyes with the back of his hand.

They're about to be overtaken by a white service van, and Lino remains silent. When it passes by, the thought of that number of boys walking for five years fades as Joe thinks of the boy, Bryce. That he and Keith, the roofer, have likely reached Red Deer by now and are in a motel. He gives in to his suspicion that Keith not only abuses Bryce verbally. He thinks of Steve, going over to the car that night to see what the man wanted, and being abducted. For three days. Steve's subsequent evasiveness, his dedication to bodybuilding, make sense now. The tail lights of the passing van recede, red beads glowing in the far darkness.

He thinks to ask Amina where she'd been before arriving at the refugee camp, but when he recalls the scar on her shoulder, he decides not to. "What happened to those twenty thousand boys?" he asks Lino.

"Some of them, like me, are here in Canada. Others are in the United States. But most are still living in refugee camps," Lino says. "So many of us perished, Joseph. Thousands of boys were taken by crocodiles. In a single day, while we were crossing a river. I myself saw it happen. It was terrible, let me tell you. And then thousands more took sick along the way, and died. We had no medicine, nothing, some of us didn't have clothes. We were so thirsty all of the time, and so even though we knew what would happen, we still went to the water holes and so many were carried off by hyenas and lions."

His eyes find Joe's in the rearview mirror. "Land mines. Some were shot. I don't like to dwell on the details."

"Lino almost died many times," Amina chimes in.

"Yes, many times. Once I was saved when a woman took pity and gave me a cup of water. Another time, something inside me said not to go with the others, but to go my own way. There was this one boy—I had walked with him from the start. I couldn't persuade him to follow me. And so he went with the others and that day he was killed by a land mine." Lino is quiet then, his strong profile illuminated by the dashboard lights, and his eyes are unblinking as he stares at the road.

"But the hardest thing was being tired. All the time. So many people would say, 'Oh, I can't go any longer without resting for a little bit, wake me up when you're going to leave.' But of course, Joseph, they never woke up. Just when I too wanted to lie down in the shade I would hear about someone I knew being in a place fifty miles away. A cousin, or someone from my village, and this gave me the strength to go back where I had just come from, or to go on to another place. To Kenya, into Ethiopia, back to Sudan, then Kenya again."

It comes to Joe that he's heard about this. The Lost Boys. He recalls seeing something on the news, the army of naked boys, their eyes huge and illuminated by thirst and hunger, their emaciated bodies mottled with dust.

"I was eleven years old when I heard, finally, about my mother. I learned she was at Kukuma with two sisters from my father's second wife. And so I went there immediately. Some soldiers gave me a lift on their truck. And then, years later, Amina arrived. "But that is her story, and perhaps one day she will tell it."

After a moment Lino says, "I'm sorry, Joseph. Maybe I have talked so much, I thought, you have told me your story, and I will tell you mine."

"The Lost Boys," Joe says. "You're one of the Lost Boys of Sudan."

"Yes, that is what they called us," Lino says. "But you see, I am no longer lost."

"That happened some time ago," Joe says.

Lino nods. "Yes, long ago. In 1983, that's when it all began, but I ran from my village five years later. I am told that many of the university students in the cities were rounded up and sprayed with paraffin and set on fire. I prefer to believe that my brothers were not among them."

Joe steers his imagination away from the thought of flesh searing, the pain. Human torches. "Why did it happen?"

Lino's sigh is loud and long. "People used to say, 'They want us to be a different colour.' But in the end, it is not very complicated. There was a war, and whatever bad thing you can possibly imagine happens during war, and I myself, as a small boy, have seen it all. Amina has experienced more than you can imagine, Joseph. And it is still going on to this day."

"Okay, okay," Amina sings out. "You will stop now." Joe takes it to mean that Lino should stop talking, but as he slows down and pulls over onto the shoulder, he realizes she meant he should stop the car.

She has prepared food, she tells Joe, her features animated. "Tea," she says and lifts a metal Thermos for him to see and taps it. "I also have a rice salad and bread."

"Amina, say, *sandwiches*," Lino commands.

"I learned to speak English at the refugee camp. There was no such word as *sandwiches*," she tells Joe, struggling to pronounce it. She dives forward into a bag between her feet and comes up with a plastic container. "You see? Bread. Bread, with bananas and peanut butter. But first, you must wash."

"The doctor wishes us to be hygienic," Lino says.

Amina opens the car door and leans out, water splashes against the ground. Joe gets out and goes over to her, drops to his haunches and cups his hands. She's about to pour water into them from a two-litre Coke bottle, when Lino comes up to his side, takes it from her and motions that Joe should follow him down into the ditch.

In turn they wash their hands, the water gushing from their palms to splatter the grey earth the colour of charcoal. Joe breathes deeply of the cool wind sweeping across the foothills, smells what he takes to be iron and ice. This handwashing is for his benefit. They likely think he hasn't been near water for days. He welcomes the shock of the cold wetness against his chapped face, rubs it in, his new beard scraping against his palms.

They stand for a moment looking out across the land, grey-mauve in the light of the moon. Joe thinks to ask Lino if he's seen the antelope, and whether they are similar to the antelope in Africa, when Lino says, "Amina will go back. When she is finished studying medicine she will return to our homeland. She will become a surgeon, as she wants to heal the effect of war on the women and girls."

Joe hears the sound of an oncoming vehicle and turns to see its headlights, the steady swift trajectory boring through the dark. The traffic coming this way is more frequent than it was earlier and he wonders if Lino has noticed. Lino seemed to think that his Canadian brother might not know enough to pull dry grass to start a fire, and he might also think he'd given up too quickly on hitching a ride. After hearing Lino's story, he understands why he would return on the chance of picking him up.

"Will you go back too?" he asks Lino, thinking of the woman he's waiting to marry.

Lino's face is lit by the headlights now and the question goes unanswered as his eyes widen in disbelief.

The sudden shriek of tires is a jolt of electricity zinging through Joe and he turns in time to see the collision, the car crashing into the rear of Lino's car, climbing halfway up its trunk and falling back, the shimmer of beaded glass shooting outward in a silvery aura. It happens like that, all at once, the deadening whomp of the impact, Amina's arms flying up as she's flung backward and then pitched forward, her head and shoulders bursting through the windshield.

Oh, God, no. He thinks he hears himself scream as he takes off at a run, but as Lino runs past him and up the side of the ditch he realizes it is Lino, screaming Amina's name. Lino stops abruptly only steps away from the car, his feet drumming the ground in a staccato of anguish. Then he darts forward, stoops to try to see into Amina's face, which is flat against the hood. With a leap he's on the car and kneeling, his legs on either side of her head as he begins to bash at the web of glass encircling her shoulders.

Joe goes to grab for his phone, realizing as he does, that it's in his jacket pocket, and the jacket is on the back seat.

"Get into the car," Lino yells. "Go. You will help her to pass through."

Steam rises from the car that crashed into Lino's car, its hood sheared off, the exploded airbags bulging through the broken windshield. Metal squeals when Joe wrenches open Amina's door, pieces of glass fall to the ground, a spurt of beaded glass flies onto the floor now as Lino batters it loose. The back of Amina's seat is gone. It has broken off and tilts into the rear of the car. Her body hangs from the dash, her knees bent and resting on the floor, the silver Thermos of tea to one side of her leg.

It's not possible that she is alive. Her arm is limp at her side, fingers curled, and he sees the pale skin, the creases in her upturned palm. When he wraps his arms about her hips he feels her heat as he lifts her, carefully, while Lino begins to ease her through the cleared windshield. When she is almost through Lino turns her body so that she is face up, gathers her by the shoulders and is about to slide her across the hood and carry her in his arms, when Joe calls for him to wait. He smells gasoline now and thinks of the intense heat of the exhaust pipe, the possibility of a fire. He's seen the blood, the wide gash on Amina's forehead, the flap of skin pushed up revealing bone; her squashed nose.

As he gets out of the car he looks in the back of it for his jacket, when he doesn't see it, he assumes it's buried beneath the broken seat. Then he sees another car stopping, parking across the broad shallow gully of the median, its lights on, someone running across that stretch of land. Maybe they'll have a cell.

He feels Amina's slenderness, her lightness, as they carry her down the slope of the ditch. When they lay her on the ground her head lolls to one side, the flap of skin gaping open and revealing the ivory wetness of her skull. Her eyes are closed. Likely she didn't know what happened. No air bags. No seat belt. No headrest. Lino drops to his knees beside her, reaches to touch her hair and pulls his hand away as though frightened. Then he curls into himself, covers his face with his hands and begins to rock.

Joe peels off his hoodie and spreads it across Amina's

body, thinking, she's already gone. The blood has left her face and there's an absolute stillness that is deeper than sleep. He looks up and imagines a flurry of tiny white moths in the shape of a body, a swirl of limbs, hurrying off into the night. *Absent from the body, present with the Lord.* Or just absent.

"I've called 911. They're sending an ambulance," a man says and when Joe looks up he cannot see him for the glow of the cellphone in his hand.

"It's too late for the guy in the other car. It doesn't look like he made it," the man says.

Asleep at the wheel, or drunk. It serves him right. The thrust of anger pushes through Joe's numbness.

The man is about to be joined by a woman now, teetering down the slope on high heels and Joe wants to shield Amina from their gaze. When she arrives she wraps her arms about herself.

"It looks as though this one is dead too," the man says to her.

"Oh, my God," the woman says and covers her mouth with her hand.

That is what people say, oh, my God, in circumstances when other words fail to come. For an instant there was Joe, Lino and the infinite silence emanating from the wreckage. That minute fraction of time following the impact, before Joe began to run. Just as there had been an instant of time before he'd seen his mother's canvas sneaker in the police officer's hands. As there was between the ticks of the mantel clock in the dining room downstairs when he lay awake listening for that pause between the seconds when everything and nothing seemed possible.

Oh, God, no, Joe breathed out in that moment following the crash. Instinctively he had reached beyond himself
to utter a prayer. He pleads now for Amina's death not to
be. That her sudden paleness is shock. He wants this, not
as proof that there are such things as miracles. He pleads
for the sake of the boy, Lino, walking for five years in search
of his family, that the mercy finally given to him, by God,
by fate, will not be withdrawn.

More people begin to appear, colourless, like phantoms
drifting toward them. In the far distance the wail of a siren
rises, circles like a hawk riding the air currents far above
the foothills. Joe reaches out, Amina's skin cool as he places
his fingers on the artery in her neck. He presses lightly at
the base of her jaw and feels nothing. He slides his fingers
down, near to the spoon-shaped indentation of her throat,
and that is where he feels the unmistakable flutter of her
pulse. He shuts his eyes for a moment, holding tight inside
his intense and rising joy.

He touches Lino on the shoulder, then tugs at him and
when Lino uncurls, he puts his arm about his bony shoulder and draws him close so that their ribs touch. Joe
begins to weep for the swelling inside, for the boy he'd
been when he grew aware of the light shining around
him, warm and the colour of honey, and how it had
infused his limbs. When he was eleven years old and felt
love for the first time, which he feels surging in him now.
He takes Lino's hand, presses his long black fingers into
Amina's neck with his own. "Do you feel it?" he asks after
a moment.

"Aha," Lino says quietly in what sounds like a great and
long sigh of relief. "Aha, Joseph, I do feel it."

Then, as the first of the police cars arrive, Lino rises up on his knees, anxiously looking for them to come.

The air is cold against the wetness on Joe's face and draws his skin tight. He wipes at it with his arm and says to himself, thank you. Thank you that he is again able to feel love for another human being.

"You are going to be okay now, my little sister," Lino says, and as if to reassure him Amina opens her eyes and looks at him, and then at Joe.

"There was a car accident, but you will soon be okay, Amina. Don't you worry. The ambulance is here," Lino croons.

"My handbag," she mutters.

The words are barely spoken, but Joe understands.

When he goes up to the car, the ambulance attendants are hurrying toward it, and he shouts to gain their attention and points to Amina and Lino, and they veer away from the highway and go on down into the ditch.

Both sides of the highway are lined with vehicles now, and police cars are parked across the two lanes, the headlights illuminating the people gathered around the other car, the swirling blue and red lights laying bare in flashes the shattered glass scattered across the pavement, pieces of twisted metal. Joe looks for the man with the cellphone, wanting to tell him Amina is alive. He wants to fall to his knees, his teeth chattering now, the shock setting in.

Ten

LAURIE AWAKENS IN THE MORNING on the lounger, still wearing the fox jacket, the top half of her body sticky with heat while the bottom is cold and her muscles cramped when she struggles upright. She groans when she sees the cut-out bits of postcards and photographs, the scraps of newspaper and McDonald's wrappers scattered about on the floor. The collage covers the dinette table. She remembers her impulse to glue the pieces down, telling herself that hot water would soften the glue enough to scrape the image off before Joe would return. And then she'd decided to leave the collage intact, as a reproach, wanting Joe to see it and know how she'd filled the time while waiting for him.

She awoke during the night to the sight of the green light glowing from the bedroom and knew why she hadn't been able to sleep there. It was as though a creature had taken refuge in the room and was giving off its last breath. But up front in the cab, the two empty seats were starkly lit by the parking lot lights and emphasized the feeling that she was the only person on the planet still breathing.

Compared to the house, the Meridian is a cigar tube. The house with its wide oak trim, ten-foot ceilings, the stone basement, Verna's clock chiming the hour—yes, even that clock, much as she had resented it sometimes—gave weight to the conviction that she was exempt from destruction by earthquakes, floods and killer weather. But, nonetheless, the sturdy house had not protected her from heartache. Like other women all over the world, she had listened for the turn of Joe's key in the lock, his footsteps on the stairs. And sometimes when he'd climbed into bed beside her she'd smelled someone, a woman, on his skin. The thought was another one of those things she'd crammed into a jar and put up on the shelf beyond reach.

Alfred's cut-out face looks up at her from the floor between her feet. You've been good for Joe, he says.

"Yes, Dad, but has Joe been good for me?"

She'd used Alfred's face, Joe's, their torsos, hands, legs, along with the postcard images to create a collage profile of her own mother's face. The hours had passed swiftly while she snipped Joe and Alfred free from picnic and dinner tables, from veranda chairs and campsites, all the while thinking that in the morning she would regret having destroyed the photographs.

But she doesn't. Rather, as she stands at the dinette looking down at the collage, she's surprised at how much she actually likes what she's made. The picture Verna took of Karen, her pregnant mother, lies on one side of the table, Laurie's guide to creating her rather long and slender nose, her straight ash-coloured hair. In the collage, patches of photographs torn from the newspaper have become her hair. Her mother's mouth is open wide, and narrow strips of news stories radiate out from it and across and over the edge of the table. She picks out random phrases from the streamers of words—*fairly urgent, predicted it would, which means*—things her mother might have said. *I thought, the world*—of you, she finishes. There had been a silver seal on the tissue paper, and it's become her mother's eye.

When she'd finished the collage, she'd laid the tissue paper over it and squeezed out the remainder of the glue, and spread it thinly with her fingers. Overnight the glue had dried like a varnish, rendering the tissue translucent, what she'd hoped for, and her mother's face seems to come forward through the tissue in the way it does through the fog of her imagination. Joe's mouth smiles out from her eyelid, a daisy of splintered postcard images adorns her cheek, the body of a red-coated mounted police officer, topped with Alfred's face, dangles from her ear.

She fingers the narrow red ribbon that had bound the photographs, stiff with glue now, looped and flattened in a bow at her mother's throat. When Alfred gave it to her he couldn't say for certain if it had belonged to her mother or not, as all the Rosemont Place girls had worn them beneath their collars. It was part of the uniform they were made to sew when they first arrived, the smocks being different colours, but all of them had the white picture-frame collars and the red ribbon tied beneath it. Intended to draw the eye upward and away from their embarrassment, Laurie concluded. Soon after Verna died, Alfred, while out walking along the river, had come across the ribbon washed up in a flotsam of debris, and when Laurie introduced herself into their lives, he knew, he said, why he'd kept it all those years.

She's surprised by her creation, the words especially, and wishes now that she'd thought to cut the newspaper strips into something complete for her mother to say. Made her the kind of mother with patience enough to explain, to advise, to be playful, everything her grandmother was unable to do. Unless you were a dog.

A vehicle passes by in the parking lot and she turns away from the table, figuring that later today she'll soak a towel and lay it on the collage and clear it away. Right now her stomach is reminding her of the twenty dollars fate put in her pocket, and the promise she'd made to herself to indulge in a substantial breakfast. Her breath reeks like a barn, the stale pizza, she concludes. And although she washed her hands last night, the sour smell of the garbage can still clings to them.

More than breakfast, though, she longs to be clean, for warm water against her skin. She goes to the bedroom and changes out of her jeans and sweater, puts on the brown track suit, clips up her hair, and gathers several toiletries and puts them in the tote bag. When she presses the button on the panel beside the door, the Meridian steps unfold with a resolute whirr. Before leaving she pats her pocket, assures herself that she's got the sock, and the twenty dollars rolled up inside it; the lanyard with the ring of keys hangs from her neck.

Judging from the few vehicles in the parking lot, she'll likely be among the first in Walmart this morning. The door swings open and she braces herself for the cheerless smile of the white-haired greeter and is relieved when she doesn't see him in his usual spot. Nor is he hovering near the shopping carts, with the roll of stickers. Instead she's confronted by a rack of geraniums parked just beyond the entrance. The sparks of crimson draw her over and when she smells the pungent odour she can't help but regret the loss of her backyard garden; forgetting that her anticipation of it in spring was quickly defeated by indifference when it ultimately failed to live up to her expectation.

She feels watched, turns and sees the greeter and a female employee leaning on their elbows at the customer service desk, looking her way. Letting her know that they know she's in the store. She hurries off along a frozen food aisle, the frigid air raising goose flesh, through the chockablock of kitchenware, toward the back of the store and the washroom. Along the way she must skirt a wire bin filled with toss cushions and a tower of DVDs that weren't there yesterday.

She notes the sign on the washroom door declaring that no merchandise should be taken beyond this point. Although she hasn't any, she hesitates, thinking of the toiletries she brought with her in the tote. As she enters she's met by the push of warm moist air smelling of disinfectant, gratified that the floor looks freshly mopped and that the row of sinks, although mineral-stained, appear to have been cleaned, too. She sets her tote in a sink and takes out the jar of sculpting face cream she'd bought the first day in Regina, satisfied by the clink of heavy glass when she sets it down. Then she takes out the new cake of soap rolled in a washcloth and her small towel, toothpaste and brush.

She's about to turn on the tap when she realizes the sink doesn't have a stopper, but a metal screen, of course, it wouldn't. She berates herself for not having thought of this, and is crestfallen that her plan for a warm water sponge bath has been thwarted. She picks at the edge of the screen with a fingernail, thinking she might stuff the drain with something, but is unable to lift it. A nail file, something to get underneath it, she thinks, and when she sees herself in the mirror she takes out one alligator clip, her hair falling down the side of her face.

After several attempts to hook its teeth under the screen, she succeeds in pulling it loose. Then she jams a corner of the washcloth into the hole, works it down tight into the drain and turns on the tap. "All right," she says, congratulating herself, as the water rises up the sides of the sink.

She glances at the door before unzipping her track suit jacket, then quickly peels off her sweatshirt and drops both onto the counter. She's startled by her face in the mirror, the crackling energetic person she knows herself to be is an ashtray this morning. Thumbprints of blue beneath her eyes, her mouth looking like a dried-out squeegee. She straightens her shoulders and sees a slightly muscular tanned and freckled woman in a lace full-figure brassiere, in recent years a staple of her wardrobe. At near to a hundred dollars apiece, she had the foresight to buy several before she couldn't.

Her breasts pop free from her bra when she unhooks it and it dangles from her arms as she dips the towel in the water and works up a lather of goat milk soap, the scent a pleasant twist in her nostrils. Just as she's about to sponge the acrid worry smell from her armpits, the door opens, and the woman she saw at the customer service desk enters the washroom, her eyebrows rising at the sight of Laurie's nakedness. Quickly she looks away, her face tightening as she goes into the nearest cubicle. Laurie hears her mutter.

Sent to check on her. She slides her bra back up her arms and fastens it, her face growing warm. Likely the parking lot has video surveillance and the security men saw her dip into the garbage can last night, which accounts for the keen interest in her this morning. She glances at the ceiling. Surveillance here, too? Well, at least she gave them something worth peeping at. She yanks the washcloth from the drain. Moments later the toilet in the cubicle flushes and when the woman emerges and comes over to a sink, Laurie is dressed.

"You're from the motorhome, aren't you? The manager would like to talk to you. Come by customer service and ask for him," she says while washing her hands. Then she flicks them dry and begins to pluck at her hair while looking in the mirror. "This washroom is here for the use of our customers. And it's certainly not a place for you to take a bath."

"Where's the sign that says that?" Laurie asks. Her sarcasm startles the woman who stares at her, her mouth open.

Laurie gathers up her toiletries and tosses them into the tote bag with more force than she needs to, energized by her smart mouth, surprised to find her younger self so instantly there.

When she goes through the paint section there's a man supposedly perusing paint chips who has been sent to watch her too, she concludes, as are the several people wheeling carts along an aisle in groceries. The greeter stands near the entrance, his hand rising to his hip as she nears him. He turns toward her when she passes by. She's in the foyer, the door swinging shut, and his failure to call out *Thank you for shopping at Walmart* is a stone pitched against her back.

"Steve, it's Laurie," she says, almost shouting, when he answers the telephone, and for a moment she's unable to continue for fear her voice will break. Then he tells her that he's heard from Joe. He expects to see him by the end of the day.

"Hitchhiking," she exclaims and grasps the receiver with both hands, presses it hard against the side of her head as though to transmit the information more directly into her brain.

"That's what he said. He called from the road last night, around Brooks. You're in Regina, I take it, in a motorhome. So, what's up with you guys?"

"We're broke." Laurie looks out beyond the windows of the mall foyer at the parking lot, filling with vehicles now. Groups of people hurry toward the entrance, children running on ahead. When the door opens, the chilled grey air washes across her face.

"So I gathered," Steve says.

"Did he tell you that we've lost the house?"

"Jesus. No. Where's Joe's dad?"

She senses he's holding his breath. "In Deere Lodge. We didn't have much choice. I mean, what else could we do?"

When he doesn't reply she tells him about having sold several pieces of jewellery for their gold, Joe having sold his vintage pinball machine. Verna's mantel clock.

"Everything's gone. Including the Explorer, and my car." Her little boredom-buster, which sped her away from scenes of inertia and the pervasive question of what was she doing here? In the world. With her life.

She's stuck in Regina, she tells Steve, without money, waiting for Joe, not knowing where he was. "And I think I'm about to be evicted from the Walmart parking lot." When she becomes aware Steve hasn't said anything for several moments, she says, "Steve? You there?"

"I'm here," he says.

"How did Joe sound to you?"

A woman's voice interrupts and their connection is severed as she instructs Laurie to deposit more money. She digs frantically through the sock for dollar coins and then feeds them into the pay phone.

"Steve?"

"It's me," he says. "Listen, there must be a Western Union somewhere in Regina."

She remembers seeing a sign at Safeway, she tells him.

"I'll send you some money. I'll go down to the one here and you'll have it within an hour. Put some gas in that thing. You could make it here in a day and a half. Stay in a motel tonight. Call me when you get into town and I'll tell you how to find me."

"I think it's obvious Joe would rather I don't come," she says and holds her breath while she waits for his reply.

If you ever think about leaving Joe, I want to be the first to know, Steve once said. In the bar at the Ramada Inn where they met whenever he was in town. Where they'd spent long afternoons eating one another up, the sex hot and hard, and sometimes she was left with bruises on her breasts, and a soreness down there. She wonders now if too many years have passed. If Steve even remembers having squeezed her hands, not letting go of them until she had promised.

After a moment, Steve says, "Look, you get here, and then you and Joe can figure things out. I don't like to see you stuck like this, Laurie. But I'm staying clear of whatever's going on between you and Joe. Dakota and me, we've got something going for us and we have a deal that we both keep away from trouble."

"I understand," she says.

She's a source of trouble he wants to avoid.

At Smitty's she sips at coffee, the remains of breakfast set aside, surrounded by the din of happy people; the waitresses scurrying by, some of them stopping to chat with customers. Beyond the window, an elderly couple make their way across the parking lot, the woman holding back for the sake of the man using a walker. Alfred was right, she thinks. There's just no way a person can use one of those and look dignified. But he'd taken to the Yak-Traks quickly enough, they were the cat's meow he'd said, and had lifted his feet at the door for her to stretch them onto his boots. And he liked the ski pole she'd given him to poke his way along the icy walk, while linking his other arm through hers. She smiles at the thought of his strategic stops along the way to point something out, giving himself a moment to rest, to swipe at the briny icicle drip at the end of his nose. *How're you doing, Dad? Had enough, Dad? Should we turn around now, Dad?* Sometimes she suspected she had married Joe so she could claim Alfred as her dad too.

She feels winded suddenly, remembering how Alfred had struggled to be free of her and Joe as they'd dragged him across the yard. Pleaded with her not to let Joe do this, while Joe fought to pry his hands from the door frame of the Explorer and wrestle him inside. Joe, shouting for her to get behind the wheel when Alfred made a lunge for the other door in an attempt to escape.

She snatches up the receipt the waitress left on the table and her tote from the seat. As she slides out and up from the booth the bag hits a glass of water and sends it flying. She's aware of people staring, the water streaming over the edge of the table, a young waitress rushing toward her with a cloth. To hell with Joe, to hell with Steve.

The Meridian starts immediately and she adjusts the seat, the steering wheel, still feeling the heat of anger as she eases out into the traffic lane and drives toward the lights at Gibson Road. Beside her is the silver fox jacket and parka crammed into the oversize bag from Clara's Boutique. Although she knows the right-of-way lane is wide enough for the Meridian, her palms begin to sweat as she inches into it, then waits to check for oncoming traffic, her view obscured by a tour bus making a wide turn at the intersection from Gibson Road.

She's vaguely aware of people at the bus windows, seniors from an assisted living complex, she guesses, being taken out for a morning of shopping. There's not as many fender-benders when some of them come on the bus, the woman at the information desk said. You would not believe the parking lot on seniors' day, you're taking your life in your hands. Only last year someone got run over, was dragged under the car up and over the median before the yelling of bystanders registered in the old man's brain. By the time he stopped, the woman was dead. The woman being his own wife. Apparently his bowels were loose, he was anxious to get home and took off before she was fully inside the car. She hung onto the door, then fell.

Pride, the last thing to go, Laurie thinks. Like Alfred, stuffing his soiled Pampers behind the bed, thinking she wouldn't notice. The bus makes the turn, and the long line of cars waiting to gain entrance to the mall begins to move forward. The food court and washrooms will be busy all day.

When there's a lull in oncoming traffic she turns onto Gibson Road, and in anticipation of having to turn when she reaches Albert Street she forgets to signal, cuts into the outside lane to the immediate blast of a car horn. A moment later the car swerves round the Meridian and guns on past. No giving her the finger, though. Good morning to you too, she mutters, aware that her foot has begun to tremble on the accelerator.

She's never driven anything this big and had been taken by surprise by the responsive steering. Now, as she approaches the lights at Albert Street, she's surprised when she barely touches the brakes and the motorhome lurches to a dead stop and sends the bag flying from the passenger seat onto the floor. The light changes and she eases forward more carefully. Only several blocks down the street she nears the strip mall, and next to it, Clara's Boutique. The motorhome lists to one side, as she glides up onto the uneven curb and stops.

The brass bell tinkles when she steps into the store. There's a fustiness to it she hadn't noticed yesterday. A different woman is behind the counter, a middle-aged woman with a pen tucked behind her ear, dark short hair framing an angular and unsmiling face. She glances at Laurie briefly, looking business-like in a grey pantsuit and white blouse. But Laurie notes her tie, red with yellow palm trees and an elephant.

"I'm not quite opened yet. But go ahead and have a look around," the woman says.

"I'm not shopping today."

"Okay," the woman says carefully and takes in the huge bag at her side.

Laurie hefts it onto the counter and the woman cannot conceal her interest. She sucks at her bottom lip when Laurie holds up the fur jacket and lays it out on the counter. Then Laurie pulls the blue leather parka from the bag and drapes it on the counter beside the fur. The softness of the leather brings on a twinge of regret that she didn't wear it more often.

"They're both like new," she says.

"But they're not new. And not in season, either, unfortunately," the woman says, calculating their worth. She peers at the label on the parka, then fingers one of the toggles.

"That's deer antler," Laurie says.

"I'd have to store them for months. But they *are* in pretty good shape," the woman concedes, then she picks up a binder beside the cash register and opens it, plucks the pen out from behind her ear.

"Your tie is great, by the way."

The woman feels for it, then looks down. "Oh, that. It's my party tie. I just couldn't seem to get going this morning so I decided to wear it." When she smiles, her angular severity is gone.

She lifts a section of the counter and comes out from behind it to reveal her whole self, holds up her foot to display her ankle boots, obviously hand-painted, grey, with red tongues, pink laces and a pink and orange sunset on the sides, framed by palm trees. "Someone brought these in a week ago and I couldn't resist."

Nor would Laurie have been able to. "Wild."

"I have to fight with my daughters to get to wear them," the woman says and laughs and ducks back behind the counter, her attention focused on the silver fox now as she runs her hand across it.

Laurie glances about the store to gain courage, noticing that the display on the far wall has been changed since she was in, the pantsuits gone. In their place is summer wear, shorts and tops, sundresses, straw hats. "How much will you give me for the jackets," she asks.

"Oh," the woman says, her lightheartedness fading. "You must not have an account with us." She shuts the binder and puts it back beside the cash register and then leans forward on the counter and clasps her hands.

"It works like this. If you want me to sell the jackets you have to open an account. We take clothes on consignment. If they sell, we'll give you a credit and you can use it to shop in the store. If they don't sell within six months, we donate the clothing to charity. That's the agreement. How does that sound?"

"At this moment the last thing I need is more clothes. You wouldn't be hiring, would you?" she hears herself ask, her voice gone hoarse.

The woman is startled, and looks down at the jackets for a moment, glances at Laurie, then away.

"I'm running a family business here," she says finally, as though entering midway into a talk she's been having with herself. "My daughters work for me. I wouldn't make anything if I had to employ outside help." After a pause she says quietly, "Do you need to find a job?"

Yes, she *wants* to find a job, Laurie realizes. She wants to do something other than wait for Joe as she has throughout the years, doing nothing of consequence behind the reception desk, except be there, a pretty presence trying not to notice the pile of growing unpaid invoices. Staying after work with Joe to help clean and assess the damage and restoration of a used motorhome he'd bought for less than nothing and planned to resell, though he never got around to it. The most taxing part of her job had been payroll, the government forms that needed filling in at the year end.

So far, the friendliness of the people in Regina is appealing. Even at Walmart, no one came to physically haul her out of the washroom and hustle her through the door. No, the woman said, go to the service desk and ask for the manager. That man, Pete, leaving the lawn chair just in case she could use it. Maybe she'll stay on here, disappear in the crowd at the food court, be immersed and carried along with the chatter of recipe sharing, the comparison of physical ailments and treatments, places to stay down south. She'll learn to gripe about the price of oranges at Safeway. And of course, line up along with everyone else to buy a lottery ticket, her retirement savings plan. Stay for a time, anyway. Until Joe realizes he can't live without her and comes looking for her and the Meridian. She'll need to find another place to park it, hook it up to services. Perhaps a trailer court on the outskirts of the city. Maybe she will. And then, she cannot hold back her tears any longer.

Clara, proprietor of Clara's Boutique, takes Laurie to a room at the back of the store and she's seated on a plastic lawn chair now, explaining her circumstances, a mug of coffee in hand. Her tremulous voice is muffled by the racks of winter coats and jackets, the shelves lined with boots and shoes. Clara fusses about clearing away the hill of coffee whitener from the small round table in front of Laurie, and then the scatter of it across the floor. Laurie shook the can of whitener too vigorously and sent the powder flying everywhere, apologized too profusely, too loudly, and with so much anxiety that Clara set her hands on her shoulders and steered her over to the chair saying, "It is not a problem. You don't know how many times I've done that."

One by one, Laurie takes the jars down from her shelf and opens them, begins by telling Clara of having to sell Alfred's house. It never was her house, she knows that now. As much as Alfred tried to make her think it was, there was always the ticking of Verna's damn mantel clock, that perpetual reminder of the sacrifice she'd made while trying to rescue Laurie's mother from drowning. But the largest of her regrets is that Alfred will be forced to live the remainder of his life in that confining room in Deere Lodge.

She tells Clara about Joe's growing aloofness, his anger, his smashing things. Joe, Joe and Joe.

"I think he's been sleeping around," she says finally.

Clara has listened without speaking the whole time, arms crossed over her party tie and leaning on the small refrigerator. Now she plucks several tissues from a box on top of it and drops them into Laurie's lap.

"Men," she says as though this is the sum total of Laurie's lost life. She says it without bitterness or wry humour, but with resignation.

"I know there's a trailer park somewhere, but not exactly where. I can find out," Clara says when Laurie asks. "And if you're serious about staying, I do know someone who *is* hiring."

When the brass bell tinkles from the front of the store she touches Laurie on the shoulder lightly. "Stay put. I'll be back as soon as I can."

Laurie was always certain Joe didn't suspect anything about her and Steve's periodic leaps into bed. But she wonders, now. Perhaps the same evidence that caused her to suspect him had given him reason to wonder—absentmindedness, aloofness, the vagueness of his explanations for being away for long periods of time. But she doubts that. From what she's learned of men, most are clueless about anything that goes on beyond a three-foot radius from themselves.

When Clara returns moments later she has a city map that she spreads across Laurie's knee, shows her the route she's already marked in red, the way to get to Value Village in the north end. The manager, Tracy, is expecting her.

"I called," Clara says. "If everything works out, you could do your orientation today and start work tomorrow. Tracy's always looking for someone reliable."

Then Clara gives Laurie a piece of paper with her address and telephone number. "I live just around the corner from here, only two streets away. You can park in the driveway for now." With a wave of her hand when Laurie tries to thank her, she says again. "It's not a problem. My daughters' boyfriends will just have to park on the street."

When Laurie gets up to leave, Clara studies her for a moment. "Have you ever shopped at Value Village?"

VV Boutique is what Sandra calls the chain of second-hand stores, of which there are several in Winnipeg. Wives of doctors and lawyers shop there, Sandra said. They bring their own bags, with the names of exclusive shops on them, so no one will know.

"Yes, I have," Laurie says. She'd gone once with Sandra, and hated every minute. The clawing through other people's cast-offs. The types lurking about in the store, entire families of carb-enriched people waddling about, Goths and some theatre students, but mostly the overweight, the grungy, the poor. It takes time to find the good stuff, Sandra said. Take all the time you want, Laurie said, and waited for her in the car.

"Okey-dokey, you're qualified, then," Clara says. "I may close early today, so if I'm not here, you know where to find me."

Laurie is approaching the bridge on Albert Street, referred to on one of the postcards as being the longest bridge in the world to cross the smallest body of water. It spans a narrow creek on one side and the man-made lake on the other, where she can see people walking along a path beside the water. From the bridge, the grass edging the lake is like brushed suede, and the lacy treetops in the park beyond the lake path are like crochet. A fountain shoots a fan of water high into the air. She's almost halfway across the bridge when she comes upon city workers in Day-Glo vests seated on stools with jars of paint open on the sidewalk around them, oblivious to the traffic going by while they concentrate on hand-painting the intricate pastel designs on the balusters, the small glazed columns that look slightly Egyptian.

Yes! She's buoyed by the number of people riding bicycles along the bridge, the dogs loping beside them, their tails flags of exuberance. By what looks like a Fisher Price city arranged on a floor mat of green parks and a lake bobbing with geese and kayaks.

Although she's still on the same street, the scene changes when within a few minutes, she comes near the commercial area where the green glass towers dominate the skyline. She peers in their direction down a broad and welcoming tree-lined street, and promises herself to find that park with the buffalo. But there's a certain dull grittiness to the buildings along Albert Street now, aging and in need of paint—a tattoo and body piercing parlour, a used bookstore. The street narrows as she approaches an underpass; she touches the brakes and drives down under it, leery of the sudden darkness and the guardrails so close to the side of the Meridian.

When she emerges from the underpass she begins counting the number of streets until she reaches Clara's red circle on the map, relieved then to see the name of the street where she's supposed to turn. According to the map spread across the seat beside her, she must continue along that street until she comes to the next set of traffic lights. When the light changes she rounds the corner, thinking that this must be a warehouse district, given the number of slightly sinister-looking red brick fortresses along the way. She drives past buildings fronted by fences in which debris is caught. Beyond one fence, tall weeds grow through an apron of pavement around a closed-down gas station. When she reaches the traffic lights, she turns north onto another main artery and travels along it for several blocks. You'll soon see Value Village, on the left, set back on a corner. You can't miss it, Clara said.

And indeed Value Village is hard to miss, a large square cinder-block building painted bright yellow and blue. While she waits to turn at the intersection, she eyes the parking lot and notes the few vacant and rather narrow looking spots. When the light changes, she decides to drive past to search for a place to park on the street, though as she does so, she becomes wary of the growing number of dilapidated storefronts, the security bars on dirt-encrusted windows that are piled high inside with what appears to be a haphazard assortment of junk. Only yesterday while walking along Albert Street from the shopping centre, she observed that there didn't seem to be any discernible plan to the kinds of business being carried on side by side. Here, there seems to be one single trade—used goods. On the sidewalk in front of one of the small rundown buildings there's a display of furniture and several people stand among it, watching as a man plops down into a couch as though testing its springs.

She's fortunate to find a parking spot large enough a block and a half down, and now as she hurries back past the used furniture display, she tries not to look at the people, all of them appearing to be native. Two men emerge from the store, one of them carrying a floor lamp and the other, the shade. As they begin to cross the street toward her she finds herself calling out to them, "Hey, that's a great-looking lamp." Cheerful. Preparing for the interview with the manager. Prepared to be generous and accepting, as likely most of the people she'll be working with will be native.

The men stare at her. Then the man holding the shade calls out, "Okay then, thank you very much."

This will work, she tells herself.

When she steps inside Value Village she's stopped by the sheer vastness of the space, it's like a curling rink. The employees, men and women in red vests, move among the racks of clothing at the front of the store, and none of them, that she can tell, are native. She becomes aware of an odour that reminds her of school, when the janitor would sprinkle dustbane over someone's sickness to hold down the smell. On one side of the store near the front is a roped-off area where people line up in two rows waiting for the fitting rooms, which are like washroom cubicles with clothing flung over the tops of their doors.

She goes over to the nearest cashier, a young woman with spiked bleached hair and several nose rings, the sight of them making her eyes water. "Could you tell me where I might find the manager? Tracy," she adds to give weight to her request.

"You must be Laurie," the young woman says, her friendly smile revealing a mouthful of crooked teeth.

"Yes, I think she's expecting me." Before Laurie's finished speaking the young woman has picked up a telephone. Her amplified voice booms out, "Tracy, your person is here at number five."

"There she is," the cashier says, and Laurie turns to see a determined-looking short blonde woman in jeans and T-shirt, come charging along the aisle.

"Clara sent you over? Laurie, right?" Tracy says and extends her hand. She squeezes Laurie's hand so hard her rings cut into her fingers, and she can't help but wince.

"Sorry, I tend to do that," Tracy says with a little laugh. "You made it over here fast. Good. I usually give my spiel first thing, but we're so busy today I'm going to take you straight back to production and show you where I need someone to start work, like, right now, if possible. That way, if you decide the job's not for you, I get to save my breath."

Just then another voice reverberates over the intercom as someone calls out rather impatiently for receivers to come to the loading dock.

"Wait here just a minute. I've got to see about that. There's a big delivery coming in right now," Tracy says and takes off at a sprint toward the back of the store.

While she waits Laurie wanders over to a rack of goods set up beside the cash register, and thinks, even here, while waiting to go through to the checkout there's something to keep the eye busy. A tea set—oriental china, a pot and several cups arranged on a matching tray—not as pretty as her Japanese tea set was, and not priced as high as she had priced her own either, she discovers when she turns over the pot.

A small piece of porcelain catches her eye then, what seems to be a jam or honey pot, given the tiny spoon sticking out from the lid. She's about to reach for it when Tracy returns, followed by two young men who must hurry to keep up. The men shoot on past Laurie toward a large open doorway at one side of the store where she sees another set of doors opened to the street and the truck backed up in front of it, a man unloading boxes.

Tracy stands beside her, watching for a moment. "You could likely work in receiving. You have to be able to reach and lift. Most of the guys around here are pretty small. When a load comes in they tend to head for the washroom and I've got to go and haul them out." She rolls her eyes.

No jewellery, no cosmetics, not an unfriendly person, but not friendly, either.

"Come with me," Tracy says, continuing to talk rapidly over her shoulder while they go through men's clothing, the shoe department where there are more shoes lying about on the floor than there are on the shelves, and then along the side of a large open area that is a clutter of used furniture and exercise equipment; Laurie thinks of the elliptical trainer she almost had to beg someone to take away. These are what are called the side departments, and housewares is the largest of them. Around five thousand items make it to the floor in a single day, Tracy says, as they head toward the swinging doors leading into what she calls the production area.

Laurie is stopped at the sight of a row of workers standing on both sides of a long wide table, some of them wearing protective masks, all of them wearing gloves. She's overwhelmed by the noise of a huge ventilation fan sucking dust and lint, the bad smells, up through the roof. Some of the sorters use box cutters to slash open bags of clothing, while others tear them open with their hands, dump the contents on the sorting table and paw through them, quickly discarding soiled and torn garments into a barrel beside them. The workers take hangers from the rod that runs the length of the table, drape apparel on them, then hang the clothing on the racks parked behind them. When those racks are full, someone appears to wheel them away to the pricing area.

"Is the stuff washed?" Laurie asks. A dumb question, she knows as soon as she speaks.

"Are you kidding?" Tracy shouts, louder than is necessary to be heard.

"I just wondered. Because you'd think there'd be more of a smell, but there isn't. This place smells pretty clean," Laurie says.

"Really? That's good to hear. The minute I get home, let me tell you, I'm in the shower." Tracy plucks at her T-shirt and wrinkles her nose.

"So what happens to the rejects?" Laurie asks flailing about for something to say.

"They're sold for rags and other things," Tracy shouts. "And whatever we can't sell on the floor is recycled. It goes to Africa, Asia, South America."

"For charity."

Tracy shakes her head vehemently. "The people there buy it. You know, anything that's too worn, maybe needs to be mended. People wear that stuff. However, a portion of what we make here in the store does go to charity. This is a for-profit not-for-profit business," she shouts. "We employ twenty-five people back here in production, people who might not get a job otherwise, and in the front there's another fifteen or so part-timers."

Again a voice calls out on the intercom and Tracy stops talking to listen. "I was expecting this. I'll be right back," she yells and takes off.

Laurie walks along the table to the end, where a man has wheeled a rack of clothing and is now fastening price tags to the items. He turns as she approaches, as though expecting her.

"How do you know what price to give it," she asks, thinking the man looks Mexican.

"Oh, it's pretty standard. Except for the high-end labels, they're a couple of dollars more. We try and keep an eye out for them, but sometimes we miss something. But not often," he says and indicates a poster board tacked to the wall above his work area.

Style & Co., Peter NyGaard, Jones NY, Perry Ellis Portfolio, Kenneth Cole, IZOD, Liz Claiborne, all labels Laurie would recognize in an instant. If she worked here, her experience would be useful.

"We actually get more stuff that's low-end. There's so much of the cheap stuff going through here, we can't keep track of it."

She sees him ticket a jacket now, without seeming to even look at it. "And that? How did you know how to price that?" she asks.

"Oh, this one was easy. Feel, it's wool. The general rule is, the itchier it is the cheaper it is," he says and grins.

"Do you get first dibs on anything? What if you see something you'd like to have. Do you get a deal?" she asks.

"No way," he says. "We're just like everyone else. We put the stuff out on the floor and if it's still there when our shift is over, then, okay. We buy it. And we pay the same price as everyone. There's no special deals." He says this so emphatically, she wonders if he suspects that she'd been sent to trip him up.

Laurie notices a particular sorter looking at them, a man without a face mask. She takes in his undernourished appearance, straggly and uncut red hair. He might be seventeen or he might be seventy-seven, it's hard to tell from his haggard features. He's a kid, she decides as she watches how quickly he works, swings a garbage bag up onto the table, slashes it open and spreads the contents about and begins to sort, his gloved hands flying. He senses her watching, and their eyes meet. And then he laughs. At her. She's stung by the realization that the abrupt convulsion of his thin shoulders, the tiny spurts of wryness are directed at her. At what he sees in her. And at what he concludes she's thinking and deducing about him. You know nothing, he tells her without saying a word.

She turns away feeling caught in the act of pretending she wants to work here. The mountains of plastic bags are stacked up on either side of the table as high as the ceiling. Pull one out near the bottom and the sorters would be buried in an avalanche. Of vomit. That's how she sometimes thought of the garage sale, the inside of the house regurgitated on the veranda, spilling down the steps and across the lawn, the excess of an all-night party gone out of control.

Laurie hasn't heard Tracy come up behind her and is startled when the woman shouts, "Come on. I'll take you into the side departments."

Which prove to be two smaller spaces beyond the clothing sorting room, what look to be caves hollowed out of a solid mass of junk. A dishevelled and confused-looking man holds an armful of shoes and glances up at Laurie as she goes past, as though in a plea for help. Beyond him several women chatter loudly while they unpack boxes of housewares, books, mirrors and bedding piled up the walls and around them.

"So, are you interested?" Tracy asks when they emerge through another set of swinging doors into the furniture department, which is relatively calm and pleasant-smelling.

"Yes," Laurie says, thinking that she owes it to Clara to at least finish the interview.

Within moments she is sitting beside Tracy's desk in a small windowless office, perching on the edge of the plastic chair Tracy directed her to, while Tracy explains the salary, pleased to be able to say that it's slightly above the minimum wage, to explain the option of company benefits, the hours, the future.

"Anyone who wants to can make it in this company," she says and Laurie gets the feeling she wants to say, *Look at me. I've made it.*

"It doesn't matter what your experience or education is, if you want to, you can make it here. You could become a supervisor. We've got two of them out there right now," Tracy says. Laurie nods at the appropriate moments, regretting not having been honest, impatient for Tracy's spiel to end.

"Well, that's it, then. When you come to work at nine tomorrow, be sure to wear closed-toed shoes. You'll have the vest to protect your clothes, but don't wear anything good to work. You'll likely spend the first half of the day filling out personnel forms," she says then slaps her hands against her thighs as though to say, well, that's done! and rises from her chair. "Laurie, welcome to Value Village."

Her welcome reverberates as Laurie goes back toward the entrance. Welcome to the dead end of a shopper's world, where three dollars will buy you a tea set that you can then put in a garage sale and sell for four. But even if you don't sell it for four dollars, but only three, even if you sold it for less than what you paid for it, you still had the pleasure of discovery, of imagining making a pot of orange pekoe tea at the end of the day, setting the pot down on a small table beside your chair, adjusting the lamp to fix the light directly on the page of your book, lifting the pot and feeling its weight, the tea, a steaming amber liquid, rising up the inside of the cup. You might only make tea in that pot once, or not at all. But it doesn't matter, because it is the imagining of what you might do that is the real pleasure of spending.

Through the span of windows at the front of the store she sees that the sky has cleared now, as it did yesterday around noon. Too piercingly clear and cloudless, not what she would have liked for driving. From what she remembers of their arrival in Regina she knows that the ramp to the highway is only a short distance from the Safeway where the Western Union is. The sun will be behind her all the way to Winnipeg. She's almost at the door now, almost out of the store when she remembers the jam pot and sees it there on the rack at the first cashier. She goes over and picks it up and sets it on her hand, admires the bands of colour around it, each one printed with apples, peaches, grapes, pears. The lid is shaped like a strawberry and when she lifts it and sets it back down, the porcelain makes a satisfying little grating sound. She could fill it with pebbles, tiny polished river stones, present it to Alfred when she sees him. It's small, but she can see it on the bureau, brightening his room.

Eleven

THE TAXI PULLS UP BESIDE the wrought iron gate across the entrance to the driveway, the bronze fish symbol on the gate assuring Joe he's got the right address. With some effort he gets out of the cab, stiff from the long bus ride from Calgary. When the taxi leaves, he stands on the side of the street looking after it, catapulted into daylight, the sky, the inlet far below, all rushing toward him and making him light-headed. He turns his face up to the fine drizzle of rain, and inhales deeply. Thank you, he breathes.

The gate is electric, he discovers—someone will need to let him in. When he sees the panel on the stone wall, he goes over to it, finds the intercom buzzer beside the code pad and presses. While he waits he takes in the upward sweep of the grounds beyond the gate, the lawn interrupted by raised flower beds cascading with vines and flowering creepers, wet and vivid with dashes of colour.

Throughout the years he'd kept up with Maryanne and Ken's energetic accounts in newsletters, the successes and failures of their television ministry, their reports of last-minute bailouts by God, doors opening, doors closing; the adventures and misadventures of their only child, a daughter, Cerise. But he wasn't prepared for their prosperity. His thoughts scatter as he hears Maryanne's exclamation of pleasure when she says, "Joe." She must see him on a monitor, he realizes.

She waits at the front entrance, a woman in her mid-sixties, trim and fit in an off-white wool pantsuit, the ruffles of the neck of her turquoise blouse a foam of silk. He follows the drive through a grove of Japanese cherry trees, their leaves polished by the rain. When he emerges at the front of the house, she raises both arms and hails him. Her hair is silver-blonde, as it has been all the years he's known her, although she wears it smooth and shorter now. An Asian man rises on his knees in the garden, and beyond him sheets of water flow across plates of black shale, bushes are clipped in the shapes of large and small deer. A bird calls out. Welcome to Janat Aden, Joe thinks with a smile. The Garden of Eden. Maryanne rushes toward him, and she enfolds him in an embrace.

"Hey, guy, you have no idea what it meant to us when you called the other night." She squeezes him hard before releasing him. When he steps back he sees the tears in her eyes. "You look exactly the same, Joe."

"Ha," he says.

"Well, almost the same." She laughs as she takes in his three-day beard, the orange juice stains on the front of his white hoodie. Then she presses her fingers against her mouth and says, "We'll talk, for sure. But not yet, okay? Once Ken gets home, we'll talk." Ken has been kept late at the television studio with an unexpected meeting.

She links her arm through Joe's, draws him toward the entrance while explaining that she's just got home and hasn't had a chance to remove her makeup. Which accounts for her exaggerated features, Joe thinks. Her bright peacock blue eyelids and thickly coated lashes, rose-coloured lips that go on farther than her smile. When he steps inside the house he's aware of height, the ceiling far above, daylight flooding the entranceway and a large room beyond.

She leads him into the kitchen, into the sheen of steel and polished granite; then surprises him as she peels off her wig and drops it on a counter. She rakes her fingers through her short, wiry grey hair. When she sees his look, she laughs. "You didn't think it was real, did you?"

He grins, but doesn't reply, thinking that her teeth are whiter and more perfectly shaped than he recalls them being, and wonders if the miracle, the yellowish patch of filling in her molar, is still there. Muted voices draw his attention to the small television suspended from a corner cupboard, the image of Pastor Ken leaning into the space between his chair and the man seated across from him in a television studio. "Ouch, that must have hurt. Sometimes God just hauls off and socks it to us, right?" he says in reply to something the man has said. "I remember one time Maryanne and I were in an airport. Man, oh, man, if you're ever going to lose it, it'll be in an airport." He relates an incident from their private life, a vacation, a clash of wills. Maryanne watches, lost for a moment, a pucker growing between her eyebrows while she gnaws at her thumbnail.

Joe remembers Ken's kinetic energy, how even when he's sitting, he's not sitting still. Sometimes they'd played touch football and Ken would get carried away and lay on a tackle. He dislocated a boy's shoulder once. But Joe hadn't experienced any roughhousing, or Ken's spurts of impatience while they were on the camping and canoe trips, or during the outings when Ken played surrogate father. Rather, Joe remembers Pastor Ken calling out the beginning of a line of scripture as they paddled from island to island, and him finishing it. *I can—do all things through Christ, who strengthens me.*

"That's last week's program. I haven't had a chance to watch it," Maryanne says now. She turns off the television. "Let me fix you something to keep you going until dinner."

He's had soup and a sandwich during one of the many bus stops along the way, he tells her. *Amina, say sandwich.* He expects she will ask about Laurie, why he's come on a bus, but she doesn't.

"Well then, let me give you a tour of the house."

He follows as she clacks across stone floors from room to room, several of them unoccupied. Her daughter's suite, she says as they stand in the doorway looking into a sitting room of bamboo furniture with jungle print cushions; what appears to be a mosquito net hangs from the ceiling around the bed in the room beyond it. Although Joe has seen pictures of the fair-haired and sunny-looking girl at various stages of her life, he's never met her. She is away, studying communications in a Christian college in the States. "And, I hope, finding a great guy," Maryanne says and laughs. And Joe recalls that she'd met Ken at a Christian college in Chicago. He thinks of Crystal, and where they might be now after twenty-some years of marriage. In a falling-down church in the country, taking care of a small and aging congregation. Or some place in Africa, teaching English in a refugee camp to people like Lino and Amina. But he doubts that.

"Do you ever hear from Crystal?" Joe asks as he follows Maryanne down a hall toward another set of rooms.

"I sure do," she says, then turns and looks at him. "Why do you ask?"

"I don't know. Sometimes I wonder," he says.

A thought passes across her face, and then she says, "Well, she seems pretty satisfied, happy, now. It took some time, though."

She turns away and leads him farther down the hall and stops in front of one of the guest rooms. This room, she says, has been done in red mahogany. "This is where you'll sleep tonight. You'll be in good company." Tim LaHaye and Jim Kennedy have slept in the four-poster bed. Kennedy, the evangelist, she explains, surprised that Joe wouldn't know who the man was. Then she laughs and says, "He snores like you would not believe. We could hear him all over the house."

Near the end of the tour she takes Joe to the gym where she and Ken work out to a fitness program every morning. Beside the gym is another small room, tiled, and holding a sauna and Jacuzzi. There's one more room, she says, in a way that suggests she has saved showing it until the last, and for a reason.

They go up some steps to a large open space with windows the full length of the house, revealing the side of the hill and the dripping, green tangle of vegetation beyond. Joe hears soft music, water trickling across stones. He sees two young women at the far end of the room seated in front of computers.

"Hey gals, I want you to meet one of my favourite people," Maryanne calls out, and they both rise and come toward him, soft-complexioned blonde women whose tailored white blouses are tucked into their narrow beige skirts, both wearing necklaces of polished wood and seashells that clack pleasantly when they shake hands with him. He recognizes their radiant smiles; the music playing is a treacle of praise songs like the water trickling over stones in a fountain at one corner of the room—peaceful, but only for a short time. After that it has him gritting his teeth.

When they return to their desks, Maryanne takes him around the room to show him the "product" stacked up on the floor-to-ceiling shelves. The merchandise she calls *product* is all natural, she explains. There are herbal remedies to be rubbed into the skin, ingested and inhaled or immersed in. Products to be worn, to clean the house, to fend off cancer and help cure it, to prevent the physical and mental effects of aging. She explains that years ago, when they were so poor they sometimes had a hard time making rent, she took on the product, just as she had once invested in gumball machines, ten of them, placed in the lobbies of various institutions in Winnipeg. The money they'd earned from gum dispensers had helped finance some of the church outreach programs and supplemented their income. When she took on selling product, they had financial stability for the first time in their married lives.

She goes over to a shelf and takes down a plastic bottle and shakes it. "I'm going to fix you a drink before dinner, and you won't believe how good you're going to feel." Again, her eyes sweep over him. "Listen, while I go and see about dinner, why don't you have a shower?"

Call Alfred, Joe reminds himself moments later when he's in the bathroom of the mahogany guest room. He leaves the shower running and returns to the bedroom to get the cellphone, and is stopped short at the sight of a shirt and pair of pants, socks and underwear lying across the bed where he'd tossed the phone.

The phone is on the bedside table now, and beside it his watch and wallet, and, he notes, an electric shaver. The clothes he shed and left on the chair are gone. The bathroom door was open and there was no way Maryanne could have come in and left the room without having seen him in the buff. The thought is unsettling as he turns off the shower, winds a towel around his waist and goes back to the bedroom. He sits on the bed and calls his father, then listens to the telephone ring in his room at Deere Lodge. The two-hour time difference makes it near to nine o'clock in Winnipeg, late to call, he knows, and yet his stomach clenches as the telephone continues to go unanswered.

What are his wishes regarding his father's health care, the supervisor will want to know, if he calls the desk. In the event of impending death due to pneumonia, the friend of the elderly on their final ride. He's heard it can overcome the old within hours. Likely what the supervisor meant to ask was did he want his father to be taken to the hospital, or be made comfortable at Deere Lodge while he succumbed. What would Alfred want? It's a question that demands a certain history of openness in order for him to ask. He lets the phone ring longer in the event Alfred is in the bathroom, each ring shriller than the last.

"Hello, Joe," Alfred finally says, his voice hollow and far away.

"How did you know it was me?" Joe laughs too loudly with relief.

"Who else would it be?"

Joe wants to tell Alfred about the accident, but it is too much information, he knows. He would need to sort through his father's confusion, just as he had when he was a child. He would come home charged up over something and be made to speak slowly. To begin again. To explain, and his urgent need to tell his father what had happened, would dissipate. He'd soon learned that it was less frustrating if he kept things to himself.

"You sound better. Your cold doesn't sound as bad," Joe says.

"I am better. They did their best to make me think I wasn't. Gave me a shot. I told them, you stick another needle in me and I'll stick you-know-what in your ear." His voice is strong and clear.

"And you're wearing your dentures."

"Damn right, I am. So, you must be in BC now."

"Yes, I'm in Vancouver." Joe waits for him to ask when he'll be back. In several weeks, he had promised. And then you'll come home. If Alfred should ask, he'll have to tell him the truth. I don't know when I'll be home. It would finish Alfred to know about the house. He listens to the silence, a hollow echoing sound. I want to go home, he imagines Alfred will say again.

"Be sure and give Laurie a hello from me," Alfred says.

"I will."

Again there's a silence. And for a moment Joe thinks his father has set down the phone and forgotten they were having a conversation, as he sometimes does.

"Say, Joe. They took away my chair," Alfred says.

"Your what?"

"My chair. They took it. It's gone. I guess that means there'll be no more trips to the moon."

Joe winces at what he takes to be a moment of senility. "I'm in Vancouver now, Dad. I'll call again tomorrow. Likely in the morning."

"You what?"

"I'm going to call you tomorrow," Joe repeats.

The silence is once again long. Dad, Joe thinks. The word embodies so much more than what it distinguishes Alfred as being. To Joe it has become the age-pebbled texture of his father's skin, his body a fusty narrow closet filled with forgotten things. The word, *Dad*, has always released a whirlwind of conflicting emotions. From the moment he'd opened his eyes, Alfred had been his father, and he guesses that's the way it's supposed to be. But his father had been a bachelor for almost as many years as he'd been his father and Joe regrets now not having been interested enough to want to know, who are you?

"I love you, Joe."

"So do I," Joe says. "I meant, you, that is. I meant to say that I love you too."

"Well, good. At least we got that straight," Alfred says.

It has stopped raining and as Joe sits across from Maryanne and Ken at the table over the remains of dinner, the setting sun lights the water beyond the window where a ferry plies toward the terminal at Horseshoe Bay. If it weren't for the trail of its wake, it would look to be standing still. The view, the Lexus in the four-car garage, the late model

Land Cruiser and Jaguar, how in hell do they afford this? Joe wonders.

He looks about the room again, at the white loveseats at the far end of it, arranged around a large square glass table; the watercolours on the walls are at odds with the vivid curios on side tables and lined up on shelves, the objects they'd brought back from countries such as Russia, Turkey and Israel, where they'd gone with TV crews to record the stories of born-again Christians.

"Hey Joe, I've gotta say that despite what you've been through, you look great," Pastor Ken says, as though Joe, clean-shaven and wearing the clothes Maryanne left out for him, is in need of reassurance. Ken swirls the last of his white wine in his glass, looking into it, preparing his thoughts. Getting ready to speak, Joe thinks.

Ken is florid, thick in the neck and gone completely grey, although his hair still shines; he wears it slightly long and in an attractive way. It occurs to Joe that maybe it, too, is a wig. He looks fit though, judging from the swell of pectorals beneath his polo shirt.

Throughout dinner neither one strayed near the reason why he might have come, or why Laurie wasn't with him; rather they gave him a lengthy account of their recent trip to Ukraine where there was an underground church of born-again Christians, living in the spirit. Technology was taking the gospel to countries farther and faster than ever before, and it wouldn't be long now, Pastor Ken said. China, North Korea. And then we'll all be swept away, Joe thought. They'd also been to Poland, Pastor Ken went on to say, a hard nut to crack, given how ingrained the RC church was in their history and culture. And Polish people were stubborn. But they'd met with members of a small Baptist church in Warsaw. "Maryanne made a haul in Poland," Pastor Ken added.

"Dinnerware," Maryanne jumped in to explain, telling Joe about the twelve-piece set of china she'd bought in Krakow for next to nothing. "And I didn't know Poland had such great crystal."

"I was thinking of your chairs," Joe says now with a grin to let them know that he's teasing. "When you lived in Winnipeg." Reminding them of the lime-green knit cloth Maryanne had come across in a fabric store. She'd covered the seats of their dining room chairs with it and the knit had pilled so badly the chairs were mats of fuzz. It became a joke between them, Maryanne saying she had to go home and shave the chairs. Reminding them of their shared history. Hoping that she might think back to the day on the balcony when he wound up halfway across the room, without knowing how he'd got there.

"Winnipeg was not good to us," Maryanne says. Her thoughts turn inward as she twists at a large silver ring. She's put on a lounging costume for dinner, a velour sweater and pants the colour of shiitake mushrooms, and her pale skin is a sheen of hydration, free of cosmetics now. Joe thinks of the products, and the youthful look of her skin.

"The innuendo, the terrible things that were said about Ken, almost finished us," she says with a bitterness that surprises Joe, and he thinks she may be referring to the split that came in the church when they began to focus on miracles; the boisterous and unrestrained worship they'd claimed to be spirit-led.

"Honey, those times are over," Pastor Ken interrupts briskly, leaving Joe to wonder what else she might have said.

"Yes, honey, they are."

They've always called one another *honey*. Maybe that is why he came to call Laurie the same. Maryanne's earrings, crescents of mother of pearl, swing against the side of her neck whenever she moves. Joe turns away from the sight, surprised by the thought that he'd like to put his mouth there.

He wants instead to talk about being with her that hot summer afternoon soon after his mother's death, kneeling at the Come to Jesus Chair. About being in a semi-wakeful state, his heart like a sparrow crashing from rib to rib. He was receding into a time before there had been time, and his name was being breathed out into the gases that would become the universe. *God has a wonderful plan for your life.* Of course he would pick that up and run with it, given that he'd been made to believe he was remarkable. The miracle birth.

But what *had* happened on the balcony? Over the years he'd told himself that he might have been high on the toxic fumes of the chair's metallic paint, and passed out. Or God had looked on him with mercy and given him what he'd most needed at that time. Rapture, ecstasy. Whatever it was, he'd experienced the same thing when he'd felt the flutter of Amina's pulse.

"It looks like Vancouver, on the other hand, has been good to you," Joe says now. "You sure do live on the right side of the city."

"And why not?" Maryanne asks. "I remember those seat covers, Joe. What a joke, they were. You know, there was something wrong with us having to live like that. Since we've left Winnipeg we've learned that God doesn't want his children to be poor. We're first-class citizens, not second class. What kind of advertisement would we be for God if we lived in a shack and went around in rags?"

"Amen," Pastor Ken says.

"God *likes* to give things to his kids," Maryanne continues. "But we have to ask. And he wants us to be specific. You wouldn't believe how our ministry grew once we learned to be specific." She goes on to say that after Joe had called them, they'd specifically asked God to send him to them. "And here you are."

Sent. Drawn. That's what he'd been feeling.

"Listen, Joe, you've been lying heavy on our hearts for some time now," Pastor Ken says. "So much so, that one night I just couldn't get to sleep for thinking about you. And so Maryanne and I came to this room, to that very table over there." He nods at the arrangement of white loveseats around the glass table. "We agreed to pray until we were at peace about you. Before we knew it, it was morning, and the sun was shining down there on the water, and I said, 'Well, Lord, I'll just put Joe in your hands now. I'm going to leave it up to you.'" His voice cracks with emotion.

"Hey there, honey," Maryanne calls out gently, and hands him a serviette.

"Thank you, honey." He laughs, obviously embarrassed. "It's what I do now, Joe. I cry at the drop of a hat. About a year ago I had what's called an ischemic happening and I've been left with this. I've become a blubbering fool. But, hey, that's all right. I don't mind. God can use tears too, eh Joe?" He dabs hard at his eyes and then balls the serviette in his fist.

He's ill, Joe realizes, noticing that he has pouches of soft flesh beneath his eyes, that his features are bloated, his fingers curled against the table are swollen.

"I want to show you something," Maryanne says to Joe. "You see that rug over there?" She indicates the carpet on the floor beneath the glass table. "Come and have a look at it."

Joe stands beside her taking in the pattern of animals on the area rug, what look to be gazelles bounding along the borders, reclining among fern-like trees, the colours rich, oranges, reds and browns on a dark blue background.

"I've had it for years. Wherever we've gone, I've taken it with us. I'll decorate a room around it if I have to. But I'll never part with it. Once, when we were at rock bottom financially and the apartment we were in was just so awful, I was hungry for something to brighten up the place. And so I asked God for a rug."

Maryanne sits down on one of the loveseats, and Ken, who has joined them, sits on another and indicates Joe should do the same. As he does, he recognizes the large and well-worn Bible on the table, beside a box of tissues. It's the same Bible that was on the homemade pulpit when he and Steve broke into the church.

Maryanne continues her story. "And God said to me, 'So you want a rug. Well, Maryanne, you've got to be more specific than that. Just what kind of rug do you want?' And so I went out and looked at rugs. I found one. But it was way too expensive and I was ashamed to ask for so much, and so I told God the size I needed, and the colours I preferred, and let it go at that.

"I don't know why I was surprised, but I was, when not much later a delivery man came to the door. He had something for me, but wouldn't say what, or where it came from. He'd been paid to deliver it on the condition that he didn't say. And it was this carpet," Maryanne says. "When I unrolled it I couldn't stop crying. It's a Balouch rug, Joe, it's from Iran. The rug I thought was too expensive, was also a Balouch rug from Iran. But get this, Joe," she says and leans toward him. "This one is *midnight blue*. Midnight blue has always been my favourite colour, and God knew that. You see, I was willing to settle for just a rug, but God wanted me to have the absolute right one."

"Praise the Lord," Pastor Ken says. "I never get tired of hearing that story."

Joe fights the growing pressure in his chest as he pictures Lino as the Lost Boy he saw on television so many years ago, standing beside the journalist who seemed at a loss for words to describe the child's situation. The boy was a walking skeleton, naked; his taut mouth stretched across his face, baring his teeth. He looked stunned, as though he didn't recognize the man pointing the camera at him or the stammering journalist as being human, as his own suffering had turned him subhuman.

"Midnight blue," Joe says.

"Yes. But what that really says is that God delights in blessing his children. And he wants to bless you. You're his kid too."

"With a Jaguar."

"That's Cerise's car," Pastor Ken says. "She worked hard for that, she earned that. Look, Joe," he says and then takes a deep breath. "God wants more for you than a washed-up trailer business. What kind of advertisement is that?"

"God wants you to be part of our ministry," Maryanne breaks in to say.

"Me?"

He can hear their breathing as he holds his own breath. Sent. Drawn. Fuck. He senses their growing unease, but remains silent.

"You know what, honey, I think Joe and I need a moment here," Pastor Ken says.

Maryanne gets up without a word and leaves the room.

"What we need, Joe, is a moment of prayer. Shall we?" Pastor Ken says.

When Joe doesn't answer, he says again, "Shall we?" and it is not a question. Then he closes his eyes and begins. "Our dear father. Our heavenly and almighty God and Father. Maker of heaven and earth. You have said that when two or three come together in your name, you are present. Come now and sit with us. Thank you, Jesus."

His voice deepens and grows strong as he goes along. Then he raises his head and hands, his palms open, to receive what words should come next. For his thoughts not to be his thoughts but something from on high that will leave Joe euphoric and brimming with hope, his fears, anxieties, uncertainties banished. After a time Ken falls silent, and then begins to whisper-pray, *la, la, la, la, tickle, tickle,* his tongue making little clicks.

Joe stares down at his hands, the muscles in his neck taut.

You know, Joe here needs, wants, your will, tickle, la, la, reveal, hold, lay, open, display, give to Joe. To Joe. La, la, la, la, click, click. He opens his eyes and blinks, as though surprised to find himself where he is, and his hands fall to his knees. Then he turns and looks at Joe. "You know, I haven't even asked about your father."

It takes a moment for Joe to reply. "My father is fine. He's going on ninety-six years old now."

"Oh my, ninety-six. That is just so amazing. And Laurie?" Ken's voice drops as though her name is a cause for deep sorrow.

Joe chooses not to answer. "You remember when we talked on the phone, I said I was going to Fort McMurray to see Steve. And that's what I thought I would do. And then I met these people who gave me a ride."

And as he tells Lino's story of having walked for five years in search of his family, Ken's head begins to droop and his chin comes to rest on his chest. His eyes close, but sometimes he sighs, makes a sympathetic sound to let Joe know he's listening. As Joe relates the accident, he sees the shower of glass flying toward him, Amina's head and shoulders erupting through the windshield, he hears Lino cry out her name.

When he's finished, Ken expels a long breath of air, as though he's been holding it the whole time. "Wow, oh, wow," he says. Then he looks at the ceiling and says loudly, "Sometimes you need to yell at us, right?" He turns to Joe. "Big Daddy just gave you a shove in the right direction. He's chased you down like Paul of Tarsus. And here you are. Do you need a bigger light or a louder voice?"

Just then Maryanne enters the room carrying a tray. With dessert and tea, she tells them. She sets the tray down, and begins setting mugs and bowls of sorbet on the table, and as Joe watches, his churning thoughts settle.

"Honey, you missed hearing what happened to Joe," Pastor Ken says.

"I heard," she says quietly and begins to pour.

"Just what would you have me do in your ministry?" Joe asks. "My father's in great shape, but I sure don't see moving him to Vancouver."

Maryanne looks at him, the glass teapot suspended in the air, in it a swamp of red flowers and leaves. "Of course not. But you'd be able to get to Winnipeg now and again to see him. It wouldn't be easy, I know. But remember those first disciples, they were willing to leave everything and everyone in order to serve the Lord. Even their families," she adds and resumes pouring.

Pastor Ken tosses the crumpled serviette on the table. Then he sits forward on the loveseat, as though about to call a meeting to order. "What we need, Joe, is for someone to pray over the mail." The cheques, the money orders, the requests for literature. "And we need to get organized in there. We've got to be able to get back to people sooner. The turnaround time is much too slow." The volunteers they have now, who sort the mail, work in the call centre and prayer room, need to be organized.

"You're so good with people," Maryanne says. With him on board, she says, she would be able to let one of the two girls moving product across the country go.

"I don't think so," Joe says, startling them as he gets up from the loveseat.

"Joe, wait," Pastor Ken calls out to him as he leaves the room.

Within moments Joe is striding along the winding driveway through the Japanese cherry trees, feeling the pull of the grade in his thighs. He rounds a curve and sees the gate below, realizing then that someone will need to let him out. The last bit of sunlight glazes the water in the inlet, and the spaces between the wrought iron bars on the gate look solid, like clear glass.

He turns and takes in where he's been, the sheen of water flowing across the black shale plates, bushes whose branches bend to the earth beneath the weight of giant, pastel flowers, the row of tall cedars beyond them. He's seen a documentary on the various places where the Garden of Eden might have been, on a mountain in Turkey; between the Blue and White Nile rivers; the great saline reed bed where the Euphrates and Tigris rivers merge. There's a muddiness there that matches the muddiness of the sky, and so it's impossible to know where the water and sky meet. A concave swelling of water, of longing to forever be children walking and talking with God at the breezy end of the day. He's seen another place where the Garden of Eden may have been, and like in the Joni Mitchell song, it's a paved-over parking lot.

He looks up at the ten-foot height of the gate, at the spear-shaped tips at the tops of the bars, thinking that somehow, he'll climb over it. Then he hears a buzz, then a click, and when he pushes on the gate it opens. Maryanne calls out, her voice distorted and loud, but he gets the message. They'll be praying for him. Good, he thinks. Everyone needs to be prayed for. The goodwill embodied in a prayer goes somewhere, and like a moth, it finds a source of light.

Twelve

Five years later

WEEDS BURNT BY THE SUN crunch beneath Joe's feet as he walks along the side of the highway, the metal water bottle clipped to the belt of his shorts pinging rhythmically against a pocket rivet, as though counting his steps. In the far distance a murky haze has begun to rise on the horizon and he fixes his eyes on it, thinking it is like silt at the bottom of a fishbowl. I don't know. Maybe it's rain clouds. But it's almost too much to hope for, given that he's got his tinderbox of a motel room in Winnipeg to look forward to, the air conditioner conking out just before he left to go to Brandon.

The intense heat this summer is like the heat of that last summer he had with his mother. The same water restrictions, newscasters reporting with a heightened urgency the record amount of water being piped into the city from Shoal Lake, the sightings of funnel clouds. He recalls the swish and chug of lawn sprinklers coming to life after dark, his mother's obvious flouting of the water restriction making him wild as he ran through the spray of water clad only in his underwear, and she watched from the veranda, the sphinx shape of her stiff hair a silhouette, her cigarette rising and the spark flaring into a pocket of light around her mouth.

He dreamed of her last night. He awoke to the smell of the damp earth beneath the footbridge in Brandon, the algae rimming the duck pond in the park just beyond, and he remembered his mother had come to him. She was not warm and solid, but not a ghost either. She made a hollow for him with her arms and he set his forehead against her breastbone and stayed there. For how long, he can't remember. But he does remember that when it ended she'd taken his face in her hands and pressed her mouth against his, hard, for a long moment, as though she was telling him it was important that he know something. He'd thought she meant to tell him he was forgiven for breaking into the church. For being away from the house with his father when she lost her life.

He's returning to his room at the Palomino, the last of the cheap motels along Pembina Highway to offer a small kitchen. When he'd heard from Pauline that Clayton had split with his family and had returned to his hometown to die of cancer, he took a bus to get to Brandon quickly, and then he was just there, a presence beside Clayton's bed until he died. Nothing was said between them, only Clay's eyes taking him in, and then closing.

In the years since his business went bust, Joe has helped build two houses for Habitat, one in Calgary and another in a small town south of Winnipeg. Joe, a rough carpenter, clean-shaven, his hair a brush cut, a pencil stuck behind his ear. Joe, stacking food at the Food Bank, long-haired with his scruffy jeans gone through at the knees, blending in, steering clear of gratitude.

The sun is behind him now, and the air is thick with the scent of sage. All around him are coulees, shallow bowls of sunlight set down among the humped beige land. A wilderness just beyond the highway that he's driven so many times, failing to notice the moguls, the tall and silvery sage, ribbons of ragweed the colour of rust, stiff and tall. He's nearing a dugout pond now, one of several he's passed, all of them looking like mirrors set down on the earth.

"I don't know," he says. Maybe if he cuts across that field he'll eventually wind up somewhere close, or not close, to Winnipeg. *I don't know* has become his new mantra, what he says to himself when he gets up in the morning. Not knowing where he'll be tomorrow or the next year used to fill him with dread. What he feels now is a certain weightlessness, that one small step is a giant leap of possibility.

Sometimes he takes the bus past the old house, thinking he'll see Laurie, but so far he never has. One year, a strip of earth had been turned up along the front walk and bushes had been planted, surrounded by the fresh look of cedar bark chips, and the next year, the bushes were gone, and the sidewalk had been taken up and interlocking bricks put down in a random pattern of red and grey that looked like shadows. He was glad again that he'd given the house to her. Glad that she'd been there for his father at the end.

He cuts away from the highway and goes down the slope of the ditch, the dried reeds slashing at his bare legs. He ducks between the strands of the fence and heads out across the field when, within moments, he's surprised by a flock of Franklin gulls rising up all at once, the air filled with their complaints. And it comes to him then, that the dream of his mother had nothing to do with forgiveness. Rather, with her cold, hard and long kiss, she was telling him that he should know that he is alive, while she is not. He stands for a moment to watch the gulls turn across the eastern sky, and remembers seeing the doe and her yearling at the beginning and end of the day through his last winter at the Happy Traveler. Then, in spring, something told them to leave, and wherever they went, it was the right place to be.

Acknowledgements

I would like to acknowledge the assistance of the Carol Shields Writer in Residence Programme at the University of Winnipeg, the Saskatchewan Arts Board and the Canada Council for the Arts during the writing of this novel.

And a special thanks to Anne Collins for asking all the right questions.

SANDRA BIRDSELL, among Canada's finest fiction writers, was born in Manitoba, and lived for many years in Winnipeg. Her novel *The Rossländer* was nominated for the Giller Prize, and her bestselling novel *Children of the Day* was longlisted for the International IMPAC Dublin Literary Award and won the Saskatchewan Book Award for Fiction. She is also the author of three collections of short stories, among other works. She lives in Regina.

A Note About the Type

The body of *Waiting for Joe* has been set in Adobe Garamond. Designed for the Adobe Corporation by Robert Slimbach, the fonts are based on types first cut by Claude Garamond (c.1480–1561). Garamond was a pupil of Geoffrey Tory and is believed to have followed classic Venetian type models, although he did introduce a number of important differences, and it is to him that we owe the letterforms we now know as "old style." Garamond gave his characters a sense of movement and elegance that ultimately won him an international reputation and the patronage of Frances I of France.